RICHES TO RAGS

Sandra White

ISBN 978-0-9817521-1-2
      0-9817521-1-X

Published by Mirror Publishing
Milwaukee, WI 53214
www.pagesofwonder.com

Printed in the USA.

Sandra White, Ed.D., has had a lifetime interest in writing, and at one time was a journalist with The Midland Daily News in Midland, Michigan. She later entered the training and development field and spent most of her career life in that arena. After her retirement, she resumed writing. Her first novel, The Album, was published in 2003. Ms. White currently resides in Springfield, Missouri.

To
NAMI
The National Alliance on Mental Illness

Prologue

As she cradled Molly's limp body on her lap, she looked at her friend's lifeless hands. Hands more yellow than flesh-colored, veins running down the back like small blue ropes barely covered by yellow parchment. Molly's fingers were long, and although gnarled like joints on an aging apple-tree limb, they were slender, and she could imagine how pretty they once had been. Her nails were an oval shape. That is, what was left of them. Most were broken or torn, and red and ragged cuticles covered half of each nail. Two long fingernails—one on each hand—were grotesquely black with layers of grime caked underneath.

She couldn't take her eyes from Molly's hands, now more ugly than beautiful. Even so, she could still picture them once very lovely. A long, long time ago. Before the illness. Before the poverty and all the bad luck. Before the street.

Molly's lashes were long and lay gently on her cheeks, cheeks filthy with dirt. Tear-washed tracks traced down her cheeks, marking her face with signs of her final tears, her final sorrow.

When she found Molly just past dawn, Molly's lavender-gray eyes were open, as if she were staring in wonderment at something especially exciting. But she knew Molly rarely found anything special. Nor had she ever seen her stare at something she found exciting. A few times, though, very, very rare times, Molly's lavender-hued eyes had looked right at her, and she saw warmth and compassion. Brief moments when the curtain of Molly's illness seemed to rise, and she had a glimpse of who Molly really was. Of who she used to be.

And then there were those times—those wonderful times—when Molly spoke to her, guided her, as if she were her protector and not ill at all. But those times were so few—"precious and few," as a songwriter once penned.

Most of the time Molly didn't look at anyone; she looked at the ground, kicking whatever lay in her path, mumbling unintelligible nothings. Oh, she would get excited. But excited only with something in her own world. The world inside her head. A world that didn't include anyone else.

She had closed Molly's eyes gently, as if she feared hurting her friend if her trembling hands scratched those beautiful eyes or pushed too hard on the thin, gray, creased lids. As if Molly could feel anything now. As if anything could have hurt her more than the street had already done.

Wisps of gray hair with an occasional strand of brown curled out from underneath the misshapen dirty felt hat Molly always wore pulled down as far as it would go. She had never seen Molly without her hat, and she didn't remove it now. It would have seemed like desecrating her friend's memory.

She gently touched Molly's hair and marveled that it would still curl, stiff as it was from God only knows how many days, weeks, or months—maybe years—it had gone unwashed, accumulating the dirt and dust of the street. The street that Molly called "home."

She wondered if her name really was Molly. Probably not. Come to think of it, Molly had really never told her her name. Others had.

"Oh, that's just crazy Molly," or "Do you see old Molly over there? Watch out or you'll turn out just like her."

It was a beautiful morning, not a cloud in the sky. A perfect day. The temperature was in the mid-fifties, and a gentle wind rustled the tiny green leaves just beginning to sprout on the trees lining the street. The breeze blew scattered paper and trash, remnants of the night before when the homeless lined the alleys and sought refuge in abandoned doorways—and in each other.

The air smelled almost clean as the new day approached, its refreshing scent drifting over the usual fetid stench of garbage and waste that was the trademark of the back alleys in this part of Valeria. When she inhaled deeply, she could even smell the wonderful fragrance of bread from Percy Lyons' Bakery three blocks away.

It didn't seem right that Molly was lying here like this on such a beautiful morning. She fought her urge to pull her by the arm and say, "C'mon, Moll, time to rise and shine. Isn't it a purrr-fectly gorgeous day?"

Instead, she flicked away a tear before it dropped on the still body of her friend. Not that Molly would have noticed. Another escaped before she could brush it away, tracking down her cheek, crossing three rows of light brown freckles before it found its way to the tip of her upturned nose and off onto Molly's still hands.

In the distance, she heard the shrill haunting noise of a siren. She raised her head and listened keenly to determine just how close it was—and if it was coming her way.

Yes, it was. And it was getting closer.

She leaned over and kissed Molly on the forehead, lifted her from her lap, and laid her ever so gently on the hard ground. Then she grabbed hold tightly of the small gold cross Molly wore about her neck, and tugging firmly, she broke the slim gold chain and dropped the cross and chain into her pocket.

Then, looking back just once more at the woman lying amidst a pile of tattered boxes and rusted cans heaped beneath a faded and torn green awning, she walked hurriedly away.

Chapter One

"Well, Merritt, what do you have to say for yourself?" demanded Sister Mary Margaret in her most authoritative voice. Authoritative and firm, but, nonetheless, gentle. She tried always to be gentle with the children. Even the most exasperating ones—ones like Merritt Hall. Her emerald-green eyes reflected her gentility, and even the severity of the black and white attire of her Order did not overpower the kindness of her oft-present smile.

Sister Mary Margaret, principal of St. Agnes Academy, truly respected three traits above all others—after a strong faith in God, that is: a fine mind, a healthy curiosity, and an independent nature. Young Merritt Hall had all three. In abundance. Sister's dilemma was how to teach a nine-year-old to constructively channel these virtues.

Merritt sat straight on the chair across from Sister Mary Margaret, her lavender-gray eyes cast down, her navy and white uniform smoothed demurely across her lap, her wavy light-brown hair brushing softly across her round cherub-like face.

Merritt was all too familiar with Sister's office, familiar with this chair with its stiff dark-brown leather upholstery, this chair so high off the floor that her feet in their new shiny black patent-leather shoes dangled. Since her feet couldn't reach the floor, she swung them back and forth, back and forth, watching the light from the window reflect in their shininess. It made her smile.

Merritt loved things that shone—like the gold cross she wore, the cross her mama and daddy had given her just last month for her ninth birthday. Every day as she fastened the gold chain around her neck, she'd look at its shiny reflection in the mirror, and it made her feel special. Very, very special.

She was thinking about the day her parents presented her with her treasured piece of jewelry. Her birthday. What a wonderful day that had been.

The birthday party was a gala affair for such a young girl. An almost formal celebration. Piles of elegantly wrapped gifts were stacked on either side of the birthday girl as she sat in her place of honor at the end of the massive dining room table, her eyes dancing with excitement. She wore a lavender ruffled dress with a wide silk purple sash and lavender rosebuds embroidered across the bodice. Her shining lavender-gray eyes almost matched her party dress. They glistened with just a bit more gray.

Huge bouquets of lilacs adorned a large ornate buffet, their sweet heady fragrance filling the room. The flowers' color matched Merritt's dress, and she wore a sprig of lilac in her hair.

Lavinia Hall sat beside her daughter. Lavinia wore a soft ankle-length blue gown, the blue enhancing her pale-blue eyes—eyes set rather close together on her narrow face. Her golden blonde hair, stylish with rows of waves and turned softly under at the ends, lay gently on her thin shoulders. A fringe of curly bangs rested on her narrow forehead.

Lavinia was a tall woman, almost as tall as her husband, David. Her tall erect posture, coupled with her patrician-looking countenance, gave her an almost arrogant, austere look. But there was nothing either arrogant or austere about Lavinia Hall. A devoted wife and mother, she was the warmest, most caring woman one would ever meet.

David Hall sat opposite his young daughter, at the other end of the table, watching her adoringly as she excitedly unwrapped her birthday treasures. He loved this child almost to the point of worship, and his happiest times were when he was making Merritt happy.

David was a big man with wide shoulders and large hands. Strands of his full head of brown hair often drooped down over his large gray eyes, and his wide mouth seemed forever in a smile. Although his hair was unruly much of the time, and his warm smile was loaded with boyish charm, his attire spoke of elegance—and of affluence. Born into and reared in poverty, he now dressed in the finest clothing he could find—rich woolens and linens, fine cottons and extravagant silks.

David Hall was a very wealthy man.

But none of his wealth mattered to him like this child—this girl so small he often wondered how she could possibly be the progeny of him and his tall slender wife. Then he would recall his own mother, a tiny women, her small stature made even more so as she became stooped through years of thankless toil. Esther Hall died when her son David was in his teens. Although he was told she died of tuberculosis, David always felt his mother died of complete and total exhaustion.

9

The other birthday-party guests seated around the large mahogany table beneath the multitiered crystal chandelier, its prisms reflecting a rainbow of colors, ranged from the very young to the very old, representing a wide range of relationships—close relatives, distant relatives, friends, and neighbors. Most had been guests of the Hall's before.

Although their home reflected well the family's riches, the Hall's household was vibrant and friendly. People of every social status—and those with none—were always warmly welcomed through the Hall's front door. Parties were common and very well attended.

Merritt had observed her other birthdays much the same as this one. And each year she was just as excited as if it had been her first experience as the guest of honor.

Overdressed children—little girls in their layers of ruffles with bows as large as their tiny faces adorning curls that bounced with their every step, and little boys looking mildly uncomfortable in starched shirts and clip-on bow ties—were escorted to the elegantly carved front door of the Hall mansion by the drivers of their families' lavish and expensive automobiles. A few were accompanied by their mothers, one or two by both parents, family friends of David and Lavinia's.

Although most of the party guests appeared to be of the same social strata as Merritt's family, a few were not. But the welcomes were the same. A big smile from Merritt and her father, and a hug from Merritt's mother greeted the little boy with the hole in the knee of his pants the same as the one arriving in the silver-gray Rolls Royce. One little girl had on the school uniform she wore to St. Agnes. It was the only "good dress" she owned.

Once the children entered the foyer of the house, they were engulfed in the excitement of their surroundings, and hole-in-the-knee-of-the-pants became instant friends with starched-shirts-and-bow-ties—ties quickly askew.

After a time of play and entertainment, they were seated at the dining table to share in the beautifully decorated birthday cake and ice cream. Each serving of ice cream was molded like a basket and overflowing with fresh strawberries. Lucy Mae, the little girl whose best dress was her school uniform, was so awed by the confection, she had to be persuaded to eat it.

When sticky fingers and frosting-smeared faces were added to the children's laughter, it was time for the birthday girl to open her gifts—a time-consuming task, as Merritt took her time carefully untying each ribbon.

"Hurry up, Mimi, we want to see," shouted several of the children in unison. "Do you like it?" each would inquire as she opened their special contribution to the assortment of gifts.

"Of course I like it," she'd reply to each inquiry—often adding, "especially since it's from you."

Merritt had opened all her gifts when her father took from his pocket a small gold-foiled wrapped box bearing a gold sticker embossed with the name, "Tiffany's."

"Isn't she a bit young for such a valuable piece, David?" Lavinia had inquired when her husband showed her the purchase he made the last time he was in New York. "She's only going to be nine and not always too careful with her things. What if she loses it?"

"Then she loses it," replied David matter-of-factly. "It had such a lovely simple elegance about it, I decided I must buy it for Merritt— no matter the cost."

"You're a good man, David Hall," said Lavinia, kissing him warmly, "and a wonderful daddy. Merritt will love the gift. I know she will."

Lavinia Hall smiled at her husband, knowing his generosity had no bounds. So different from his own father.

Jim Hall never gave his son David a cent he didn't have to give him. And much of what he should have given him for essentials like clothes and food, he withheld. "You work for it," had been his directive to his young son.

So work he did.

By the time David Hall was thirty-five years old, he presided over the largest publishing empire in the country. The printed word ran in his blood, started as a boy when he stood shivering on the street corners of Hayden, peddling the *Hayden Press* to shop owners hustling off to ready their stores just as the sun was starting to color the eastern skies.

David used remnants of his daily supply of newspapers to line his boots in the winter, to keep his feet further from the holes always a part of the shoes his father would bring home to him from God only knows where, when David's growing-boy feet could absolutely no longer squeeze into the last holey pair. And he wadded papers to

11

fill cracks around his window in the attic room he called his own in the old ramshackle house where he lived with his father, mother, and five sisters for the first fifteen years of his life.

But his industriousness did not go unnoticed. Although only a boy, David Hall was given tagalong assignments—told to accompany "Big Jack" when he was assigned to cover news at the police station, or to shadow Elmore Horn when the paper's chief reporter had a big lead.

David knew as much about the newspaper business as anyone at the offices of the *Hayden Press* before he reached the age of twenty, and although he never finished high school, he made just the right moves at just the right time. Before his thirtieth birthday, David Hall was the wealthiest newspaper-publishing mogul in the U.S. Before his fortieth, he was one of the ten wealthiest men in the country.

And he shared his wealth generously.

As Merritt carefully removed the small gold cross surrounded by tiny gold carved leaves and tinier-still gold flowers from its box, her eyes shone with delight. "Oh, Daddy, it's so beautiful. I've never seen anything so beautiful."

"Here, honey, let me clasp it around your neck for you," offered her mother as the children—and even some of the adults—"oohed" and "aahed" as she lifted the chain with its cross from the box.

With the chain firmly clasped around Merritt's small slender neck, she walked around the table and let each of her guests examine the piece. When she reached her father at the far end of the table, she jumped into his arms and hugged him with all the strength a nine-year-old could muster.

"I love it, Daddy. I'm going to keep it on forever."

Apparently, she really intended to do so. Only with a great deal of coaxing could Merritt be persuaded to remove her treasured gift at the end of the day.

"Here, honey, let's just lay it in this little glass dish by your bedside. You don't want it to get all dull from your bath," explained her mother. "It'll be here for you to put on first thing every morning."

"Well, all right," relented the child. "I don't want to make it un-shiny. It's just so beautiful," she said again, gently touching the cross as her mother placed it in a small crystal dish on top of the bedside table.

Since that day, just one month ago, Merritt had carefully clasped the chain around her neck first thing in the morning. Some nights she couldn't bear not having it close to her, so she wore the cross and chain to bed, clutching it often in her sleep. Just as she clutched it now, thinking again about her birthday.

Then she heard Sister sigh. A really big sigh.

Sister Mary Margaret placed her hand on Merritt's shoulder, firmly, but not unkindly. "What are we going to do about you, child?"

"Who's 'we,' Sister?"

"You know very well, Merritt. Me. Your teachers. The 'we' who don't always understand why you say the things you do. Especially since it so often gets you into trouble."

"Am I in trouble now, Sister? Just because I didn't agree with Sister Alice!" she exclaimed incredulously. "How can I agree with her if what she says doesn't seem to me to be true? How can I, Sister?"

Sister Mary Margaret didn't answer. She turned her back to the child and looked out the tall floor-to-ceiling window framed in dark wine-colored draperies someone long ago deemed appropriate for the office of the principal of such a prestigious school as St. Agnes Academy. The window faced a beautiful garden filled with the colors of a wide array of blooming botanical masterpieces flanking walkways the students at St. Agnes had favored for three generations. Two of the older girls were walking there now, along with one of the teachers.

But Mary Margaret wasn't seeing the garden, or the girls, or the teacher. She was seeing herself. Long before she was principal. Long before she was Sister Mary Margaret—and she flinched with the memory.

She had been Callie McDowell then. Mischievous and fun-loving. Her long black tresses flying as she ran, which she did most of the time, and her bright green eyes snapping with challenge when something—or someone—stood in her way.

That's how Callie was before the accident—the accident that took away her mother and father and changed her life forever.

"Stop running, Callie Marie, right now!" ordered her aunt. "It isn't right that you should behave like a wild banshee with your mother and father just buried. You ought to be ashamed of yourself!

"I can't imagine what my sister was thinking letting you run wild like you do. I'll have you acting like a proper lady in no time, however. For starters, I've enrolled you in St. Agnes Academy. There you'll be with young ladies who are your own kind instead of spending

13

so much time with these—these urchins who always seem to find you."

She said the last nodding toward the door where she had just escorted out two of her niece's friends and sent them on their way.

"Aunt Grace, I don't want to go to St. Agnes. I want to go to Hillsdale just like I always have. And Jimmy and Laura aren't 'urchins.' They're my best friends."

She was so angry her green eyes seemed to spark, and bright spots of red burned on her cheeks.

"You *will* go to St. Agnes, and you'll do exactly as I say. Your permissive father isn't around anymore to encourage your freethinking ways. As granddaughter of Horace Laughlin, you have a position in life to uphold, you know. You're certainly a step above—several steps above—these so-called friends of yours."

"I don't believe that, Aunt Grace, and I don't believe it's right for you to say it. I'm not going to let you make a snob out of me. The family doesn't need another one. You're snobbish enough for all of us."

With that pronouncement, she turned to flee from the room. But not before Grace Laughlin grabbed the arm of her teenaged niece and slapped her across the face so hard it sent Callie reeling.

That memory caused Callie McDowell, known for over forty years as Sister Mary Margaret, to flinch as she brought her hand instinctively to her face. The memory pained her still today.

"Sister? Sister, are you all right?" questioned young Merritt with concern, noting the distress on her principal's face.

Merritt's voice broke Sister Mary Margaret's reverie. It also broke her resolve to discipline this child—this child who would never be a conformist, never cease to challenge. This child with such a strong sense of what was right. Who even now expressed concern, not for herself, but for her principal, who apparently was showing the pain she was reliving.

"I'm fine, dear," she said softly, again placing her hand on the child's shoulder.

Merritt looked up at her with her wide lavender eyes. *Such wisdom and intelligence in those eyes*, Sister Mary Margaret thought. *So far beyond her years. Where did such a young girl gain so much depth? I'll probably never know, but I do know I'm not going to be the one to stand in her way.*

14

She sat down in a chair facing Merritt and met her direct gaze. "I'm going to ask you to do something for me, Mimi," she said, using the name she had heard Merritt's friends call her. It made the little girl smile. She liked Sister Mary Margaret and would be only too happy to do something for her.

"It's really just one thing with—let's see—one thing with three parts. First, I'd like you to apologize to Sister Alice for disagreeing with her so openly in class. Wait now until you hear the rest," she added, holding up her hand to silence the child, who had begun to frown and was about to voice an objection. "The apology. That needs to be taken care of so you can go back to class and get on with your learning.

"The second part—this is very important for my job as principal here. Please, please try to state your opinions with a little less arguing. You can disagree a bit more discreetly, Merritt. I know you can if you try. It isn't necessary to be so belligerent—so angry—about everything. Just make your position known and *listen* to the other person's viewpoint.

"And third, don't *ever* let anyone talk you out of standing up for what you believe to be right. Do you think you can do that three-part favor for me, child?"

Merritt had begun smiling again as soon as Sister told her to stand up for what she believed was right. She bounced off the chair, almost tipping it over in her exuberance.

"Sure. I can do that. I *will* do that. I really don't like the idea of apologizing to Sister Alice, but I'll do it anyway. Just for you.

"But what's *discreetly* mean? I know what it means not to act so angry and to listen better. I just don't know about discreetly."

Sister Mary Margaret smiled and blinked back tears. How this child got to her. Maybe it was because she knew if she had ever had a daughter, she would have hoped she would be a feisty one like Merritt Hall.

"As long as you understand what I meant by not getting so angry and doing a better job of listening, I think you'll do just fine. I'll explain *discreetly* another time.

"It's our agreement then?" She offered her hand to Merritt, and the child clasped it, excitedly nodding her agreement. Not exactly a hand-shaking contract between two business-minded adults, but almost.

"Now back to class, young lady."

"Yes, Sister."

With a skip and a smile, Merritt rejoined her fellow fourth-graders in learning—and in challenging all obstacles that came her way.

Chapter Two

In reality, obstacles for Merritt Hall were minimal. She was, after all, the only child of a wealthy family—bright and beautiful. She whizzed through all twelve grades at St. Agnes with top honors and graduated from the University of Michigan *summa cum laude*.

Her next academic challenge was medical school.

Merritt had decided she would be a doctor when, as a small child, she watched a veterinarian seemingly bring back to life her adored cat, Fluffy, who had tangled unsuccessfully with the neighborhood German Shepherd.

The child was devastated when she saw the mass of blood-covered gray fur. To make it worse, Merritt was engulfed in guilt because she was the one who had left the door open and allowed her cat—which never went outside and was certainly not up to the conquest of a dog ten times its size—to disappear across the spacious lawn in front of her home.

But instead of succumbing to her fear for her pet and what seemed to her parents to be an inevitable outcome, she insisted on taking Fluffy to the vet *and* to watching as Dr. Williams struggled to save the small cat's life.

"You'd better wait in the waiting room, honey," suggested Dr. Williams, nodding towards the well-furnished room where there were books to read and toys to divert young pet-owners' minds from their worries.

Dr. Sam Williams was a very kind man and had genuine concern for the children who lavished so much love on their pets. His warm brown eyes reflected his caring as his large hands gently probed the injuries of the small gray feline, its weak mewing barely audible.

David Hall tried to usher his daughter out to the waiting room as the doctor suggested, but she'd have no part of it.

"Please, Daddy, Fluffy's mine, and you told me it was up to me to take care of her. And I didn't," she said with a sob, tears streaming down her face.

"Sweetheart, it was an accident. You probably should have watched her more carefully when you opened the door, but accidents happen. Dr. Williams will do all he can for her, you know that."

"I know he will, but Fluffy needs me in here. She'll be better if I'm here. How can I learn to be a really good doctor if I run away from hurt?"

David looked at Sam Williams and shrugged. "I guess we stay," he said with resignation.

"Okay, David.

"So you plan to be a doctor, huh Merritt? A vet?" he asked, hoping that engaging the child in conversation would help take her mind off watching Fluffy die before her eyes.

"I'm not sure yet. Maybe. Or I might want to be a people doctor."

"Well, I guess you have a few years to decide," he said with a smile as he continued his healing efforts.

Merritt didn't say another word—just watched, silently crying, her father's hand gently resting on her shoulder.

Miraculously, Fluffy didn't die. Dr. Williams' efforts were indeed lifesaving, and Merritt enjoyed the companionship of her pet for many more years.

She never wavered in her determination to be a doctor, and for some time she was certain she'd be a veterinarian and save small children from broken hearts—just as Dr. Williams had done for her. But long before she was ready for medical school, she decided upon being a "people doctor," a family physician.

Merritt was accepted into Harvard Medical School. And there she met Barry Davis.

Merritt and Barry met in a study group and were instantly attracted to one another. Both newcomers to the group, each sat on opposite sides of the periphery, brows furrowed with concentration as questions bounced about the room.

"Okay now," said Stephen Nitzkowski, organizer of the group, "does everyone know everyone else? You really need to know whose brain you want to pick. Now for the new ones. That's Donald Masterson over there—better known as 'Dooley,'" he said, nodding towards a tall bespectacled young man sitting by the wall, his chair tilted back precariously. Dooley and the others in the group exchanged nods of introduction.

"And that's Merritt Hall," said Stephen, nodding towards the other newcomer to their midst. Merritt smiled and nodded in return. "You two, make a point of meeting the others," advised Stephen. "Trust me—you'll need them."

Stephen was a third-year medical student and knew how vital the study groups were to surviving the rigors of medical school.

Barry Davis had been introduced to the group the previous week, so as soon as the two hurried introductions were made, the group delved into the mysteries of the circulatory system, their topic for the day. Names of veins and arteries rapidly replaced the names of the group's participants.

Merritt was quiet that first day, her head bent over her notes as she wrote extensively, recording answers to questions the group members tossed at one another. She did as Stephen suggested, however, and made her way around the room as the group disbanded for the day, meeting the other members, her mind whirling with countless bits of information.

She shook hands and smiled, gathering names she hoped she'd recall the next session.

One hand didn't release hers immediately as did the others, who hurried to be on their way. "Hi, I'm Barry Davis," said the voice that went with the firm-gripping hand. "Could I interest you in a cup of coffee?"

"I really shouldn't. I'm so bogged down in the books, sometimes I feel like I'll never stay caught up." Merritt smiled warmly at this tall handsome young man who was still holding her hand tightly in his, thinking, even as she was explaining why she really shouldn't take the time to join him for a cup of coffee—*I'd really like to get to know him. Darn these books, and double darn the professors. These assignments border on impossible!*

"C'mon. The coffee will help keep you awake for hours of studying. I'll tell you what; I'll throw in the price of a ham sandwich. You can't study without nourishment. And if you say, 'yes,' I'll even let go of your hand."

Merritt had to laugh at his persistence, enjoying his attention. "Okay, it's a deal. I need a very big sandwich, though, because I have very big mound of reading to digest yet tonight. And thanks for the return of my hand."

So arm in arm, Merritt Hall and Barry Davis stole away for the first of many hours together. Theirs was a whirlwind romance—when the demands of medical school allowed it to be a romance at all.

Merritt adored Barry's rugged handsomeness, his blue eyes that sparkled when he laughed, his mass of wavy auburn hair, his endearing smile, and his tall athletic body. Barry Davis had been a track star at Notre Dame, and his tall, lithe frame was firm and disciplined.

19

For Barry, it was love at first sight. He was overjoyed that this lovely young woman's personality was just as delightful as her appearance. Merritt had never lost the charm she had as a child—nor the spunk, the determination Sister Mary Margaret had so admired. Barry admired it, too. That and her brilliance.

Barry Davis thought Merritt Hall was the most incredibly beautiful woman he had ever seen. Her unruly brown hair and full-lipped smile—and those lavender-gray eyes! Barry had never seen eyes like Merritt's.

Merritt's small stature belied her strength. She handled the demands and rigors of medical school without faltering. If more studying was required, then that's what she did. Sleep scarcely seemed a necessity.

Sometimes Barry was overwhelmed with it all. But not Merritt. She had an uncanny ability to stay focused and march steadily towards her goal.

During their third year of medical school, in the fall, doctors-to-be Merritt Hall and Barry Davis were married at a small ceremony in the chapel on the campus of St. Agnes Academy, with only family and close friends attending. Following the ceremony conducted by Father Patrick O'Hanlon, Barry's former roommate at Notre Dame, the couple stole away for a brief weekend honeymoon.

It was all they had time for before rejoining their fellow classmates in their challenging duties on Monday morning.

Chapter Three

After what sometimes seemed like a lifetime to both, Drs. Merritt and Barry Davis opened their practices—hers as a general physician, his as a surgeon. Their lives were busy and hectic—and incredibly happy.

No matter how demanding their schedules, no matter how tired each was when the last patient was seen, they found time for each other. Quality time. Time that gave substance to their love for one another.

Just when it seemed as if they couldn't possibly be any happier, little Megan Marie Davis was born.

Now they were truly a family.

Megan was a delightful child, doted upon by both her parents, but possessing a naturally charming and sunny disposition. Her small round face, framed with auburn curls like her father's, was usually brightened by smiles. Her lavender-gray eyes would sparkle with happiness when her parents entered the room.

Sometimes when Merritt closely held the small body of her child, it seemed she would burst with love.

Megan's extended family was small; there were only her maternal grandparents, David and Lavinia Hall. Merritt and Barry had no siblings, and Barry's parents had both died very young. Merritt had cousins, children of David Hall's sisters, but only two lived close enough to visit, and that seemed to be only during the holidays.

But lack of family members didn't diminish the attention little Megan received. David and Lavinia both cherished the child, and their gifts were boundless. Merritt feared their home would be totally overtaken by stuffed animals and dolls.

"No more, Dad. I mean it," ordered Merritt, begging her father to curtail his generosity. "I've already taken a car full to the children's ward at the hospital a couple of times."

"It's so hard not to buy for her, honey. I love to hear her laugh and squeal when I pull some new toy out a bag. She's just so darned adorable," he said as he tossed his laughing granddaughter into the air and caught her firmly, hugging her tightly.

"That she is," agreed Merritt, patting her daughter's auburn curls, which were resting against her grandfather's chest, "but let's limit the gifts. Okay? Promise?" she added as he nodded. "You'll spoil her rotten."

"I did the same with you, honey, and you didn't turn out so bad."

Merritt laughed as she said, "Maybe, but even you have to admit I was pretty well spoiled."

"No you weren't—you were perfect."

When Merritt said good-bye to her father that day of their friendly banter about his overindulging the two-and-one-half-year-old Megan, it turned out to be their final good-bye. Three days later, David Hall was killed when his plane went down over the Atlantic. There were no survivors. Nor did anyone have a clue why the airplane crashed. It was there in the sky flying its predetermined flight plan one moment and gone the next.

David Hall left millions to his wife and daughter, and a flourishing publishing empire to two of his sisters. He had been a very wealthy and generous man—an exemplary husband and father. Now he was gone, leaving his wife and daughter enmeshed in grief.

Not long after Merritt said good-bye to her father for the last time, she began to have headaches, severe headaches, similar to some she had experienced earlier in her life—but of greater severity and longer duration.

The headaches changed Merritt, and the life of the family that had seemed, for a short while, the ideal family, spiraled down and down until shattered spirits and broken hearts replaced happiness.

***

Barry sat across the breakfast table from Merritt, watching his wife, her lovely eyes veiled in pain, her hands on her temples, applying pressure, circling around and around.

The early morning sun bounced off the white walls, filling the entire room with a brightness that was almost ethereal—a contradiction to the grayness of the mood pervading the home of the young couple.

Barry sipped his coffee while watching, worrying—almost feeling her pain, it was so strong. Merritt's coffee remained untouched. Neither of them said a word. The only sound was the playful chattering of Megan as she sat in her Jenny Lind high chair, spooning her oatmeal into her small round mouth to the best of her young-child ability.

Suddenly the quiet was broken by the "clang, clang" of Megan's spoon on the tray of her high chair.

"Megan, stop that!" screamed her mother.

Megan, not accustomed to having her mother shout at her, began to wail loudly. Barry quickly removed his crying daughter from her high chair and carried her into the playroom, gently hushing her cries.

"Shh, honey, it's okay. Mommy's just not feeling well. She didn't mean to shout at you." He sat in the rocking chair at the edge of the colorful braided rug that covered the center of the room, and holding his young daughter close, he rocked back and forth, continuing with his soothing sounds as he rocked. Soon Megan's cries ceased.

When Megan was happily playing with her dolls, Barry left her in the care of Katie Brady, the young woman recently hired to care for her while he and Merritt were at their respective offices. Megan adored Katie, and soon her little-girl giggles were ringing off the walls of the warm and colorful nursery.

Barry stopped in the doorway to the breakfast nook and watched his wife. Her head was on the table, nestled on her folded arms. The wall clock ticked its measured cadence, the only sound breaking the silence hanging over the room like an unwelcome shroud.

"Merritt," he began, "We need . . ."

"Do it, Barry. Just do it."

"Do what? What is it you want me to do?" asked Barry as he sat down beside her, lines of concern etching his face. "Honey, what's happening to you?"

Merritt raised her head and looked squarely at her husband. In a voice so soft, it was almost a whisper, she said, "I don't know, Barry, but I'm scared. And so ashamed. I just screamed at my own baby." Her voice cracked as she said the last, and large tears rolled down her cheeks and splashed on the table. "How could I, Barry? What kind of a monster am I?"

"Honey, you're no monster," comforted Barry as he wrapped her tightly in his arms. Merritt's entire frame shook with deep rending sobs. "Listen, Merritt. Megan's okay. She understands her mommy isn't feeling very well this morning. Right now, she's in the nursery playing with Katie as if nothing happened. She'll forget the whole thing within the hour—I'm sure of it."

"But we need to take care of you. What is it that you want me to do?"

Merritt pulled back from her husband's embrace and again looked directly into his eyes. "Call Dr. Gustave Halverson at the Meadow Lawn Psychiatric Center.

"Sit down, Barry, I want to tell you something about me nobody knows. Except maybe my mother. And she denies it."

Merritt took Barry's strong warm hand in hers, and again tears welled up in her eyes. "I hear voices, Barry—frightening voices."

Barry again enfolded her in his arms as she quietly sobbed.

"Shhh, shhh, honey. It'll be okay. We'll find someone to help you—this Dr. Halverson, if that's whom you think you need. You're still grieving over your father's death, that's all. It was a God-awful shock to all of us, but it must have been terrible for you."

Still hiccupping with her swallowed sobs, Merritt nodded, appearing to agree with Barry in his assumption that her father's death precipitated her current state. She didn't tell her husband that she had heard the voices before—a long time before David Hall had taken his ill-fated flight.

That first time, years ago when she was in college, was still fresh in her memory—the first time the voices had haunted her, and she felt she was on the brink of madness.

***

Merritt stared at the wall seeing nothing. Then she closed her eyes. Tightly. That's when she saw them. The nightmarish figures that went with the voices. Quickly she opened her eyes, and their lavender-grayness again stared at the wall.

Merritt preferred the nothingness. She was only a girl, a college junior, and was terrified by what was happening to her.

Why am I seeing things, hearing things? I have never been so afraid. Oh, how I wish Daddy were here. But I don't dare ask Mother to send for him. I don't want to have to tell her about the visions, the voices. It would frighten her too much—just like they frighten me. Please, God, don't let me be losing my mind.

Merritt fought back tears of terror, and she choked on a sob.

"Merritt honey, the doctors agree you've just been working too hard," said her mother. "You really don't need to push yourself so, you know. It's okay if you're not first in everything. You are just trying to do too much."

Lavinia gently touched her daughter's hair, smoothing back the brown curls tumbling across the stark-white hospital pillow. "Aren't

24

the flowers gorgeous," she said, nodding towards a huge bouquet of lilacs and daffodils that covered the top of the dresser across from Merritt's bed.

Merritt turned her head towards the voice of her mother and forced a smile. A pair of tears escaped and slid slowly down her cheeks on to the pillow—on to its white crispness smelling mildly of disinfectant.

"Why the tears, Merritt? Don't you understand? You're going to be okay."

Lavinia Hall's voice choked with the last statement, and she had to struggle to hold back her own tears.

The doctors had indeed said her daughter had a breakdown because she overloaded herself with far too much work. Both her mind and body had simply collapsed. The consensus of the pooled expertise of the medical group was that young Merritt Hall, a brilliant and dedicated pre-med student, would soon recover fully.

This is what Lavinia told Merritt's father when he called from London, where he was negotiating a major publishing agreement. Frantic, he was ready to take the next flight home until Lavinia and Doctor Harold Morrison, whom he trusted implicitly, informed him his only child was the victim of overwork and would soon be her old exuberant self.

It was eighteen months after her "breakdown" that Merritt met Barry Davis. There had been no sign of any problems for so long—no nightmares, no voices—that she, too, was convinced her collapse had been nothing more than overwork. Overwork and her innate intensity.

With Barry in her life, she had seemed to be able to do even more with no adverse affects.

***

Barry phoned his office and Merritt's, leaving messages for Merritt's secretary that Dr. Hall-Davis was ill, and she'd need to reschedule appointments. He told his secretary and "right-hand-man," Mary Blake, that he'd be running late. "Do the best you can, Mary. I have surgery scheduled for 1:30 this afternoon, and *that* I plan to make. I think this morning I only have a couple of follow-ups, is that right? Great," he said as Mary confirmed his recollections. "Ask Hy Matthews if he would take them for me. Tell him I'll return the favor anytime. Thanks, Mary. Don't know what I'd do without you," said

Barry.

Mary Blake knew he meant what he said. He was a great boss, always appreciative, and she had been able to tell he was really troubled about something of late. About what, she had no idea.

Next Barry called Dr. Halverson. The doctor agreed to see Merritt that morning.

Dr. Gustave Halverson had known Merritt's parents, and Merritt remembered that David Hall held the doctor in high regard. "Gus is the best there is in his field," her father had declared. "He has a remarkable balance of an incredible comprehension of the mysteries of the human mind and an overflowing amount of compassion."

Barry, too, had heard David's praises of the doctor and knew Halverson was exactly whom he wanted for his distraught wife, a feeling confirmed as he sat across from him in a room that seemed more like a den in someone's home than a psychiatrist's office. It was homey—clean but mildly disheveled. Just like Dr. Halverson himself.

Professional journals lay scattered on a pale-oak coffee table—a piece of furniture like newlyweds might pick up at a second-hand store to furnish their first apartment. Open books lay on his desk next to a pile of yellow lined writing pads. A large Philodendron, its leaves curling downward as if begging for water, sat on the table next to the chair where Dr. Halverson was seated.

The short gray-haired doctor sat forward on the brown leather chair, his feet stretched out in front of him. He held a note pad in his lap, scribbling a few words while never taking his eyes from the young couple seated on the brown leather sofa across from him. Barry was amazed at this feat, Dr. Halverson's ability to write while never looking at his writing.

Gus Halverson quickly summed up what he saw—a distraught young woman, her eyes glistening with unshed tears, eyes swollen and red from tears shed earlier. Her hands were clasped tightly in her lap. Every inch of her body spoke of the tension torturing her. Next to her sat her young husband, lines of concern marring his handsome face.

Barry Davis towered over Gus Halverson, who was barely half-a-head taller than Merritt. The doctor had taken a step back to look into Barry's eyes as they shook hands following their introduction, and Gus liked what he saw. Warmth and compassion. *This is a good man, and he loves his beautiful and vulnerable young wife. Good! I have a feeling she needs it.*

"I was so terribly sorry to hear of your father's death, Merritt. David Hall was such a fine man—and a good friend." Merritt just nodded in agreement, knowing that words would cause the inevitable tears to start anew.

"And how is your mother doing?"

"Not too well," said Merritt, her voice quiet and husky. "She seems to be having a lot of trouble accepting the fact that he's gone." She gulped the word "gone" in a half-sob, and Barry tightened his grasp around her shoulders.

For a moment, Dr. Halverson watched her struggle with her emotions, her pain, then he spoke in his soft gentle voice. "Tell me about it, Merritt—tell me about your hurt."

Openly sobbing now, enfolded in Barry's arms, she gave the heart-rending account of how she was a horrible mother, screaming at her baby, of how terribly tired she was, how she couldn't sleep— and of the voices. The horrible voices.

Dr. Halverson listened without a word. At times, he would jot down a few words on his writing pad—never taking his eyes off Merritt. When finally her outpouring ended and her sobs lessened, he reached over and took her small slender hands, clasping them in his large ones. "Merritt, first, you need rest. I'm going to suggest we admit you to the hospital—a small hospital over in Lodenberg where you'll be away from your own patients and fellow doctors. Just a week for rest and evaluation. You're grieving, child, and I'm guessing that you're keeping too busy to let it run its course."

"But I can't do that, Dr. Halverson," she argued—forgetting the doctor's request that they call him "Gus." "I'm a doctor, and I have responsibilities to my patients. I can't just disappear."

"You won't be disappearing, honey," reasoned Barry. "Marsha will call your patients. You know she'll be glad to. I know you have responsibilities to your patients, but how about your responsibility to yourself, Mimi?"

"And to this young man, who obviously loves you very much," added the doctor, "and that wonderful little girl you've been telling me about."

So with reluctant resignation, Merritt agreed to a week at the hospital in the small neighboring town of Lodenberg—a week that stretched into two. The stay left Merritt rested, with new coping skills and medications to help her deal with her grief, her exhaustion—and the voices.

Merritt again went at her life with vigor—and a new peace. A peace that, unfortunately, was not long lasting. A year later, almost to the day, she was again so distraught, she went to see Dr. Halverson. This time he admitted her to the Meadow Lawn Psychiatric Center. She stayed one month. She then declared herself "well" and would not stay another day.

Chapter Four

How ironic that Merritt's only remaining parent had, herself, parted with reality. Lavinia Hall simply couldn't get over her husband's death. Although she had once beautifully fulfilled the role of society hostess, as she was called upon to do as the wife of the wealthy David Hall when he was alive, she so totally succumbed to her grief that she never again hosted or attended any social function. Including those involving her family or the managers of her late-husband's publishing empire.

Lavinia became so withdrawn that she ceased to care for herself and her home. Her increasingly secluded lifestyle eventually seemed to affect her mind. After months of escalating deterioration, Merritt had no choice but to place her mother in a nursing home. An excellent nursing home—one with all the accoutrements anyone could have hoped for, as well as the finest staff possible. The best care money could buy.

But if Lavinia was aware of the change in her surroundings, she certainly didn't indicate it. She went through the robotic lifestyle she had become accustomed to in the months since her husband's death—since life, as she had known it, ended.

She spoke little, expressing only the minutest of needs. Most of her days she sat knitting—knitting the same pink bootie over and over. As she finished it, she savagely ripped out the stitches and started over again.

The nurses and attendants were uneasy about Lavinia's knitting needles when they saw the anger in her face the first time she tore apart the small pink bootie with such vengeance. But once the yarn was again rolled into a tightly wound ball, Lavinia would exude the same calm and peaceful childlike countenance they were accustomed to seeing on Mrs. David Hall. So when Merritt pleaded with the staff to let her mother continue with her pointless knitting, they acquiesced—on the condition that she knit only where she could be closely supervised. Merritt agreed.

***

Merritt's head pounded fiercely. She wished the noise outside would stop—begged that it would stop. Maybe if it did, the noises bouncing around inside her skull would cease.

But the clinic was never quiet. Located in the center of the city, it was surrounded by the constant hub-bub of traffic and activity.

Merritt sat down at her desk and buried her head in her hands, massaging her temples, fingers applying pressure, around and around. But the throbbing continued.

The voices continued.

They will never stop. I will hear these voices telling me what a horrible person I am until the day I die. Everywhere I turn, there they are—screaming loudly at me. I will never have peace.

She laid her head down on her desk and softly sobbed. Tendrils of soft brown hair sparsely laced with gray lay beneath her face and absorbed her copious tears. Her shoulders shook with her sobs, shoulders clothed in mauve silk, hanging loosely on her too-thin frame.

The room was bare and old. Faded and water-streaked paper covered the walls. The pattern had probably been pretty once, but now was a non-descript design of a non-descript color, streaked with rusty brown stains where water had trickled down through the leaky roof.

The only decoration on the wall was her medical diploma. "Merritt Lavinia Hall, M.D.," it read. Her credentials to practice medicine—credentials surrounded by a solid-walnut frame edged with a narrow fluting of gold. Real gold. Such an elegant frame, so out of place in this old deteriorating building.

Merritt recalled when her father had her diploma framed. He took it to St. Louis to a shop specializing in fine solid-wood frames.

Specializing in expensive.

"Daddy, it's just a piece of paper. It's not what's going to make me a good doctor," she had protested.

Merritt had been an exemplary student. She earned one of the finest scholastic records ever at St. Agnes and was a straight A-student during her college years. She graduated in the top five percent of her class at Harvard Medical School.

David Hall was very proud of his daughter's accomplishments. He just knew she was going to be a great doctor. And since he couldn't declare it to the entire world, he could at least surround her credentials with the best frame money could buy.

Since money was something David Hall had in abundance, nothing brought him more pleasure than spending it on his only child.

He was going to miss that. Spending money on Merritt. She announced when she graduated from medical school that she'd take no more.

Her parents' generosity had allowed her to go to the best schools, created top-notch opportunities for her. But she was married now, and she and Barry were both full-fledged physicians, hoping to be *well-known* physicians some day. She felt it was now time to stake her claim as an adult—to take on the full responsibility for her own life and that of her family, to take care of her own financial needs.

And so she did. That is, until she became heiress to a fortune.

Even today, surrounded by the squalor of the storefront clinic, Merritt could envision her father, handsome and powerful. She still missed him. Always would. She wondered if he were still alive, would she tell him about the voices? Would she tell him she was afraid she was losing her mind?

Merritt's hand closed around the small cross hanging about her neck. She clutched it so tightly, the edges dug into her hand, leaving ugly red marks. She lifted her head from the desk and looked blankly out the window.

A steady rain had begun to fall, and the wind blew sheets of it against the window in a repeated rat-a-tat-tat. An intermittent ping joined the chorus, as water dripping through the leaky roof found its way to the metal pan she had placed beneath the most pronounced of the many spots needing fixing in this seemingly God-forsaken building.

The huge drops of rain gliding down the windows were like tears. *I wonder why the world is crying?* she asked herself.

Merritt again lay her head down on the desk, cradling it in her arms. So still was she that any observer might have thought she was sleeping.

The loud ringing of the phone broke the rhythm of the rat-a-tat and ping, startling her. She raised her pain-wracked head from her desk and reached for it.

"Dr. Hall," she said in a voice husky with pain and exhaustion. She tensed as she heard the words delivered by the messenger on the other end of the line. Quick tears flooded her eyes. Tears of sadness.

The news grieved her but didn't surprise her.

Her mother had died.

Lavinia Hall had been fading monthly, if not weekly, so when

31

she quietly died of natural causes in her sleep, no one was terribly surprised. Not her caretakers and not Merritt. Lavinia had begun to die when her husband's plane sunk in the frigid waters of the Atlantic.

It just took a while for her death to reach completion.

Chapter Five

Lavinia Hall wished for only a quiet graveside service. She had made her desires known to her daughter years before. Merritt granted her wish.

Like most of the mornings of late, the sky was secluded by haze—as if the heavy dew of the night was being sucked up into a blanket to be pulled back up into the heavens as the day advanced. Merritt shivered as the damp chill inched its way through her body.

She felt a hand grasp hers and knew before she looked up that he had come. How good Barry's hand felt as he clasped her cold clammy hand in his. Doctor Barry Davis. Her husband.

She smiled a moment, remembering how concerned they had been about Dr. Davis and Dr. Davis, concerned their patients would be too confused. So she had retained her maiden name—at least professionally. She had remained Dr. Merritt Hall.

"Thanks for coming, Barry," she said, looking up at him, forcing a weak smile.

"Lavinia was my mother-in-law, Mimi. I loved her—just as I loved you. Just as I love you still."

Pain was evident in his voice as he said it, and he clasped her hand even more tightly. Merritt looked down, unable to face the hurt in his kind eyes the color of a summer sky, afraid she'd give way to the tears she was just barely keeping under control.

Clinging to Barry's other hand was Meggie. Young Megan Davis with the same lavender-hued eyes as her mother, eyes now downcast, kicking softly at the dirt patches surrounding the plot where her grandmother was about to be buried.

Oh, Meggie, how I long to take you in my arms, thought Merritt. *I love you so. How did it end this way?*

But she knew the answer to her own question. A child terrorized by her mother's outbursts, her mother sitting with her head in her hands, sobbing and screaming, "Please make them stop, please, please. It hurts so."

A child too young to understand.

"But Mommy, there's no one here. No one's hurting you." Sobbing herself—choking, heart breaking little-girl sobs.

Helpless to aid her mother, Megan became afraid of her—ran from her, from her touch. Months of nightmares when she awoke

33

screaming in terror, followed by tearful promises from her mother that it wouldn't happen again, promises that were always broken, left the once outgoing happy-go-lucky little girl shy, serious, and fearful.

Barry was torn between the little girl both he and Merritt loved so deeply, the baby they had hoped for and treasured, and his wife.

The once brilliant and stellar Dr. Merritt Hall.

But it wasn't only for her brilliance that he loved her so. It was for her depth, her intense passion for everything she encountered. And her compassion. Merritt's compassion was evident to every patient she treated, whether the very wealthy or the very needy. They could see the caring and concern in her eyes.

But what Barry loved most about Merritt was her commitment to what she believed to be right. When there was a cause that needed support—or her voice—she was there heart and soul. It became *her* cause. And she never relinquished her stand, no matter what the opposition.

She could be unyielding, but gentle. Incredibly gentle. She was the gentlest physician he had ever seen. And the most gentle parent.

Until her wild outbursts and ravings so terrified Megan that she ran from her mother and hid when she heard her approach.

Barry was caught in the middle. If only Merritt would seek help. She surely knew, just as he did, that something was terribly, terribly wrong. That she was ill—ill in a very confusing and frightening way. Barry knew she could be helped. Dr. Gus Halverson had helped her so much. Barry thought he was wonderful, and so had Merritt—at the time.

But now Merritt would have no part of it.

"Dr. Halverson isn't going to be able to help me, Barry. I'm beyond help. I'm not going to have him tell me I'm going insane. I am smart enough to figure that out for myself!" she screamed at him, as she fled from the room and from the house when Barry begged her to seek help.

That time she didn't return for three days.

Barry had even threatened to forcibly commit her, force her to go through the myriad of tests she needed, tests that could result in answers to why this brilliant physician seemed, at times, to be a hysterical madwoman.

But he couldn't go through with it. Couldn't bear the thought of his wife being forcibly restrained, robbed of her independence. So he would hold her, shaking and sobbing, until she wore herself into an exhausted sleep.

Sleep that sometimes lasted for days.

Although he didn't understand Merritt's reticence to seek help, he always gave in to it. After all, there were still good times, treasured good times.

***

Before long, however, the good times were only in their memories.

Merritt's life as a prominent physician ended. First she lost her privileges at the hospital, and then, her practice folded. Her patients couldn't depend on her. Some even came to fear her.

It was a sad heartbreaking day when Dr. Merritt Hall closed the door to her office for the last time. Cartons filled with her belongings had already been packed and were on their way to her fashionable home in Melville Heights. Home. Where she lived with her husband and daughter.

But this had been home, too. This was where she cared for the sick she had grown to love. And she loved them all, even Mrs. Culpepper, who flatly refused to follow the diet Merritt prescribed again and again. Instead, Ada Culpepper came to the office regularly, her puffy gray-tinged face twisted in agony, her chronic gastritis fighting the exotic highly spiced foods she just couldn't seem to leave alone.

Merritt's eyes strayed to the long wall opposite her desk. The pale-blue paint had faded slightly, just enough to outline the various-sized rectangles where, until three days ago, framed photographs had hung—photos of those who were so dear to her.

Many pictures of Megan had adorned the wall, the wall that now looked as empty as she felt. Megan with her large lavender eyes and irresistible little-girl smile. There had been a picture of Barry, as well as one of her and Barry together on their first wedding anniversary.

It was her favorite photo, taken on a skiing trip. Although the photograph showed them carrying their skis, the snow glistening brilliantly beneath the cloudless sky, they had spent most of that holiday in the chalet. Just the two of them, loving the privacy of being alone together.

There were other photos, too. Others whom she loved. It had always been so comforting to her when, on a particularly hectic day, her eyes would stray to her wall of photos, and she would feel renewed strength.

Strength that sometimes encouraged her to push herself far beyond what would have been normal human endurance.

But there were times when she gained no renewal from her photos. Times when nothing could encourage her. Times when nothing could calm her.

In those instances, her agitation reigned, and she would rail at her patients, causing them to vow never to return, or at her nurses, driving them to tears and, eventually, driving them to accept positions with other physicians.

Sometimes she would collapse in tears—uncontrollable tears. Then her receptionist and dear friend, Marsha Givens, barely keeping her own tears at bay, would call Barry, and he would leave his own busy practice and come to comfort his distraught wife and bring her home to rest—frequently for days.

Sometimes the days stretched into a week or two.

Marsha was soon canceling more appointments than she was scheduling.

Still Barry remained by Merritt's side. He remained until her behavior affected Megan. Until Megan became completely terrified of her own mother.

Barry felt he had no choice but to remove his daughter from Merritt's presence for a while. Initially, that was all it was to be. Follow the doctor's advice and keep Megan away from her mother—until they both were better.

But Merritt didn't get better. She just got worse. Barry knew she wouldn't get better without help, and she continued to refuse help.

How Barry wished Merritt had been less of a fighter, more like her mother rather than the determined independent she was. She was so like David Hall with her, "I'll do it my way with no help," attitude.

The first few weeks after Merritt locked the door to her office for the last time were difficult, emotionally grueling. She would walk through her large home every hour of the day and night, eyes cast down, speaking to no one, not even her child. Or she would lie in bed and weep. Hours and hours of uncontrollable sobbing.

36

Barry would come into the bedroom to console her. He would sit by the bedside and hold her hand as he fought to control his own tears—and his fears.

"Oh, Mimi. Darling, please. Let's call Dr. Halverson. He can help. I know he can help."

But his entreaties only seemed to make her worse.

Sometimes he'd try the firm approach.

"Okay, Merritt, this has gone on long enough. You're allowing your life to be destroyed—not to mention mine and Megan's—by this insidious condition you have. But it can be handled. So let's go find someone to help us handle it.

"For God's sake, Merritt, you are the most intelligent and strongest-willed woman I've ever met. Use that strength now and face this thing. We need help."

Barry's voice would inevitably falter as he implored her to allow help. It always came out as a desperate plea and often ended with him begging her, "Please, Mimi. Please."

But Merritt turned a deaf ear to his pleas. Her condition terrified her, and she felt that facing it would only heighten her terror.

She became irascible and hysterical much of the time, almost catatonic the rest. It was during this time that the damage being done to Megan reached its apex. The charming, laughing child became a high-strung, frightened girl subject to her own bouts of hysteria.

Barry, so engulfed in the tragedy that was his family, decided to follow the recommendation of his child's pediatrician, his close friend, Dr. Hal Loomis.

"Barry, Megan can't take much more," said Hal. "She's a little girl who's living in hell. She adores her mother but is terrified of her. She feels so guilty about her fear that she's beginning to blame herself for Merritt's condition. She's a mess, Barry, and if you don't decide to do something drastic pretty damned soon, she'll be in such bad shape, she'll never get better. Your kid deserves better than that. She's too young to suffer this much."

"I know, Hal. I know. I just don't know what to do, that's all. I try to be with her as much as possible, but I can't totally abandon my practice. I have patients depending on me, not to mention my partners. They've been great about picking up the slack in recent weeks, but I don't know how much longer I can ask them to do it."

Barry ran his hand back through his thick auburn hair and sighed deeply. "Tell me what to do, Hal. I just can't think anymore."

"Get Megan out of the house before it's too late. Get her away from Merritt, Barry—just until Merritt accepts some help, takes some medication. You know as well as I do that your wife has classic symptoms of schizophrenia. Why she refuses help, God only knows. I certainly don't," he added, emphasizing his anger at his friend's wife, whom he loved dearly and had always respected as a top-notch doctor.

A large portion of Hal's anger was simply directed at life—life that would so devastate his friend, who now sat with his head buried in his hands having to make a decision that, whichever way, would seriously hurt the ones he so loved. But Hal knew the only thing Barry really could do was to take his advice.

Take Megan away from her mother.

And that's exactly what Barry did. That same day.

Because of the little girl's fragile state, Hal hospitalized Megan for a week. That week gave Barry a chance to find a suitable place for him and his daughter to live. Time to discretely move some of their belongings. Just some, because he prayed the arrangement would only be temporary.

Merritt was nearly beside herself with grief and hysteria when she realized what Barry was doing.

"How can you leave me now, Barry? How can you?" she screamed. "And take Megan? You can't take Megan away from me. I'm her mother. She needs me. And I need her," she sobbed.

"Can't you see? I have to. Meggie is near the breaking point. My God, Mimi, she's just a baby. She can't take this. She loves you so much, she can't bear to see you in torment like this.

"It's only temporary, darling. Let's get you better, and then she'll be back here safely nestled in her own bedroom. All better. No longer sad and afraid all the time. Little girls shouldn't have to be sad and afraid all the time, Merritt," he added, his voice breaking.

Hearing Barry's words, Merritt seemed to physically sag. Barry took her by the arm and gently guided her to a chair—a cream-colored chair, her favorite, so large it all but swallowed the small woman. She looked as forlorn and helpless as a lost child.

Barry felt his heart would break.

"Can I see her before you take her away?" implored Merritt, her pained lavender eyes begging him. "Please, Barry."

Barry hesitated, but then remembering Hal's warning about Megan's seriously fragile state said, "No, Mimi. Hal's hospitalized her. No visitors."

"But I'm not a visitor, Barry. I'm her mother," she argued.

Again Merritt was agitated, and Barry knew that momentarily she would be screaming and sobbing. He knew it was time to leave. He walked over to his wife, who had bounded out of the chair with the declaration of her parentage, and wrapped his arms around her.

"I love you, Merritt. I love you more than I ever dreamed I could love anyone. You are the most wonderful person on the face of the earth, and I thank God daily that you are my wife.

"But you are ill. Is that your fault? Of course not. But your refusal to allow help, to take medication, baffles me. Why, Merritt? Why? I love you so, but I love Megan, too—as I know you do. I just can't take the risk of that wonderful child being destroyed by something she can't even understand.

"You'll have full-time help here, and I'll be by regularly. When you get better—really better—I'll bring Megan home.

"Be well, darling." He kissed her deeply and longingly, turned, picked up the last suitcase and walked out of his home, away from his wife.

Merritt saw Megan rarely over the next few weeks. After each visit, Megan would become a sad and distraught child.

By mutual agreement, the visits became fewer and fewer.

Although he checked on her well-being daily and stopped by often, Barry Davis never moved back to his and his wife's lovely home in Melville Heights.

***

Merritt was very glad to have Barry here with her now, to lean on him a bit as she buried her remaining parent. She had loved Lavinia—loved her in a protective, almost parental way.

He held her hand tightly as they lowered his mother-in-law into the ground. *Poor Lavinia*, he thought. *She was simply unable to face a world that seemed to her totally void without David. Instead, she hid in an imaginary world where her husband was by her side and her daughter was an infant—a time she had loved. She felt too alone without her husband.*

Now Lavinia was gone, too, and it was Merritt who was alone.

Chapter Six

At first when Barry and Megan left, Merritt appeared to give up. She'd lie for days staring at the ceiling, refusing food, not even speaking to her nurse, Melanic Harris. Patient and determined Melanie Harris.

After several weeks, perhaps due to the rest and the mild sedatives she finally agreed to take, Merritt improved. Not profoundly, but noticeably, nonetheless. Barry's visits helped, and so did those of her many friends and colleagues. Friends like Helen and Jake Barney, and Marsha Givens. On the days when Marsha didn't see Merritt, she called her. She had truly grown to love the gifted and dedicated doctor she worked with.

As the weeks progressed, Merritt continued to get better, in spite of the fact she was alone. Some days her longing for her daughter was so strong, and the emptiness would cause her such physical pain, she would double up in agony. She never let Barry see those extremely painful moments, however. She feared he might interpret them as a relapse.

Sometimes, it was difficult for Merritt to fill the empty days. But as she diligently took a new medication, she felt better, her headaches subsided, and the voices diminished. She spent less time resting—much less time, and boredom and restlessness plagued her. She begged those hired as help to simply go—to let her take care of herself.

Barry was reluctant to listen to his wife's arguments that she was now "fine," that she didn't need someone else to care for her night and day. But when even her nurse reported that Merritt really no longer seemed to need a caretaker, that she was monitoring and taking her medication, even the newest the doctor had prescribed, that she was sleeping through the night, arising seemingly rested and calm, Barry conceded that perhaps Merritt was ready to "try it alone."

So Melanie Harris was released, and Merritt began to again tend to her own needs. She so wanted Barry to see how well she was, to return to their home. With Megan.

But Barry kept putting her off. "Soon, darling. Soon." He was pleased at Merritt's progress, her seeming return to normalcy.

But he also saw that *Megan* was healing slowly. He guessed it might be months—many, many months—before he could safely ensconce their child in their home again.

One day, he seemed particularly cheerful as he stopped by to see Merritt. He smiled as he opened the front door, the door still bearing the solid-brass nameplate, *Merritt Hall & Barry Davis, MD's.* Every time he opened the door, a pang of sadness engulfed him. How he wished he could still call this home.

But today, even the sadness seemed less. He was excited.

"Mimi," he called as he stepped through the door. "Where are you, honey?"

Merritt walked out from the living room, her finger marking her place in the book she was reading. She read many books these days, grateful for the time they consumed, eager to keep her mind working.

"Don't you sound chipper today," she said, smiling as he kissed her warmly. "An easy day?"

"No, just the opposite. It was horrendous. But I am feeling great. I've run across a great opportunity for you, Merritt. Let's sit down, and I'll tell you all about it."

They went into the kitchen, hand-in-hand, like young lovers. An observer would never know that each carried a spot of indescribable ache inside. They each poured a cup of coffee and sat across from one another at the antique golden-oak table where they had spent thousands of moments in the past.

As Barry sat down in the all-too-familiar ladder-back chair, he leaned forward and took Merritt's slender hand in his, noting anew the delicate grace of her hand, her slender fingers. He leaned close to her, his face almost touching hers.

"Mimi, what do you think about going back to work? Now let me explain before you say anything," he said, anticipating her objections, seeing the confusion in her eyes, watching the smile leave her face, and feeling her stiffen.

They both knew she would never open her practice again.

Merritt Hall had been a good doctor, a very good doctor, and the pain of that loss was monumentally profound. It showed on her face now, barely covered by the quizzical expression brought about by Barry's question, "What do you think about going back to work?"

"Mimi, there's a new clinic opening on the west side. Kind of a 'rag-tag' operation, but a clinic, nonetheless. The organizers have leased the old library annex—you know, that square redbrick building in the middle of the block, just across from Durham Park? Sarah Baker from County General will be the administrator, and I understand she's begging for good doctors to join the staff. There'll be very little money in it," he added, noting an expression of interest cross her face. "They want doctors committed to helping those with few resources. And honey, there's no one more committed to helping than you. I thought . . ."

"But Barry, does Sarah want *me*?" interrupted Merritt. "She knows my story—the breakdown, my dismissal from the hospital, having to close my practice. Even my stay at Meadow Lawn. Will she even *want* me?" she asked, her voice revealing despair.

"Of course she wants you, Merritt. I spoke briefly with her yesterday. Not too long. I didn't want to make any commitments for you. But she's definitely interested." Barry came around the table to where his wife was seated and placed his arm warmly around her shoulder. "You're one of the best, darling. Sarah knows that."

So Dr. Merritt Hall joined the staff of the newly created Durham Park Women's Clinic, a facility for assisting poor and indigent women with their medical needs. A wonderful place, in spite of the old, drafty building where it was housed—where the staff baked in the summer, froze in the winter, and coped with major roof leaks during the spring and fall rains. Where Merritt was working on the rainy day her mother died.

The clinic was a godsend for Merritt. She lost herself in the needs of her clients. And they had so many needs. Many lacked the basic necessities of life. Others lived in the shadow of violence and deprivation. Many needed to be taught rudimentary hygiene practices. A large number desperately needed advice about not adding to their already too-large families.

Merritt's work again became her life. It helped ease the pain of her loneliness, of the heartache over her longing for Barry and Megan. She literally lost herself in her work. She did little else other than tend to the plight of her patients.

As she had agreed to do when she signed on with Sarah, Merritt took her medication. On schedule. On time.

At first.

As she became more and more enmeshed in the demands of the clinic, however, she sometimes forgot. Oh, she'd take the pills as soon as she'd remember, chastising herself for being so careless with her own health, her own well being—actually, her own survival.

But then, she'd forget again. And consequently, it seemed—and it probably was so—the medication ceased to be as effective as it had initially been.

Merritt's moods began to vacillate remarkably. She started to hear voices again. Not all the time, not even often. But occasionally.

Fortunately, most of the time when Barry saw her, Merritt was having a stable day. But he wasn't seeing her as frequently. Either his schedule or hers consumed most of their time. One day when he dropped by the clinic, he was disturbed with her agitation, her seeming disorientation.

After several minutes of unsuccessful attempts at meaningful conversation, Barry said, "Please tell me you're taking your medication, Mimi. You know—you *have* to know how important it is. Good Lord, Merritt . . ."

"Of course I'm taking my medication. Do you take me for a total fool?" Her anger was obvious, and she pulled away from his embrace.

"Of course I don't take you for a fool. It's just that you don't seem like yourself today, you're so . . ."

Again Merritt cut him short. "I'm tired, that's all," she shouted. "I'm just tired." This time the words were no more than a whisper.

She lowered her chin to her chest and was absolutely silent, almost as if she were sleeping. Barry felt uneasy and a familiar fear gripped his chest. Then as abruptly as she had become quiet, she lifted her head, and anger flashed from her eyes.

"Why are you always criticizing me, Barry? Why do you say things to hurt me? And why do you keep my child from me?"

She screamed the last, and Barry knew for certain that something was again wrong. Drastically wrong.

"I'm sorry, honey, really I am." He put his arms around her and drew her to him, even though she remained stiff and unyielding in his arms.

"I'd better let you get back to work, and I need to do the same. I'll stop by and see you again in a couple days." He kissed her and walked out, before she had a chance to voice any more of her groundless accusations.

Barry went straight to a phone and called Merritt's doctor. He

43

told him of the newest frightening developments in his wife's state of mind. Arrangements were made to again place Merritt in the hospital for around-the-clock observation.

She refused, just as he feared she would. They argued by phone, they argued face-to-face.

Then Barry gave up. He didn't see her, didn't contact her for quite some time.

Not until he took her hand as Lavinia Hall's casket was lowered into the ground.

Chapter Seven

Merritt continued her "see-saw-like" mental health. She would fulfill her duties at the clinic well—admirably, in fact. She had been doing so now for quite some time, and the clients loved her. She truly cared about them, picking up their seemingly lost causes as her own. Not only did she advocate for their needs whenever there was an official ear to listen, she dug into her own funds quite deeply for those who had few others to care about them.

"Merritt, honey, it isn't necessary for you to privately fund this place. That isn't why I wanted you here. I wanted you because you're the best there is," said Sarah Baker, Chief Administrator of the Durham Park Women's Clinic.

"Thanks, Sarah, but I can afford it. I have more money than I could ever begin to spend in a lifetime. Anyhow, once a long time ago, I made a promise to a teacher—my principal. I promised her I'd always stand up for what I believe in. And I believe in this place. It's a last resort for so many of these women," she added with a deep sigh.

So Dr. Merritt Hall-Davis put her heart, soul, time, energy, and money into helping to care for women who, because of their lack of resources, had not been well cared for in the past. For many, she was able to start them back on the road to good health.

Sometimes, their neglected illnesses were so severe, Merritt was unable to help them regain their health. The times when she had to tell a woman that her cancer had so completely metastasized throughout her body, it was likely no treatment would prolong her life, or that her heart condition could be terminal, were devastating to Merritt.

She would become severely depressed after she was called upon to deliver such heartbreaking news, and sometimes, she wouldn't return to the clinic for days. Sarah said nothing to her about these absences. She knew Merritt struggled with the demons of depression—plus God only knows how many other mental and emotional illnesses. Sarah greatly valued this struggling and brilliant doctor—for whenever she could have her.

One morning as Ruthie Schultz, Merritt's twice-a-week housekeeper, walked into Merritt's bedroom (thinking Dr. Hall-Davis had left early for the clinic), she found her curled up in a fetal position, totally catatonic, unresponsive. Terrified, she called Dr. Barry Davis, who in turn, called an ambulance.

After a week in the hospital, where the doctors could find no physical reason for her condition, she was moved to the Meadow Lawn Psychiatric Center. There she would again be under the care of Dr. Gustave Halverson.

***

Cautiously, Megan picked up her mother's hand and placed it in her own. How she loved holding her mother's pretty hand.

"Don't worry, dear, you won't wake her," said the nurse, her voice soft and kind. "She sleeps so soundly with the medication she's on, nothing could disturb her."

Nurse Dorothy Bly's voice sounded a bit like that of a children's librarian reading nursery rhymes to little ones, and she looked the part. She smiled at the girl sitting by the bedside, her head filled with auburn curls, bent over her sleeping parent, her thumb gently stroking her mother's hand as it rested in hers. Her pale-yellow dress made of a soft crepe seemed to flow from her small body. Although Megan was nearly a young woman now, to Dorothy Bly, she looked like a small child trapped in a confusing world.

Megan Davis looked up at the nurse and smiled. "Thank you. I didn't want to wake her."

"Well, as I said, you won't. I'm afraid she may not even wake up while you're here. Your father visited for three hours yesterday, and she never did awaken—didn't even know that he was here."

"That's okay. I don't care so much that she sees me. *I* just need to see *her*, to be near her. I really do love her, you know," she added, her eyes brimming with tears.

"Of course you do. She's such a sweet lady, why anyone would love her! And she's your mother, honey. Of course you love her," she repeated.

"Do you know it's *my* fault she's not living with my dad and me—that we're not living with *her*? We had to move away from her—just because of me."

Megan's voice broke as she choked on "me," and she buried her face in her hands. He shoulders shook with silent sobs.

"Child, I'm sure everyone did what they thought was best." Nurse Bly's own eyes filled with tears, and a look of despair clouded

46

her mature, lined face. She knew the patients who filled the rooms of Meadow Lawn left lives in chaos. This girl was obviously suffering terribly. She didn't know much about the story of Megan's mother—only that she was a physician and suffered from at least one form of dementia. Dorothy had spent thirty-seven years serving the mentally ill; the often forgotten could not have hoped for a better "angel of mercy."

Dorothy Bly was not attractive to look at—short, overweight, sparse gray hair, and ordinary blue eyes. But to those she cared for, she was a beauty. She never lost patience, she never raised her voice, and she never showed fear of the frequently erratic behavior she witnessed daily.

Dorothy placed her arm gently around Megan's shoulders. "It'll be okay, honey. And I'm sure she understands," she added, nodding at Merritt.

Megan only continued her silent sobs, her shoulders shaking convulsively. Dorothy Bly stole quietly out the door.

"Come in," said Dr. Halverson, looking up for a moment from the chart he was intently poring over. "What is it, Dorothy?" he asked as his favorite nurse stuck her head in the door.

"Dr. Davis' daughter is at her bedside sobbing her heart out. I thought maybe you could say something to console the poor child."

"Ah, yes. Megan. Do you have any idea what upset her? Is she that worried about her mother?"

"Well, I suppose that's some of it, but what she told me was that it was all her fault they're not living together—her, her mother, and her father. Sounds to me like she's on one heck of guilt trip."

"Poor kid," sympathized Dr. Halverson, sighing and shaking his head. "I'll go in and talk to her."

"I was hoping you would."

The doctor laughed. "You have me figured out pretty well, don't you, Dorothy?"

Dorothy just smiled and walked away, wondering if Gus knew how much she had loved him all these years.

Dr. Halverson knocked gently on the door of Merritt's room, but didn't wait for a reply. Nonetheless, he opened the door slowly, not wanting to startle the young woman leaning over her mother, who was lying in the throes of deep, drug-induced sleep.

"Megan," spoke the doctor softly.

"Oh, Dr. Halverson, is my visiting time over?" asked Megan as she stumbled to her feet, quickly brushing tears from her face.

"No, no, stay where you are. You're fine. I'd just like to talk with you a bit if I may."

"Sure," she replied, sitting down again and taking a tissue from her bag. "Not much point in pretending I haven't been crying is there, Dr. Halverson," said Megan as her voice cracked with a half laugh, half sob.

The doctor pulled up the room's only other chair and sat beside her. Resting his large gentle hand on her shoulder, he said, "Crying's okay, Megan. It's what we humans do when we're sad and grieving."

"I've grown up without my mother—my own mother," she said, her voice quivering. "I hardly know her, and yet we live in the same city. We should have been together. I should have seen her more often."

"You were very small when this all started, Megan. I remember the first time your mother and father came to me. She was beginning to have severe headaches, the voices were starting to torment her, and she had shouted at you—a toddler. It about broke her heart. She thought she was a monster, treating her own baby that way."

"But she wasn't. She was a good mother, and I loved her. We should have stayed together."

"But you couldn't. Both your mother and father could see that— no matter how much they loved each other. They both loved you too much to further the damage that was being done to you as a little girl. You couldn't begin to understand your mother's outbursts, and it was tearing you apart. You loved her, but you were afraid of her, too. No one was trying to keep you away from her indefinitely. Only until she was better.

"But she never really got better, Megan," explained Dr. Halverson with a sigh. "It's quite likely she never will. But we're trying—trying and hoping," he added. "Don't blame yourself for any of this, my dear. No one is to blame. Absolutely no one."

Gus Halverson got up from his chair, patted Megan gently on the shoulder, and walked to the door. "I don't know if I helped you or not. Just keep telling yourself that she loved you—still loves you *and* your father very much. And who knows, maybe some day she'll be well enough to show you how much."

Megan allowed herself a small smile. "You *have* been a help,

Dr. Halverson. I know none of what's happened to Mom is my fault—not really. It's just that sometimes it's easier to blame someone, and that someone might as well be me."

Standing, she leaned over and kissed her mother gently on the cheek. "'Bye, Mom. I'll come back tomorrow," she said softly.

"Do that, Megan," encouraged the doctor. "Maybe tomorrow will be a better day, and she won't need to be so heavily sedated. Just don't let it get to you if your visit doesn't go as well as you hoped. Promise?"

"I promise," said Megan, this time with a slight smile. She knew this kind man was doing all for her mother that she could hope for. He was the best, and she was extremely grateful to him.

Chapter Eight

Merritt sat huddled in a corner, her arms wrapped across her chest, her hands cupped over her ears, her right hand over her left ear, her left hand over her right. The sleeves on her kimono-like gown slid up her arms, revealing wrists so thin and tiny, they appeared to belong to a child.

She pressed her hands tightly, blocking out the voices. Trying to block out the voices.

But still they raged.

She didn't know who they were or why they said the things they did. Those creatures shaking their fingers at her, blaming her, threatening her. She didn't do it. She didn't make them die. Why would they say such things?

"No, no. It's not my fault. I didn't do it!"

Her cries were loud, laden with fear and despair.

At times, amidst all her indecipherable cries, she could be heard to moan, "Megan. Oh, my Megan."

"Do you know what she's denying, Dr. Halverson? What is it that so terrorizes her so?"

"No, not totally," replied Halverson. He had been Merritt's primary caretaker during this stay at Meadow Lawn, just as he had been the previous two times—always attempting to find help for Merritt that would make a difference. Always with the hope that somewhere there was something—the right treatment or the miraculous medication—that could return her life to some modicum of normalcy.

"As far as I can tell, the poor woman is going through something akin to the Inquisition, complete with threats of torture. She doesn't say much. Just bits and pieces. I'm not even sure what it is she's denying, but I do know it's an issue at the very core of her being, and it's tearing her apart.

"Of course, her cries of 'Megan' refer to her daughter, Megan Davis. She was killed along with Merritt's husband several months ago. A dreadful accident.

"Merritt was here when it happened. Both Megan and her father, Merritt's husband, Dr. Barry Davis, had visited her several times during the weeks preceding the accident. I remember clearly sitting with Megan one afternoon, trying to convince the girl she bore no blame for her mother's condition, for her sadness. In fact, we saw some real progress during those last visits before the accident.

"When we told Merritt what had happened, that her husband and daughter had been killed, we weren't certain she even understood, but she certainly understood later. She was close to catatonic for nearly three months after the whole tragedy hit her. I was afraid we'd lose her completely that time. But she came back, little by little.

"Merritt Hall-Davis is a remarkably strong woman. Very strong and very ill."

Dr. Halverson had known Merritt for a long time, and he had known Barry—also Lavinia and David Hall. As a friend, he had grieved all their deaths.

He now grieved for Merritt.

The first time Merritt was at Meadow Lawn, Barry came to see her daily. Often, he brought Megan with him.

He went with Merritt to Meadow Lawn in the ambulance that second time, after the housekeeper found her totally unresponsive, curled up in a fetal position. It was during that second time that Megan and Barry were killed in an automobile accident.

Megan, no longer a little girl but approaching young womanhood, was to begin an art antiquities program at the University of Chicago. She and her father were so excited.

It was a good day for both of them as they packed the car and readied themselves for the jaunt to Chicago.

Megan had long ago decided she didn't want to enter the world of medicine. Having already seen too much pain, she had no desire to follow in her parents' footsteps.

Megan Davis had done well in conquering the fears that engulfed her as a small child—a child torn between love and terror, reacting to the menacing mental condition of her mother.

Of course it took years and the finest of therapists to facilitate that victory.

Megan had reached the point where her mother no longer frightened her. She would visit her, often alone—more often than her father realized—and along with the pull of the love she had always felt for her mother, was immense compassion. She knew her mother was a wonderful person whose life Merritt was powerless to control.

Megan was a lovely and loving young woman, full of promise, destined for a brilliant future.

51

A future that wasn't meant to be.

As Barry pulled within ten blocks of the university, a car careened around a corner, too fast for the rain-slicked street. It struck Barry's car, head-on. Megan died instantly, Barry, three days later, never regaining consciousness.

Now Merritt was *truly* alone.

"Gus, does she respond to any of her medication?" continued the curious Dr. Melvin Calhoun, Chief of Staff at the well-known facility famed for sometimes accomplishing miracles.

"Yes, but usually very briefly. And not completely. Nothing seems to rescue her from her terrors for long." Gus Halverson looked at his fellow doctor with sad gray eyes, partly concealed by drooping eyelids and wild-looking bushy brows.

"I don't think you'll be able to list Merritt as one of Meadow Lawn's success stories, Mel. As much as I continue to hope, that lovely woman seems to be drowning in her terrors."

With a defeated shake of his head, Dr. Halverson slowly walked over to his patient. Gently stroking her hair and uttering soft, soothing reassurances, he injected a strong medication into Merritt's arm, hoping to rescue her from her tormentors, at least for now, giving her respite in deep sleep.

Merritt slept for several hours, lost in deep, seemingly restful, sleep. From time to time, her face twisted in a grimace, her body writhed as if in pain, and she emitted cries like a wounded animal.

But most of the time, she slept, never moving, never changing position. Simply sleeping.

When Merritt awoke, for a while she lay and stared at the ceiling, seeming no more conscious of where she was than when in the throes of her drug-induced sleep. But her face no longer showed signs of pain.

She turned and surveyed her surroundings, the soft-blue walls, the pink of sunset reflecting off the blue, giving it a lavender hue. Just like the color of her eyes.

Just like the color of Megan's eyes. The association brought tears to her own.

The furnishings were solid but attractive. They conveyed warmth and comfort.

The only decorations were soft pillows and stuffed animals, much like a child's nursery. Only here, the colors were not the vibrant

52

ones so often brightening the child's room, offering stimulation and cheer. Here the colors were gentle and soothing—muted colors.

Stimulation was not needed for Merritt. She needed calmness and comfort.

As she stirred, her hand went to her neck and clasped the small gold cross resting there. As she closed her hand tightly around it, she smiled.

A scene repeated hundreds of times, thousands of times since she received her first "real gold" piece in celebration of her ninth birthday. She seemed to draw contentment from the small piece of jewelry that had not left its place around her slender neck for so many years.

The nurses at Meadow Lawn learned long ago that to attempt to remove it resulted in incredible savage outbursts. So it remained, even during baths, its somewhat tarnished brightness resting against her too-white skin.

Merritt got up from her bed and walked to the window. She looked across the tip of the skyline, most of it hidden by the trees surrounding the hospital. She loved the view here, the mixture of nature's beauty combined with the architectural accomplishments of man.

She smiled, and tears rose to her eyes. She may be ill, but she could still feel aesthetic joy, still feel the presence of God.

Merritt had been a resident at Meadow Lawn for quite some time, this third visit, vacillating between total withdrawal and agitated excitement. When in her excited state, she would walk hurriedly through every available space, pound her fist in her open hand, and mutter loud nothings in anger.

Both her withdrawn state and her agitated state were generally preceded by a bout of terror.

Gus Halverson worked with Merritt many months, often watching her rest, with her long brown hair, now heavily streaked with gray, framing her troubled lovely face, her eyelids covering her striking eyes. He thought of her father, David Hall, whom he had known and admired since they were boys together. He remembered Lavinia, David's charming wife, who had struggled with reality in her own way.

Dr. Halverson recalled Dr. Barry Davis and his loving devotion to his wife—the wife who had unwittingly torn his family, his life, apart. He thought of Megan Davis, her young life, which had known so much sorrow, snuffed out so needlessly, so soon.

At times tears would well up in his eyes, and he'd sigh, wondering why he had entered a profession where, so often, the failures far outnumbered the successes.

***

After a time—several months of time—Merritt got better. Not well, but better. Maybe it was the newest medications, or maybe it was the loving care and patience of those working with her. Of those who really cared—like Dr. Gus Halverson.

Or maybe it was just time.

Gus looked at the woman sitting across from him and quietly studied her for a brief moment. Her eyes met his, their stunning lavender hue radiating more life than he had seen from her in so long, it gave him hope.

Perhaps, just perhaps, Merritt would be one of Meadow Lawn's success stories after all.

Her hair was tied back with a bow, soft-green in color. Tendrils of curls, some brown, many gray, curled softly around her face.

In spite of all she's been through, she's still incredibly beautiful, thought Gus.

Her dress was also green, a darker green than the bow, and it draped softly from her far-too-thin frame. Her face, too, reflected how frail she had become during this most recent long stay at Meadow Lawn.

Her thinness simply added to her beauty. Her high cheekbones were more pronounced than ever, her incredible eyes appeared even larger, and her tentative smile was as captivating as that of a child.

"Well, Merritt, I guess it's time for good-bye. I know it's been a long time since you've been home, and I want you to know that we're here if you need us."

"Thanks, Gus, you've been wonderful. I can't believe I'm actually leaving. I know I gave you some hard times. I'm sorry. I guess I really wasn't ready to leave last time—wasn't ready to accept the fact that Megan and Barry were gone."

Her eyes misted when she spoke the names of her daughter and husband, and she looked down at her hands folded on her lap. Then she took a deep breath, looked directly at Dr. Halverson again and continued.

54

"I'll always miss them, Gus. Always. But I know I need to get on with my life. That's what they would have wanted."

"Yes, they would have," he agreed. "And it's what we want for you, too."

Merritt smiled warmly and arose, extending her hand to her doctor and friend. Gus took her lovely hand in both of his. Merritt's fingers were long and delicate, and her nails were formed to perfection. A model's hands.

Or a physician's.

Merritt walked from the office of Dr. Gustave Halverson and out the door of Meadow Lawn to a taxi, where the few belongings she had with her awaited, and headed for her new life.

**

Merritt had sold her home, the home in Melville Heights where she had once lived happily with her husband and child, the home where she had returned as a weary but contented doctor each evening.

After the accident, she never wanted to see it again. She also had parted with most reminders of Barry and Megan. She kept no furniture, few photos, no keepsakes or memoirs.

All of this, she did just before her last admittance to Meadow Lawn.

The home she was directing the taxi to now was situated at the opposite end of town, closer to the center of the city. It was a less opulent neighborhood by far, but the house was attractive and homey. And it had been available when Merritt needed it.

Several people, directed by Merritt's attorney and lifelong friend, Jake Barney, had furnished the house and stocked the cupboards and refrigerator. All utilities were turned on and running.

There was even a new car parked in the garage.

Merritt stepped from the taxi, paid the driver, and walked slowly up the sidewalk. Her heart was pounding, and she felt afraid. *No, damn it,* she said to herself. *This is my home now and I'll be fine here. Just fine.*

The Barneys—Jake and Helen—had planned to call for Merritt at the hospital and take her to her new home. They wanted to make it a pleasant occasion for their dear friend, but Merritt wouldn't hear of it.

"Really, Jake, I'd like to go home alone. I can't have someone by my side for the rest of my life just so I won't feel any sadness. I'll be okay—really I will. I need to learn to accept my own company, and what better place to start than in my new home."

So Jake brought the key to the hospital, the key she now took from her purse and inserted in the lock. She turned it slowly and walked into the house.

Her new home. The beginning of her new life.

The foyer was bright, the sun pouring in the clear-glass windows on either side of the door. It bounced off the brass fixture hanging above and off the brick-colored tile, buffed to a glistening finish beneath her feet.

She stepped through the doorway to her left, the living room. It, too, was bright. Jake had left all the draperies open. The whole room, the entire house, looked bright and cheerful.

"Thanks, Jake," she said softly to herself.

The room smelled of new furniture. And the fragrance of roses. On the large cherry-wood coffee table there was a massive bouquet of the most gorgeous pale-pink roses Merritt had ever seen. The card read, "Welcome home, honey. Love, Jake and Helen."

Her soft smile turned into a full grin now, and she stepped sprightly through each room, delighted with what she saw. When she came to her bedroom, she flopped back, sinking in the thick puffiness of the large azure-blue comforter. She felt as if she were floating on a cloud. She stared at the ceiling and marveled at the peace that swept over her. She hadn't felt like this in such a very long time.

Chapter Nine

At first Merritt's days were filled with routine, as she relearned how to manage her own life. For a while, she was content with the predictable sameness of her life—reading, caring for her home, meeting a friend for lunch, doing a little shopping, a little socializing.

And always dutifully taking her medication—the necessary element of her peaceful, contented life.

***

It would be hard to say what changed first. Merritt began to call her friends less and less, and she said "no" to their invitations more and more. Again, she became erratic about taking her medication. It doesn't help, anyway, she reasoned. She slept long hours, sometimes for days.

And the voices returned.

Jake and Helen had not been able to reach Merritt for two weeks. "I'm worried, Jake. She's been very aloof on the phone for quite a while, but at least she answered it. Of late, I can't even get her to do that. Surely she's not out all the time. Let's stop by and see if she's okay," suggested Helen Barney.

"Sure, hon," said Jake, walking to the closet and taking out their light jackets—all they needed on this warm early-spring evening. "Maybe we can persuade Merritt to go for a drive with us. Just feel this air," he added, taking a deep breath. "It's bound to give her a lift."

The Barneys spoke little as they drove across town to Merritt Davis' home, each lost in thought, each worrying about their friend, each trying to come up with plausible reasons why she had been so out of touch of late.

When they drove into the driveway, their fears were heightened as they noticed several newspapers scattered aimlessly about the yard and several days' mail spilling out of the mailbox.

"Oh, Jake, this doesn't look good," said Helen, her voice almost a moan.

"No, honey, it doesn't. Damn!" Jake pounded his hands on the steering wheel. "Why didn't she call if she needed help? She knows we'd be here in a heartbeat.

"Well, I guess we'd better go inside—see if we can tell what's up."

"God, Jake, I'm scared. What if she's dead? What if she needed help, and there was no one to help her?" asked Helen, her concern turned to terror.

"Now Helen, don't let your imagination run away with you. We don't know the 'what ifs,' and we won't know them until we get in the house. First, let's see if the doors are open," he said, taking his wife's trembling hand in his.

Jake and Helen Barney walked up to the house, with Jake leading the way. They tried both doors and found them locked. They checked all the usual places where one might find a key and came up empty.

Actually, Jake was glad for that. He had advised Merritt, a woman living alone, to take great care.

They tried the windows, not expecting any to be unlocked. They weren't. They looked inside, the draperies and blinds were open, but in the darkness, they saw nothing.

"I'm going to call the police, Helen. We have to get inside, but I don't want to break in without the law being present."

"Will they let you do that, Jake? I mean, are they going to help you break in to Merritt's house?" she asked, finding the idea somewhat incredulous.

"I have papers in my brief case showing I have power of attorney for Merritt. Fortunately, my brief case is still in the car. I think I can persuade them that I have the right to get in, and that it's imperative we do so."

It took very little convincing for Pete Grant and Hal Blake, the two patrolmen summoned to the scene, to comprehend the graveness of the situation. They permitted Jake to summon a locksmith, and soon he, Helen, and the two policemen were entering the house—the house that Jake and Helen had prepared with such joy just a short time ago, when they hoped and prayed that Merritt would be able to find a renewed life in a new place.

They turned on lights in every room, their glow brightening the abandoned surroundings. They could find nothing disturbed in any of the rooms. They were spotless and perfectly arranged.

It looked as if a maid had cleaned the house just this morning, although Merritt had refused to employ any help this time, insisting that she needed the activity, the routine of caring for her own place.

It was the only work she had to do, she had argued when her friends suggested she accept at least a once-a-week cleaning woman.

The only sign that the house hadn't been lived in for a few days was a bouquet of dead flowers, their stems bent in dryness, their fallen petals scattered on the tabletop beneath the vase like dead leaves lying on the ground under a tree in late autumn.

As they walked into Merritt's bedroom, Helen's breath stuck in her throat, her heart pounding like a diesel motor. But her fears of finding Merritt lying dead in her own bed were unfounded. The bed was made—smooth and wrinkle-free.

"Helen, check her drawers and closet and see if you can tell if anything's missing. Maybe she just wanted to take a trip and didn't want anyone to know about it," said Jake.

"That's just not like her, Jake," said Helen as she opened drawer after drawer. Peering into her closet, she said, "If she was taking a trip, she sure didn't take much. I can't see that anything's missing. And, Jake, here's her luggage—the full set. Now I'm really worried."

"We'd better file a missing-persons report, gents," Jake said, turning to the two policemen who had been following them room to room. "I don't know what's going on, but I don't like it."

Hal Blake, the younger of the two officers—so young he reminded Helen of her nephew Bobby, a sophomore at Arrow State College—had checked the garage. Merritt's car was gone. He also checked all the windows and both doors from the inside. There was no sign of forcible entry.

As they walked out, turning out the lights behind them, the house again engulfed in darkness, Jake wondered if he would ever see Merritt again. How he longed for the days when Barry was alive, before Merritt was ill. When they were a family—his and Helen's favorite family.

The missing-persons report was filed, and a search was begun—as good a search as possible with as little information as those doing the searching had to work with. Jake had filled the assigned detectives in on Merritt's mental history, but he knew it was going to be difficult to know where to start.

Merritt Hall-Davis no longer had any living family.

Yet a diligent search was conducted, and after three weeks, the car was found. There didn't appear to be anything wrong with the vehicle; the tank was filled with at least half a tank of gas, and the doors were carefully locked. The car was simply abandoned, pulled off to the shoulder of the highway thirty miles outside Indianapolis, Indiana.

The search continued in earnest around Indianapolis, and for a while, Jake and Helen had hope. But no additional clues regarding Merritt's whereabouts turned up, and as time passed, efforts for the search diminished, then stopped.

There was simply no trace of Dr. Merritt Hall-Davis. Jake and Helen never saw her again.

***

Merritt sat in the car, in the front seat behind the wheel, just as she had for the past few days every time she stopped. Not going to anywhere in particular. Just driving away. Away from the city where she had lived for so long. Away from the new home that she tried so hard to like.

Away from the home in Melville Heights where she had experienced so much love and laughter, loss and pain.

Away from memories.

No more visits to the graves. Visits that caused her such pain that she would sit motionless, sometimes for hours before trusting herself to drive through the iron gates under the arch bearing the simple inscription, "CEMETERY." No name, just the word "cemetery" in filigree letters, all capitals.

She never wanted anyone to accompany her when she visited the graves of those she had so loved, arguing that this was her private time, her time to connect. And those who offered to accompany her— Jake and Helen, Marsha Givens, and many others who had known Merritt for so long—believed her and felt her visits to the site where her loved ones were buried strengthened her and helped her find peace.

But peace was not what Merritt found. What she found there, as she carried on one-way conversations with her parents, her husband, and her daughter, was closer to torture. The visits all but ripped her apart, and for days afterwards, she would feel the intense pain of separation from all that mattered to her.

Often as she sat in her car waiting for the trembling to stop, for her body-wracking sobs to subside, she'd contemplate suicide. The only place she wanted to be was here, in the cemetery with the others, with everyone she ever loved.

But her training to save lives, not destroy them, always won.

Even the voices did not encourage her to end her life. They only encouraged her to "go."

So go she did.

Merritt gathered so few of her belongings that those who later checked her closets couldn't find anything missing. She didn't even pack a bag. Not a real bag.

Instead, she pulled a large shopping bag from the back of her closet where it had been nestled tightly between her many boxes of shoes. She couldn't remember why she had kept the colorful Christmas bag; it was a long time ago when she'd delivered the gifts it held.

Maybe somehow she had known that one day she'd be wanting it, needing it.

Her eyes filled with tears as she placed the bag on her bed, the green and red snowflakes covering the bag shimmering through her tears, appearing as if they were moving, looking like the beginning of a child's Christmas television show, the introduction to an hour of squeals of laughter.

Taking great care not to tear the bag, she packed her clothing tightly into it. She piled her brown sweater on top of the dark-blue, and a few changes of underwear she folded carefully and stacked underneath.

Her shirts came next, brown checked and blue striped, and two white, plain with small pearl buttons, crisply starched. She closed the closet door, at the last minute grabbing an old pair of shoes—shoes that she had worn many times for walks, scuffed soft and comfortable. She wrapped them in a small pale-blue towel and wedged them carefully down the side of the bag.

Merritt smoothed the covers on her bed as she removed the bag stuffed with her belongings, closed the closet door, turned out the lights, grabbed her purse, and walked out of the house to her car.

She turned back only long enough to lock the door. The door she would never walk through again.

As Merritt drove out of town, she passed the cemetery and looked one last time at the inscription, "CEMETERY," feeling again the same pain she always experienced as she drove beneath the arch marking this final resting place for her loved ones—for Barry, for Megan, for her mother and father.

But today, she didn't stop. She didn't allow the pain to engulf her, to hold her back.

Today, she drove away—away from the gate, away from the memories, away from the pain.

***

Merritt didn't know how long she'd been sitting there, how long she had been resting her head on the steering wheel, cradled in her hands. Her neck was stiff and creaked like a rusty hinge needing oil as she turned her head. The hand that had been resting beneath her head on the steering was asleep. It prickled as she gave it a gentle shake to regain its feeling.

She looked around and saw nothing familiar. Towering over the car, over the narrow road with the gravel shoulder where she was parked, sat a huge billboard advertising bread with a multicolored wrapper that claimed to be the best and most nutritious around. Five large spotlights were spread across the length of the billboard, ready to illuminate the sign at night, not wanting a single driver to miss the message of the "world's best bread."

Merritt looked at the sign for some time. For no particular reason, really, except to remind herself that she was a bit hungry. She couldn't remember when she had last eaten, but she thought it was at least a day ago. It didn't really seem important. She often had to be reminded to eat.

Today, the billboard was her reminder.

She looked at the gas gauge. Half full—a little more than half full—plenty of gas to drive somewhere to find something to eat. But where would she go? She didn't even know where she was.

It was quiet here, along this road with the bread billboard. Very quiet. Merritt hadn't seen another car for a long time. She knew the city was close by; signs had been announcing that fact for several miles. But she knew she wasn't going to the city. She didn't know where she was headed, but did know it wouldn't be the big city. She had no desire for crowds, for people.

She remained in the car another hour, not knowing where to go. One thing she did know was that she didn't want anyone to stop; she didn't want to talk to a soul.

Then a car drove by, and although it didn't stop, it did slow down. That terrified her. Merritt tightly clutched the cross hanging around her neck and prayed, "Please, God, don't let them stop—

don't let them stop."

As if to give immediate answer to her prayer, the car again accelerated and sped away.

Away—that's where she needed to go. Anywhere, just as long as it was away from where she had been.

So Merritt picked up her shopping bag, resplendent with glittery red and green snowflakes, and her purse, stepped out of her car—the one Jake had bought new for her and left in the garage of her new home—locked the car, and walked away.

Chapter Ten

"It makes no sense," shouted Jake, pounding his fist in his hand, expressing more his frustration than anger. "How could she just disappear? People don't just vanish."

"But they do, Mr. Barney," explained Sergeant Evans, nervously pushing his glasses back up the bridge of his narrow nose. "People vanish all the time. But we're not even thinking along those lines yet. We found the car, so at least we know in what direction she was heading."

"But that was over a month ago, Evans. She might have been kidnapped. Surely you don't think she just walked away from her car."

"We don't think anything—don't *know* anything. Only that her car was abandoned. She might have gotten tired of traveling alone and found a ride with someone else. She could easily be clear across the country by now.

"But we're still looking, and we'll continue to do so for a while. You need to know, though, that as time goes by, our chances of finding her diminish. Have you considered that she might not be alive? You, yourself, told us of her mental problems. With that kind of depression, she might have just gone off somewhere and done it—killed herself."

Jake glared at this man who put into words exactly what he had been fearing these past many weeks. Then he turned and stomped out of the Central Police Station, heavy-hearted.

***

Merritt walked and walked. Many miles. She had no idea how many. Not wanting to follow the road and have a helping citizen stop to offer her a ride after she left her car, she headed across the wide stretch of land, away from the road, away from the city.

She walked a long way that first day—and the many days that followed. On the day she abandoned her car, it wasn't until close to dusk that she reached a small-town diner and satisfied the hunger that had been gnawing at her since early in the day when she sat in the shadow of the billboard.

By the time she came upon the diner, she wasn't only hungry, but exhausted. Her shoes were coated with the dust of the fields she walked across, and burrs clung to her stockings and slacks. A thin sliver of dried blood coursed down her cheek where a branch had whipped across her face as she cut through an orchard, hoping to find a piece of fruit to help abate her hunger pangs. But the only fruit she found was nothing more than tiny nubbins nestled in the middle of fading blossoms. Later, in the approaching summer and fall, the trees would be laden with fruit, succulent fruit, bending the branches with their weight.

But today, for Merritt, there had been nothing.

Part of the time, she pulled the shopping bag along behind her. Even with the few garments she had brought with her, it was heavy in her weariness, and she dragged it more than carried it.

But now, in the diner, she could rest. And eat. She sidled wearily into a booth and lifted a menu with trembling hands.

The diner, called *Billy's Family Food Shack*—so the sign hand-painted on the window announced—was cramped but clean. The tabletops were shiny, and a glass case displaying an array of pies gleamed in the reflection of the overhead lights.

A half-dozen men decked in clothes so alike, they appeared to be in uniform, gathered around two tables shoved together, deeply engrossed in a discussion about the spring planting and the prospects for a good and prosperous season. From time to time, the discussion became so heated, one or the other of the farmers would pull a wadded dark-blue handkerchief from his overall pocket to mop his brow.

A pair of young lovers sat in a booth, holding hands, their faces only inches apart as they shared an ice cream soda with two straws. A lone man sat at a table towards the back, looking intently at a map spread across the table, obviously trying to determine where he was— or where he was going.

The diner's customers didn't pay much attention to Merritt after their initial glance. Apparently the sight of a bedraggled woman covered with dust and burrs, a bloody scratch across her face, bearing a Christmas shopping bag in the early spring, didn't seem unusual to them. Or perhaps their culture of "minding their own business" outweighed their curiosity.

Merritt ate less of the "Blue Plate Special" than she had thought she would. Either she wasn't really as hungry as she felt, or the greasy meat covered with even greasier gravy curbed whatever appetite she thought she had.

But the coffee was wonderful—strong and aromatic. She bolted two cups in rapid succession before again taking off across fields and their surrounding woods, losing herself in the landscape of wherever her journey was taking her.

Occasionally, there would be a day much like the first. She would find a small town with the usual greasy-spoon diner. Once, she had the good fortune to come across one with wonderful food, crisp salads, and rolls that melted in your mouth. It was named, *Mom's*. "Mom" was a ruddy-faced older woman who poked her head out from the kitchen to joke with customers before she scurried back to her culinary duties.

Mom noticed Merritt, but was unable to make eye contact with her. Merritt's beat-down and bedraggled appearance disturbed the caring diner proprietor, but she was so caught up in the hurry-scurry business of the day, she didn't have the time to think much about her until the day was over. But that night, as she diligently brushed her long gray hair its 100 daily strokes, she remembered her eye-catching customer. *Pretty,* she thought, *but I'm not sure I've ever before seen such a sad-looking woman.*

The delectable food Mom served was wasted on Merritt. By the time she stopped at *Mom's*, she was no longer judging what she ate. She ate only to satisfy her hunger and to give her the strength to go on.

On to where, she wasn't sure. Nor did she really care.

Most days, Merritt didn't come across diners—or towns for that matter. Most days she simply wandered across central rural America. Alone.

Her only companionship, the voices resonating in her head.

Where did she find food when she needed it, this brilliant physician, born to affluence and heir to a sizeable fortune? Sometimes she found discarded produce in the fields, remains from the previous season, drying and rotting in the dirt. More often she found the remains of what someone else had thrown away. Half-eaten hamburgers and soggy cold French fries tossed out the window by some teenagers who had their fill, or some fried chicken remaining on the bones, the aftermath of a picnic in the woods.

Days of wandering aimlessly had changed Merritt almost beyond belief. She had no idea where she was. Sometimes, she had no idea *who* she was.

Other than what the voices told her.

The money she brought when she left home was soon gone, as was the purse she carried it in. She really couldn't remember if she had left it somewhere or if someone had taken it.

More important than the money in the purse were the pills. The pills that quelled the voices. The pills that kept her "well."

Merritt still carried the shopping bag, tears along the sides, the bottom worn nearly through from the dragging, the green and red snowflakes now filthy with dirt and grime. Underwear poked through the worn spots, once-clean underwear she had changed only one time, early in her journey, when she was driving and had freshened up in a service-station restroom.

She changed her shirt that early-in-her-journey day, too. Since then she had added another, on top of the first. She knew her bag wouldn't hold out much longer. If she wanted additional clothing, she'd need to wear it all.

The old scuffed oxfords, the ones she stuffed down the side of her bag just before leaving home, now covered her feet—and the two pairs of socks she wore. She had long since discarded the shoes she wore when she left home. Those shoes, although comfortable, were highly fashionable, and their purchase had given her no change from a one-hundred-dollar bill.

Now they lay in some farmer's field, plowed under, unnoticed.

If only farmer Albert Jolene had seen the shoes of black Italian leather before his machinery rolled them over into the rich soil, detective Sergeant Evans might have had a lead on the whereabouts of Dr. Merritt Hall-Davis.

But that was not to be.

***

Merritt walked across the crumbling paved road, stumbled and dropped to the wet ground, leaning against what once had been a bustling hotel, now abandoned and crumbling. Obscene words and phrases covered the boards criss-crossing the gaping holes where windows, once adorned with handsome draperies, had invited in the brilliant morning sun to brighten the mood of the hotel's guests.

Half sitting, half lying down, Merritt closed her eyes and breathed heavily with exhaustion. Her hair was plastered against her tired, drawn face, and the remains of the most recent downpour dripped from the ends of her unkempt curls, down her back, soaking further the drenched shirts she wore.

Merritt was so wet and so cold, she shivered until her teeth clattered like a marimba. Along with the rain, hail pelted her head and shoulders, followed by a strong wind uncharacteristically brisk and cold for the season.

Lying on her side, Merritt rested her head in the curve of her arm to keep it up from the puddled ground. In spite of the discomfort, wetness, and cold, weariness overtook her, and she slept. Soundly.

Merritt awoke hours later, the edges of the blue-black sky beginning to lighten. Although she awoke stiff and sore, she was no longer cold.

A man's coat covered Merritt's damp body. A coat she had not brought with her, a coat she had never seen before. It was so tattered, it wasn't much more than a rag. But it warmed her, and her shivering had subsided.

Merritt sat up and surveyed her surroundings, wrapping the coat tightly around her to ward off the predawn chill. The mornings had not given birth to coolness like this since she began her journey, and she had grown accustomed to the fresh balminess of spring mornings. But the deluge last night was accompanied by a cool front.

She knew she needed to get up and move—off the ground, away from the mud and puddles. She knew she needed to get dry.

As she rose unsteadily to her feet, she leaned against the old building. Small bits of loosened cement and brick crumbled where she rubbed against them and dropped to the ground with a "ping, ping." An unpleasant smell floated from the building—mildew and decay.

Merritt backed away from the aged structure and began finding her way across town. It was cooler away from the shelter of the old hotel, and she wrapped the coat more tightly around her and folded her arms across her chest to prevent the wind from opening the button-less garment. Her hair, still damp from last night, blew around her face, and again she began to shiver uncontrollably.

Tears arose, partly from cold, partly from the frustration of being wet and chilled and unable to do anything about it. As she rounded a corner, head down, in a quandary over how she could better her situation, she felt a hand on her shoulder. She jumped, more startled than frightened.

"What do you want?" she demanded, as she spun around, anger flashing from her lavender eyes. She turned to face a man, an old man, draped in ragged clothes many sizes too large for his frame. A grayish film covered his steel-blue eyes, and his nose was dripping from the cold. His gloved hand, resting gently on Merritt's shoulder, was huge, disproportionately large for his short stature.

His voice was husky, and he spoke in a near-whisper. "Come with me," he said. "Ya needa get dry."

Merritt followed him, the opposite way from where she had been headed—away from the city. Why she did as he directed, she had no idea. She hadn't followed anyone's directions since her last stay at Meadow Lawn. But the soft-spoken kindness in the voice of the bent old gentleman compelled her to tag along behind him.

Merritt followed her guide past the old hotel, back across the road she had crossed coming into town earlier. They sauntered across some railroad tracks, thick with rust that spoke of disuse. A few hundred yards down the tracks was a train depot, a depot, she noted as they drew closer, that appeared to have not been used for a long time.

Around the back of the depot, away from the cool winds, seven people, men and women, were huddled around a large rust-coated oil drum. Bits of charred paper floated above the crackling flames that leapt from the top of the drum, scattering on the surrounding cinders like confetti tossed about at a New Year's Eve party.

The seven, similar in their attire of poorly fitting shabby clothing, didn't look up as the old man and his newly found friend approached. The ill-clad group hovered over the fire, easing the aches and chills of the preceding night and the early morning.

"Move 'side now, jist move 'side," commanded Merritt's companion in his soft husky voice. "This here lady's gonna catch her death if she cain't get dried off'n."

Obediently, they all moved aside as he guided Merritt next to the barrel, close to the heat.

Merritt had just experienced her first episode of acceptance as a member of the community of those who live on the street in Valeria, Indiana.

The days regained their warm spring-like traits, the cold rainy night when Merritt stumbled into town replaced by warm nights and pleasant sun-filled days.

In and around Valeria, except for gathering places like the old depot at the edge of town, underneath the no-longer-in-use bridge spanning the river, or the ends of alleys with no pass-through, most of the homeless wandered the streets alone.

Seemingly displaced persons no longer gathered around rusty barrels teeming with roaring fires to warm their poorly clothed bodies. Each appeared to go his or her separate way, although sometimes in pairs or threes. Whether for safety or companionship, one could not say.

It's just the way it was.

In the daytime, some would go to into the closest branch of the public library, especially if they were seeking warmth. Unwelcome glances prevented them from staying too long, however. At night, they gathered in their unseen places with those they trusted—their homeless brethren.

A few would attempt to spend a night in the bus depot. There had been a time when all extra benches in the depot were taken as makeshift beds for the homeless, but when the city erected a new depot, overnight stays became virtually impossible—and physically dangerous for the unfortunate ones.

Merritt felt like an outsider her first few weeks in Valeria. Being part of a new community seemed foreign to her; she had become accustomed to being alone. Except for her stays at Meadow Lawn, Merritt had lived alone ever since Barry and Megan left their home in Melville Heights.

Now her "home" had no walls, bounded only by the buildings that created the parameters for the numbers known only as *street people*.

The first night Merritt was among them, she again slept soundly, with only a stack of cardboard for a pillow. Still wearing the raggedy coat wrapped tightly around her, she didn't notice until the following day that the man who went by the title of "Old Johnny" had no coat. Since the breeze had again turned warm, a southerly breeze, she no longer had need of a warm wrap and returned it to Johnny. He didn't deny it was his, and she didn't apologize for what she was sure had been a couple of cold, uncomfortable nights for her benefactor. She simply handed the coat to him with a soft-spoken, "Thank you," and a smile.

As Merritt looked at Johnny, he noted her eyes the color of wildflowers that grew in abundance along the railroad tracks—

lavender flowers—and his old heart that had known so much despair and loneliness skipped a beat.

Merritt adapted to the life style of her surroundings quite well. Most days she kept to herself, shy and cautious. Some days were really good days, when even the voices gave her some respite from their taunts.

One day shortly after her arrival in Valeria, when the voices were being particularly silent and had allowed her a dreamless sleep, Merritt was feeling quite gregarious as she looked at her companions. Dawn was just breaking, and the smattering of Valeria's street people with whom Merritt had spent the night sleeping under the stars were beginning to awaken.

Merritt remembered how she felt the previous night, stretched out on the ground with nothing to obstruct her vision of the heavens above. It was miraculous, she thought; here was the same sky that had covered her with its brightness back home.

As she gazed at the stars, she recalled doing the same with little Megan lying on one side of her and Barry on the other. They were enjoying a "camp-out" in the backyard of their upscale Melville Heights home.

The neighbors frowned upon the garish green and gold tent Barry proudly erected for their adventure—in full view from the homes on either side of the Davis dwelling. But the Davis family trio didn't care about their neighbors' censorship; they enjoyed their night outdoors to the fullest—free of work and worry, free of headaches and voices.

With the voices quiet the previous night as she lay among her new friends beneath the glorious starlit sky, Merritt recaptured some of the deep feelings of peace, contentment, and companionship that had been so prevalent on that family outing so many years ago.

The feelings were still with Merritt when she awoke. Walking up to Gert—slowly and somewhat shyly—she said, "I was admiring your lovely jewelry. It's so gay and colorful—really attractive."

Gert's bright-red painted lips spread in a wide smile. "It is beautiful, ain't it," she agreed, prancing away like royalty adorned with the crown jewels.

Merritt smiled. It felt good to make someone happy. That same feeling of fulfillment that had swept over her when, as a physician, she helped a patient who was having an especially bad day—a day one of her favorites would call "a day from hell."

She kept her smile all morning, making complimentary comments to others of her street compatriots. Some smiled at her kindness; some glared, and some growled. But their reactions didn't matter to Merritt. She was enjoying a good day. Her high spirits had barely begun to fade as night fell—when again her slumber was tortured with nightmares and fiendish voices.

* * *

Merritt slept in doorways and on fire-escape steps, with cardboard boxes serving as both pillow and blanket. Asleep or awake, she still clutched the handles of her now-totally-tattered shopping bag, the remaining contents spilling out through holes along the bottom and sides. It no longer bore any resemblance to the colorful bag designed to tote gala Christmas gifts from the department store.

Little by little, Merritt learned the names of most of her companions. Some she never saw again after that first night, when she was welcomed to their ranks. Like vagabonds of old, many of the homeless keep moving.

Perhaps they felt they could outrun their loneliness and pain.

But there was a core group, those who gathered together often and seemed almost like family—a family whose members bore little resemblance to one another, where each held unique and individual characteristics.

Old Johnny's bent frame was wrapped in a filthy navy-blue sport coat many sizes too large, the front nearly dragging on the ground as he ambled along—the same coat that covered Merritt the night she arrived in the city of Valeria. Dirty white stubble peppered Old Johnny's deeply lined face—lines so deep they looked like the crevasses down the side of a grassless hill after a heavy rain. No hair adorned his sunburned head. Not a single strand. His eyes were so light, they appeared to be a non-color, and they hid behind glasses so thick and heavy, they slid halfway down his nose—a nose badly off-center and constantly dripping.

The ponderous eyeglasses did nothing to improve Johnny's sight; in fact, they made it more difficult for the old gent to see. But he found the glasses floating in the gutter one rainy day, and he immediately added them to his treasured possessions jammed into the large bag he always carried on his back.

Unless Old Johnny was sitting, which he rarely did, or sleeping,

72

his bag was over his shoulder, riding on his bent back. When he slept, the stuffed bag was transformed into his pillow. Johnny lugged his bag in addition to the holey clothes basket filled with rags that he dragged behind him by a rope tied securely through one of the basket's holes. His load was cumbersome and likely heavy for a man of his size and age. Johnny didn't travel lightly.

Evan was as tall as Johnny was short. A wild head of bright red hair topped his long face, and short brushy red lashes shaded blue eyes, once bright, but now dull and lifeless.

From a distance, Evan appeared younger than he was, most likely because of his colorful shock of unruly hair. But up close, his age was displayed in his craggy countenance, numerous wrinkles on his heavily freckled ruddy face, and age spots up and down his also heavily freckled arms.

Bright colors covered Evan's tall, gaunt body. A gaudy green shirt, a large hole in front where a pocket once had been, covered his upper torso, gray-red chest-hair curling through the opening. Checkered pants, perhaps blue in color, or maybe purple at one time, rose three or four inches above his ankles. Now although still somewhat colorful, the threadbare pants were too grimy to really determine what color they had once been. Red suspenders completed his ensemble, one clasp missing, the free strap flapping as he walked.

Then there was Louis. Had he ever smiled, Louis might have been easily mistaken for Santa Claus. But he didn't smile. Not ever. His tangled white hair cascaded down to his shoulders, and his beard, also white, but encrusted with food and filth, reached to his portly waist. Louis wore a filthy ragged T-shirt over baggy gray pants sporting several cigarette-burn holes. A tie, decorated with many colors and breeds of ducks splashed across a dark background, was tied loosely around his neck. Louis' pants were always unzipped for two or three inches, allowing more space for his ample belly.

It was a mystery how Louis maintained his corpulent frame. Very few had ever seen him eat, concluding he must gorge himself privately whenever he found nourishment.

Another was called Danny. Danny's face was red with rash, a rash he scratched nearly raw. A wide flat nose over a nearly lipless wide mouth completed Danny's visage. Blue jeans, worn completely through at the knees, and a grimy gray sweatshirt gave Danny the appearance of a too-old teenager.

Gert's attire was mindful of a Gypsy—long red skirt billowing about her knees, a multicolored scarf draped over her long gray hair, layers of chains about her neck, and bright silver earrings, hoop style.

Her face was heavily made up, with bright-red lipstick outlining full lips, circles of rouge adorning sagging cheeks, and heavy eye make-up outlining her brown eyes, giving them a raccoon-like appearance.

Merritt's new family.

One morning, just a few days after she had arrived, Merritt awoke to a question, "What's yer name?"

Merritt turned her head to get a better view of her inquisitor. Looking through eyes still blurry from sleep, Merritt could barely make out the face hovering no more than six or eight inches from hers in the predawn semi-darkness. Fetid breath mixed with copious amounts of cheap perfume drifted to her nostrils.

She sat up with a start.

Noting earrings so large they nearly touched the shoulders of her awakener, Merritt concluded that she had been aroused by the one known as Gert. Gert's trademark was profuse amounts of jewelry—bracelets, necklaces, rings, and earrings. Long dangling earrings.

The question was repeated. "What's yer name?"

Merritt opened her mouth to speak, but could only emit a squeak. She coughed to clear her throat and again tried to speak. "Mah," she squeaked.

Before Merritt could again attempt to say her name, Gert cupped her hand over her ear and said, "What's that? Moll, you say? Okay, hon, we'll call you Molly."

From that day on, Dr. Merritt Hall-Davis became known as Molly. Molly who lived on the street.

Chapter Eleven

Merritt had days, however, when she didn't feel like Molly—didn't feel like she belonged to the community she had been deemed a part of since arriving in Valeria in the early spring. Most often, those feelings pervaded her contentment first thing in the morning, when she was greeted by a new day so unlike those that had surrounded her in the past.

As light began its glow in a narrow band along the horizon, Merritt looked about her surroundings and was overcome with feelings of being different, feelings of alienation. She didn't belong here in this unusual community of street people—no matter how kind they were!

They call me Molly, when they call me anything at all. But my name is Merritt. They are impoverished and ill. But I'm neither. I have more money in the bank than I could begin to spend in a lifetime, and I'm not ill—well, not really ill, anyway. I just need my medication.

I've only been here a few weeks. I bet Helen and Jake Barney would be thrilled to hear from me. And Marsha, too.

Pangs of guilt shot through her as she thought of her dear loyal friend and employee, Marsha Givens. She had never even bothered to tell Marsha good-bye. Merritt's eyes stung with tears as she thought of the wonderful friends she left behind. She got up from the stoop where she was sitting and walked away from the early-morning gathering of the homeless.

Soon, the whole group would be dispersing. Gatherings of the homeless at night didn't cause many problems for those who called the streets of Valeria "home," but more than two together during the day made the city fathers uneasy. The homeless sensed this, so in order to maintain peace for their numbers, they nearly always scattered by sunrise.

The stirring of those awakening from their beds of cardboard and newspapers was just beginning. Those who had opened their eyes were engrossed in stretching and yawning. No one noticed Merritt steal swiftly away.

Although Merritt had only been in Valeria for a few short weeks, she was certain she once spotted a homeless mission within three-quarters of an hour from where she was sleeping the night before—

on a pile of folded-down boxes behind *Les Osburne's Furniture Store*.

I know someone at the mission will help me call the Barneys—or Marsha Givens. Maybe they'll even help me get the medicine I need.

For the first time, Merritt found herself wishing she had taken greater care with her purse. She had no idea where she left it—wasn't entirely certain it wasn't snatched from her while she dozed during her long travels to Valeria.

I need the medications, she reasoned. Rarely during the past few weeks did she dwell on the fact that medicine was vital to keep her thinking straight—to keep the voices at bay. But this morning her mind was sharp; she was keenly aware of her situation.

Unfortunately, when Merritt emerged from the alley behind the furniture store, she turned the opposite way from the path she should have taken to find the mission. She remembered correctly—it was less than an hour from where she slept the previous night. If she had only turned the right direction.

Instead, Merritt did not find the mission until the day was drawing to a close. She wandered all day, lost in the outskirts of the city. She was exhausted by the time she reached the mission— exhausted, discouraged, and hungry. As well as very confused.

The voices in her head hammered at her all afternoon. The keen awareness that had controlled her decision to seek help early in the morning faded, and Merritt's decision-making processes were again impaired. Her head ached, and her eyes burned from the hammering assault of the voices. The headache affected her balance, and her staggering caused those she encountered in her wandering to avoid her.

When Merritt finally reached the mission, she stopped in her tracks. The sun was low in the sky and bounced off the window bearing the sign, *Westside Valeria Mission*. She peered in the window, cupping her hands around her face. Merritt didn't see anyone inside that she recognized. Nor did she remember why she wanted to come here. Gone were thoughts of Helen and Jake Barney and Marsha Givens, gone were thoughts of going home. The voices had drowned out her intentions and her plans.

The voices plagued Merritt through the next several days. She sought comfort in her street friends, found solace in the homeless community.

Even though, from time to time, she still thought of her home and the friends she left behind, Merritt didn't seek help to return—or to get her medications. She resigned herself to becoming a member of the homeless community of Valeria, to becoming Molly.

Chapter Twelve

Molly woke slowly, and for a moment she didn't know where she was. That happened to her a lot these days. She would sleep so soundly and in so many different places, confusion would sweep over her as she shook herself from the throes of deep slumber.

Sometimes, just before she awoke, she would think she was back home, back in Blythe, Missouri, at her home in Melville Heights, and she would reach out next to where she was lying. For whom?

Barry, maybe? Or Megan?

These were mornings following days when her mind had moments of clarity—when her sleep was filled with memories and dreams, not nightmares. She would awake slowly then, relishing the sensation that there was someone close by to touch.

Then, Molly would fight waking, not wanting to part with her memories. Sometimes a smile would reach her lips, as she remembered Barry's arms around her when they slept, or the warmth of her daughter's little-girl body as she lay beside her.

Sometimes a tear would escape as she remembered they were gone, and she would be engulfed in sadness.

This morning was a "sadness" morning. Her face was wet with tears shed, and her throat ached with those unshed.

It was a hot morning—sticky and sultry even before the sun was up. Molly wiped away her tears with her hands and rubbed her fists in her eyes to clear her vision. She was in a park, lying beneath a huge evergreen tree.

Now she remembered.

She had been slowly ambling through the park last night and relished the fragrance of the evergreens resting on the hot summer air. She was alone—she wanted to be alone.

The park reminded her of her childhood, of the park-like grounds surrounding the school she attended as a girl. Even then, as a child, she sometimes wanted to be alone as she wandered the paths winding through the gigantic evergreens, the fresh smell of pine tickling her nostrils.

It had been a quiet nostalgic summer night. But she knew she couldn't remain where she was now that the light rays of dawn were invading the darkness of last night's sky.

With a sigh, Molly lifted her bag, damp with the early morning dew, and walked slowly away from her resting place, her heart heavy with longing.

***

It was a brutally hot summer. Heat rose from the city streets in visible waves, and humidity saturated the sweltering heavy air. Crime in Valeria escalated as tempers ignited by the merciless high temperatures ran rampant. Sometimes the homeless were the victims of the subsequent violence; other times, they were accused of being the perpetrators.

Occasionally, they were guilty. Most of the time, they were not.

The street people had an uneasy summer, Molly's first on the street. They took great care not to gather in groups too large; many scattered. Some drifted to smaller, surrounding towns. But the smaller sites had fewer resources for the homeless, fewer opportunities for them to find food and shelter.

Small communities both resented and feared their presence. To stay more than a day or two in a place not sizeable enough to tolerate any infringement on its orderliness was risky, and more than a few of the summer's scattered street people spent a night or two in small-town jails.

A few of the familiar street group elected to stay in Valeria. Molly was one of them. Johnny was another.

Molly fared better than Johnny. Other than being taunted by a group of rude, thoughtless teenagers and being chased down an alley by a broom-wielding restaurant proprietor who discovered her rummaging through his garbage, Molly's summer was uneventful.

Old Johnny's inability to run earned him a stay in the county hospital. He couldn't outpace his aggressor and was a perfect target for a severe blow to the head—for no other reason than sheer meanness, as Johnny possessed absolutely nothing anyone else would desire.

Johnny was discovered by Riley MacRae, policeman and good friend to the less fortunate who made the streets of Valeria their home. He recognized the inert Johnny immediately and summoned the ambulance that whisked him to the hospital, sirens blaring.

Riley guessed it had been a very long time since Johnny received that much attention, but he was damned if he was going to allow the old gent to lie in the alley and die. Not on his beat.

79

The next time Riley spotted Johnny, the elderly, stooped street resident was adding to his accumulation of rags, vigorously sorting through discards behind a Salvation Army Thrift Store. The more thoughtless affluent often used the site as a dumping spot for clothing so old and torn, it was of use to no one. No one but Johnny.

Riley smiled as he watched Johnny doing what he seemed to love most—add to his stash of rags. His was certainly not a quality life. That he had lost somewhere along life's way. But he had the right to his own level of happiness, thought Riley.

And he had the right to be alive.

***

Who was Riley MacRae, this policeman so filled with compassion for a group that many regarded as discarded humanity—less-than-human individuals who'd rather eat other people's garbage and sleep in alleyways than do an honest day's work?

Riley knew it wasn't so. He had been poor—dirt poor. As had his parents and grandparents before him. But they worked hard, all of them.

His grandparents left their home in Ireland to escape the poverty that threatened their very existence, to save their lives and the lives of their seven children. And they brought their poverty with them.

Misfortune after misfortune befell the MacRaes in the new Promised Land, America. But at least here they had food—most of the time.

Riley's grandparents didn't live long enough to see their family members rise above the impecunious state that had haunted their entire lives. Both succumbed to an influenza epidemic when most of their children were still young. Two of the children were lost to the dreaded disease as well.

But the other five flourished. Aided by the church and the close-knit Irish community surrounding them, and spurred on by the memory of their parents' desire for a better life, they worked hard and studied diligently. Joseph, the youngest, became a doctor—Beatrice, the oldest, a teacher.

Beatrice had plenty of practice. She, along with her sister Kathleen, raised the boys after their parents' deaths. No small feat for two teenagers who were still terribly homesick for Ireland and fearful for their own survival.

But they treasured their parents' memories and those of their

80

two little sisters buried by their parents' sides in the charity section of the Catholic cemetery at the edge of town. So they pooled their child-rearing knowledge, their ambitious drives for success, and their strong sense of family.

They became their brothers' parents.

Their success rate was as good as that of most of their neighbors in the poor Irish-American section of Valeria they called home. They were so proud when their baby brother became *Dr.* Joseph MacRae, they could hardly contain themselves.

They were equally proud of Patrick. Never the student, Patrick opted for a more laborious career as a farm hand. But he was a good boy and contributed all his meager earnings to the care of the family.

Only Jimmy didn't make it. Attracted far too young to the bottle—and the wild life that accompanied it—Jimmy MacRae died in an alcoholic stupor. Alone.

The loss of their fun-loving brother Jimmy saddened his brothers and sisters tremendously. But he had not joined them at their table for quite some time, so they accepted the fact that they had really been losing him little by little. His death simply finalized their loss.

Four remained to reach adulthood and the lives their parents dreamed they might have when they left their homeland.

Only two of the seven children of Sean and Catherine MacRae were now alive. Riley's dad, Patrick—known fondly as Paddy—and Kathleen. Riley's Auntie Kate. Riley had been raised by his dad and his aunt, his mother having died immediately following his difficult birth.

The household of Paddy, Kathleen, and Riley MacRae didn't display much luxury. None, in fact. But love abounded, and respect for others was their credo.

Paddy had been seriously injured in a farm-machinery accident two years after his wife died, two years after his son was born. Going through life sans his right arm definitely limited his career potential, but never his attitude about life. He decided maybe he wasn't cut out for farm labor after all. Grain dust had caused lung problems, adding to his disabled status.

But Paddy didn't regard himself as disabled, only slowed down a bit. He wanted to spend more time with his young son, anyhow, and the life of an itinerant field worker most certainly didn't allow that.

So Paddy offered his services as janitor to the neighborhood police station. You can push a broom just fine with one arm, he reasoned. And his boy could be with him.

Consequently, Riley grew up in the eighth precinct station. Often riding on the shoulders of his burly one-armed dad or one of the patrolmen who came to love the little boy with black curly hair and deep-blue eyes framed by dark lashes so long he would be the envy of many a young woman in years to come.

Sometimes, Riley would just sit on a bench under the watchful eye of the desk sergeant while his father cleaned an area of the station where the child wasn't allowed. There he'd watch all manner of men and women who were unfortunate enough to have been caught in the act of breaking the laws of Valeria—and this small sensitive boy felt sorry for all of them.

At home, too, Kate and Paddy taught him not to judge the unfortunates. Sometimes, they told him, "You don't know their whole story, why they do the things they do."

Kate and Paddy remembered when their own father had stolen to feed his family. And there hadn't been a more decent and God-fearing man on the face of the earth than Sean MacRae.

Sean had wept when he placed the food, the result of his thievery, on the table; Catherine, his wife, wept with him. But he couldn't let his young ones starve. He was certain God understood that.

Both Kate and Paddy instilled in Riley the values that guided his life work on the police force of Valeria—hard work, honesty, and compassion. Everyone who worked with Riley MacRae agreed he was the hardest working, most honest, and most caring cop on the force.

He even cared about Old Johnny.

***

By the end of the summer, Molly's persona had almost totally replaced that of Merritt. If someone had called the name of Merritt or that of Dr. Hall—or Dr. Hall-Davis—it's doubtful she would have recognized it as her own, and replied.

She no longer lived in that world.

The heat wave finally broke. It had dominated the news, not only in Valeria, but in much of the entire country. Major cities had experienced loss of electric power on more than one occasion, as days of maximum air-conditioning demands taxed systems beyond their capacities.

Cool breezes drifted across Molly's face as she lay tucked beneath the shrubbery in the center of Heritage Park. She shivered slightly, even though as usual, she was decked in multilayers of clothing. She was drenched in perspiration when the weariness of the day had overtaken her, and she lay down under the clear starlit sky, curled up beneath the shrubbery still carrying the faint scent of summer blossoms, and fell into a deep sleep.

Molly smiled in her half-sleep, as the breezes gently caressed her face. The state between sleeping and waking was always the best for Molly. Even when the voices tormented her mercilessly while she slept, and pounded on and on in her head as she roamed the streets and countryside, they gave her peace as she neared awakening each day.

She touched her own face, perhaps pretending it was the touch of another. Perhaps simply trying to contain the kiss of the breeze. Her eyes opened slowly, and she viewed her surroundings. Again she smiled. She stretched, barely conscious any longer of the aches and stiffness that plague the homeless as they sleep night after night devoid of the comforts of a bed.

Molly was becoming acclimated to the life of the homeless— to the life of a "street person."

The cool breeze continued through the day, the torpid heat of the summer finally dissipated. Tempers that flared yesterday were not evident today, and the homeless returned to an easier, calmer existence on the streets of Valeria.

Chapter Thirteen

Molly walked along the street, surrounded by crowds of hurrying people. A Monday morning, most were rushing to jobs or other places of perceived importance. Several gathered at street corners to board buses, their eyes scanning newspapers to learn of any changes in the state of the country or their community that might have occurred while they slept.

A group of children congregated at one corner, waiting for the light to give them the go-ahead. They were on their way to the school housed behind the cathedral majestically towering over this section of downtown Valeria.

Molly watched the children as they bantered and played, their young voices mingling with the cacophony of honking horns and screeching brakes. The bell in the old cathedral rang, its resonant melody beckoning the young as they disappeared through the doors of the cathedral to begin their day.

She watched as the last child—a little girl, properly scrubbed and shining, her school uniform clean and starched—disappeared through the church's portals. Molly was swept with a feeling of utmost grief as she watched the children.

Oh, Megan, she anguished, *where are you?*

Molly's thoughts had become so confused, she did not always comprehend that her daughter, as well as her husband, were dead—that her daughter had been a young woman before her untimely death, her little-girl days long ago left behind.

Molly made her way along the sidewalk pressed up against the buildings, avoiding the onslaught of rushing crowds along the way. Most avoided her as well, allowing a wide path around this unkempt woman carrying a nearly empty tattered Christmas shopping bag.

It was late September.

Molly's thoughts ran rampant as she walked the streets. She felt so sad, the tears streamed down her face—a face that, after enduring the hot summer sun and wind, was tan and wrinkled. She appeared old—many years older than she was.

On the heels of her sadness, anger flared up, and she pounded on the buildings as she passed them. Sometimes her fist would pound on the plate glass windows where a store's wares were displayed, ready to entice the consumer.

More than one proprietor or store manager came tearing out their door of the establishment, ready to accost the would-be window breaker, only to see her disappear down the street—a threat to no one.

As Molly wended her way through the morning throngs, her foot kicked a small pill bottle. It rolled ahead about six inches, stopping up against a building. Molly bent to pick it up, almost causing a well-dressed gentleman to fall over her as she came to an abrupt halt.

"Watch out, you damned old fool," he yelled, catching himself before tumbling over Molly's inert body. "Somebody needs to round up all those good-for-nothing bums and run them out of town," he muttered with disdain as he continued down the sidewalk towards his destination.

Molly was oblivious to his uncaring words. She had heard them all before, throughout the spring and summer as she wandered the streets of the city.

Her concentration was focused on her find.

She shook the bottle. Three small pills rattled inside the colorless plastic vial. Round white pills.

Molly smiled and placed the bottle with its treasured contents in her pocket and walked on down the street, picking up her pace, as if she, too, now had a destination, a purpose for her early morning stroll.

Pills are good, she thought, remembering vaguely the admonition from people she knew before she left home. In her muddled memories, she wasn't certain who they all were, but she could picture two of them in her mind. One was a short man with gray hair. He had a soft voice and was very kind to her. Kind and patient.

Molly was remembering Dr. Gus Halverson. The other memory was of her late husband, Barry.

She walked until she came to the edge of the commercial part of the city. The buildings with their elegant storefronts were left behind, replaced by warehouses, small shops, and greasy diners. The part of the city where most of the street people congregated.

When Molly came to the beginning of an alley that traveled behind the buildings, she turned from her straight path and nearly ran until she came to a raised doorway behind an abandoned store. In the days when this part of the city had seen greater prosperity, before the center of commerce had spread south and east, the building had housed a women's clothing store. Now it housed only dust and rodents.

She rested on this doorstep many times over the spring and summer. So had many of the other homeless. This morning, the alley was empty except for Molly and a brown shaggy dog, so thin its ribs protruded. It eyed her warily.

Wheezing from her hurried pace, Molly sat down and removed the pill bottle from her pocket. Again she smiled. She recalled that she was supposed to take pills. It was important. They would make the voices go away. They would keep her "well."

She shook all three small white pills into her hand, and one by one, swallowed them.

Molly was walking down the alleys, checking to see if any discarded items from the rows of retail establishments could be of use to her, when she began to feel light-headed. The back doors of the buildings and the trash cans flanking the thoroughfare she was traveling shimmered like beads of water on a hot griddle, and her body was soon drenched in sweat mindful of the sweltering summer.

Molly became sick. Very sick. She vomited again and again, feeling that, surely, her entire insides would leave her body. When she finally could heave no more, she was overtaken by an incredible chill. She shook until her teeth chattered.

As Molly was in the throes of being sick, bent over a trash barrel overflowing with refuse, other street dwellers wandered down this alley so well traveled by the homeless. One of them was Gert.

Gert had rarely shown compassion or caring to any of the others. She seemed interested only in chatter, herself, and her wild garish clothes and jewelry.

But this morning, the chatterbox of their ranks held Molly's head as she heaved until the poison she had inadvertently consumed left her body. When the chills overtook her, Gert held her tightly to give her warmth, laid her down on the ground, and covered her with her own coat. Her treasured bright purple coat. She stood watch as Molly slept, weak from her bout of vomiting. In late afternoon when Molly awoke, still somewhat weak but able to get up and walk, Gert was still there.

Molly smiled at her companion, got shakily to her feet and said softly, "Thank you."

In time, Molly became well known for her gentle words of thanks. She often expressed her sincere gratitude in those soft-spoken words.

Until, that is, her illness became so severe that she rarely spoke at all.

Molly no longer trusted the advice of her memories.

Pills do not make you well.

Chapter Fourteen

Gusts of wind sent multicolored leaves swirling around Molly like confetti dropped from rooftops during a parade. As she walked, the leaves so recently adorning the trees bordering the boulevards crunched beneath her feet.

Molly wrapped her coat more tightly around her. She had her own coat now. Johnny found it for her—a right handsome black coat, a man's coat, once adding distinction to its wearer. Now it was in sad shape, one pocket ripped almost to the hem of the coat—a hem three-quarters out, adding length. The red-and-black-plaid lining hung through the tear, giving its wearer an almost clown-like appearance.

The garment was meant for a taller person and entirely covered Molly's small frame, from the turned-up collar at her neck, to her small feet—feet still wearing the old, comfortable shoes she packed in her bag when she left home. The ones she put on when she tossed her designer shoes into a farmer's field last spring. It was a warm coat, and Molly considered herself very fortunate to have it, to be protected from the chilling wind.

Molly lifted her chin and raised her head to the sky, deeply breathing in the crisp cool air of autumn. She loved autumn—always had. There were so many beginnings to this season that to many expressed instead, endings. Endings to the warmth and leisure of the long days of summer.

But Molly—Merritt—had been the quintessential student, eagerly anticipating the beginning of school year each fall. She and Barry had been married in the fall, on a day much like the one today. Beneath a clear blue autumnal sky, Doctors Hall and Davis had spoken their marriage vows.

And Megan Marie Davis had been born on a gusty October day.

As the days grew shorter and the nights colder, the number congregating in the "old town" district alleys, as the groupings of abandoned warehouses on the west end of downtown Valeria were known, grew. Some were those who had been living on the streets of Valeria for a long time, but had wandered elsewhere while the weather allowed. Molly had not seen Evan and Danny since late last spring when the air was freshly filled with the perfumed fragrance of honeysuckle. Now they returned here, to the site where she had first met them, where the homeless had first welcomed her to their fold.

Others were new, having wandered into the city during the warmer days of summer and early autumn.

One of these was a woman much older than Molly, who appeared to share Molly's mental affliction. She screamed out in her sleep and seemed perennially angry. She rarely spoke, except to mumble. It took Gert nearly three weeks to learn this one's name. Laurel. Her name was Laurel like the laurel tree, and she refused to say anything other than her name.

Molly thought it was a beautiful name.

Laurel's presence troubled Molly. In this woman, so bent, so haggard and old, she saw herself. The herself she would become. It filled her with much fear and some loathing. At times she'd wonder why she didn't return home—the beautiful surroundings from which she came.

But the wonderings would be very brief, and most of the time she had no solid recollections of home, no longer really knew where home was. And she never began to make plans to leave Valeria, hadn't seriously made plans since the day early in the summer when she searched for the mission.

Occasionally, during the worst times, she didn't even remember that she had a home other than the streets where she had spent the last two seasons.

Molly awoke, as Laurel's screams and ravings filled the night air. Or was it her own screams that had awakened her?

Only Johnny and Louis were in this alleyway tonight, along with Molly and Laurel, and they appeared undisturbed by the shrieks tearing through the stillness of the night.

Perhaps they had simply been on the street so long, they heard only what they desired to hear—even when they slept.

But as a relatively new resident of street life, Molly was awakened by Laurel's screams. The chilling sounds startled and terrified her. The fear that it may have been her own screams that ripped through the still night air only heightened her terror. She sat up and pushed herself off into a corner, away from the building and the others.

Huddling against the chain-link fence outlining the boundary of the property—a fence orange with rust—Molly shivered with fear and cold. She closed her eyes, seeing inside her eyelids the black-hooded creatures that invaded her thoughts mercilessly as she slept. Suddenly she opened her eyes wide, willing herself to stay awake so that her torturers would disappear.

Awake, she watched Laurel. Laurel didn't scream again that night.

Molly sat huddled against the fence, her lavender-gray eyes staring at the sleeping Laurel until the morning light brightened the skyline of Valeria.

***

Laurel had been on the street for more than twenty years. Her mental illness was diagnosed when she was scarcely more than a child. Her illness wasn't given a name or any promise of getting better.

Herman and Mabel Swan, Laurel's parents, were simply and brutally told that their daughter was afflicted with incurable madness. They were advised to place her in an institution immediately, before she did grave harm to herself—or to others.

The diagnosis brought these straightforward rural people great pain—pain and embarrassment. However, ignoring the professional advice they had been given, they cared for their daughter in their home for three years.

It wasn't easy, but this devout Texas couple felt it was their duty to care for their own. Why this dreadful thing had to happen to their only child, they had no idea, but they felt they were to blame.

Someone had to be to blame, and who else could it possibly be but them? Surely not their little girl with the golden corkscrew curls, big blue eyes, and dimpled smile!

They felt they must have sinned terribly, and God was exacting his recompense for their failure to consistently do good. The Swan's were God-fearing people—simple people who believed everything had a logical cause, followed by an even more logical effect.

They were being punished for their sins.

They became near-recluses on their small plot of land from which they barely eked out a living. Neighbors and relatives strongly encouraged them to institutionalize this strange girl named after the cherry laurel tree the Swans had admired on their one-and-only-time visit to the southeastern part of the United States.

Mabel was enchanted by the tree's beautiful and fragrant white blossoms. When she realized she was pregnant after that trip—a

90

pregnancy she had been longing for, for more than a decade—she decided to name the baby Laurel, if a girl.

A boy would, of course, be named Herman, after his father.

Following an unduly long and arduous labor, Mabel delivered a beautiful little girl. She was immediately named Laurel.

Laurel proved to be a nearly perfect baby—beautiful and charming. Mabel nearly burst with pride the first time she brought the baby to a Ladies' Missionary Society meeting, as the women gathered around her, "oohing and aahing" when she pulled back the blanket from her sleeping baby's face.

All agreed they had never seen a more beautiful baby. As if on cue, Laurel opened her blue eyes and looked squarely at her group of admirers. Then her tiny rosebud mouth formed what all decided was most surely a smile.

Herman and Mabel brought Laurel with them every Sunday to the small frame church with its once-white paint now graying and peeling from the hot Texas sun and ruthless wind that never seemed to cease in this far western part of the state.

Before the age of two, Laurel would bow her curly blonde head and fold her dimpled hands at just the right places during the lengthy church service. By the time she was five, her clear sweet voice could be heard warbling the melodies of the hymns—right along with her father's rich baritone and her mother's always off-key soprano.

Laurel was an excellent student, although she studied very little. Learning just seemed to come easily to her.

She was an obedient child—helpful, too. Before the sun fully arose above the horizon of the wide Texas sky, she would take a basket and gather eggs still warm to the touch of her young-girl hand.

After school, after she had trekked the dusty three miles from the ramshackle building that served as the site of learning for the meager number of children in the area, she would join her father in the unproductive fields, trying, side-by-side, to force the barren land to produce.

Or she'd work with her mother in the house, sweeping the endless supply of dust out the door—only to have it return again by nightfall.

She enjoyed the work and could usually be heard humming the tune of a favorite hymn as she labored.

At the beginning of every day, Mabel would thank her Maker

for the wonderful gift of this child.

When Laurel was fourteen, she had her first tantrum. It both startled and frightened Mabel. Nothing in her daughter's life had prepared her for its coming.

If it had happened when Laurel was two, as Mabel had expected (and been warned to expect it by her friends and relatives), she might have been prepared. Toddlers were like that, she was told.

But there was no way she could have been ready for her daughter's curses and screams, as Laurel swept her arm across the table, knocking cups and plates to the floor, most of them shattering to pieces that no amount of glue could mend.

Mabel was distraught as she viewed the destruction Laurel had wrought upon the family's few dishes—some of which she had brought to her marriage from her own mother, deceased now many years.

Sadness for her loss was added to the terror her daughter's outburst had brought upon her peaceful and orderly household.

But not Herman. All he felt was anger when he came in from the field and saw the many pieces of their dinnerware scattered across the kitchen floor, Mabel gathering the pieces one by one in her apron, Laurel hovering nearby, wide-eyed and speechless over what she had done.

Herman whipped Laurel for her outburst—the first and last time he ever laid a hand on his daughter, this child that both he and his wife had always regarded as God's wonderful blessing to their lives. Laurel's tears so upset Mabel that Herman realized he had really punished his wife more than his child. And he deeply loved his wife—this woman who never once complained about her difficult life here in this treeless land beneath the wide Texas skies.

The Swan's lives changed after that. Mabel became wary of her daughter, wondering if there would be another tantrum, and if so, what might set it off. When they became so frequent, there was no longer any question of "if," only "when," Mabel began to withdraw from Laurel—and from Herman. She became silent, rarely speaking to her husband and *never* to her daughter.

And when the doctors told the Swan's their daughter was a hopeless madwoman, Mabel totally withdrew. She even stopped attending church.

Laurel, too, became withdrawn. She'd often miss a stretch of many school days after an outburst, and she couldn't keep up with the schoolwork she missed. When she was sixteen years old, in what would have been her junior year of high school, Laurel stopped going to school altogether.

Peppered throughout her silent young life—which now was spent entirely at home—were her loud unmanageable and unexplainable outbursts.

When Laurel was seventeen years old, and the number of raging outbursts over the three-year period had become too many to enumerate, her mother escaped the chaos her life had become. Mabel Swan hung herself. She simply was unable to deal with the anguish of the changes in the daughter she adored—and the guilt she had to deal with because of her self-inflicted blame.

Herman found his wife's lifeless body dangling from the rafters of the small barn where they stored their meager supply of produce.

Knowing Laurel was the cause of his wife's drastic action, he looked upon his daughter as a murderer and turned her out of his home.

He never saw her again.

Herman's church friends totally shunned him, regarding Mabel's suicide the work of Satan. Herman buried his wife—whom he had truly loved—alone, on the edge of his worthless land.

Herman Swan died seven years later, still alone, a bitter and defeated man.

When Laurel was forced out of the only home she had ever known, she wandered, heartbroken and sobbing, to the nearest neighbor's house. Todd and Mary Griffin loaded the girl, along with the small bag she carried containing the few possessions she owned, into their decrepit old truck and brought her to the asylum for the insane, nearly sixty miles away.

Their own three children—all under age nine—waved a frightened good-bye to their parents and the neighbor girl they only vaguely knew. Only Caleb, the oldest, could remember Laurel as the girl who held them on her lap when they were only babes and told them wonderful stories that made them laugh.

She had baked cookies for him and Sarah, his five-year-old sister, when the youngest of the trio, four-year-old Cassie, was born. He had been saddened and confused when he was forbidden to even go near Laurel if he should happen to see her anywhere close by.

93

Word of Laurel's "illness" spread rapidly across the countryside. There was little else other than gossip to amuse the farmers and ranchers in this remote community, so gossip they did. Especially the wives.

All agreed their children should distance themselves from this strange—maybe dangerous—girl. Who knows what she might do to them.

Todd Griffin would not, however, refuse entry to his unfortunate young neighbor when she came pounding on his door, nearly incoherent. He shooed his children into the other room, and sitting across from Laurel at the old chipped green-painted dining room table, listened to the story of how her father had packed her bag, shoved her through the door, and locked it behind her—without a touch or a simple good-bye.

Todd's timid wife stood off to the side, watching the door to the bedroom, ready to snatch her children if they should dare to come out. Her lank dishwater-blonde hair hung partly in her face, as she warily watched the life-important conversation going on between her husband and this girl she had grown to fear.

Mary Griffin could see the muscles working in her husband's jaw as he listened to Laurel's tale. She knew he was angry.

Todd Griffin was a quiet gentle man—introspective and private. As did Herman Swan, Todd worked hard on his land to try to make some kind of a living for his growing family. Most of the time he realized it was a hopeless task, but he continued to try.

Tenacity was his middle name, his father had always said.

And although Todd had admired Herman Swan's diligence and drive in tending his own barren land, he didn't like him. He thought his neighbor, nearly twenty years his senior, stiff-necked and self-righteous.

Now he thought him cruel as well.

Todd couldn't understand Laurel's problem any more than the others, but he certainly didn't think she was dangerous. And she didn't deserve to be shunned for something she probably couldn't help.

When Laurel had finished her tale of what amounted to "parental disowning," he turned to his wife and said in his soft Texas drawl, "Get your handbag, Mary, and tell the kids we'll be gone today. We're taking Laurel into Amarillo. There's a place there where they take care of people with her kind of problem," he added, nodding towards

Laurel, who sat quietly, her shoulders still heaving from swallowed sobs, her eyes cast down, fixed on her hands folded on her lap.

"Tell the kids they'll be alone today. And, Caleb," he called to his eldest, "the chores need to be done."

Caleb came to the edge of the doorway and stood tall—as tall as a nine-year-old small for his age could. "Yessir," he responded proudly. He had never before been given sole responsibility for the place, and it made him feel very grown-up.

"Make sure the girls do their share, too," said Todd, smiling. He knew his son wouldn't take advantage of the situation. Caleb had a gentle nature and watched over his younger siblings with a protective vengeance.

"But Todd," interrupted Mary, having listened to the exchange between her husband and son in horror, "don't you think I best stay home with the children?"

Not that she was worried about leaving the children alone. They had done that before—although not for an entire day. Widow Johnson lived but three miles away, and Mary knew the children would go to her in a dire emergency.

But she was horrified to think she would be sitting next to this crazy girl all the way to Amarillo.

"I want you along, Mary—just in case she has some needs on the way. You know, woman needs."

So that settled it. Todd, Mary, and Laurel climbed into the truck and headed for Amarillo.

Before leaving, Mary stooped down and hugged her little girls. "Be good now. And do what your brother says. Okay?" She gave them a big insincere smile.

Inside she was seething. How could her husband do this? Why couldn't they just send Laurel on her way?

But she crawled into the truck, taking great care to sit as far from Laurel as she could. With a wave to their children, Todd and Mary Griffin set off down the dusty road on their way to Amarillo.

When they dropped off the sobbing troubled teenager, the Griffins felt they had fulfilled their Christian duty. But as they drove away, Todd kept glancing back. He felt he could have done more, knew he should have done more. This was a child—a sick child. He felt guilty, but what more could he do?

Mary didn't care. She just wanted to go home, to get back to her own children, away from this frightening place.

For nearly two decades, Laurel resided in this warehouse for humanity regarded as "imperfect but acceptable" by those making such judgments. Most of the time, she simply sat, appearing more like a vegetable than a person.

But at times, she demonstrated some of her youthful vigor, as she was allowed to roam the gated grounds and benefit from the fresh air. Laurel also retained her intelligence. Contrary to Herman and Mabel's beliefs, their daughter had never lost her innate brilliance. It was only the confining structure required by attending school that she couldn't handle.

That and the fear of an *episode*.

Laurel's doctor kept her supplied with books to read and paper and pencils to write with. The pencils they collected from time to time, for fear she might inflict some damage to herself or someone else. But when she was having a series of good days, she wrote endlessly.

During her episodes, she was locked in a room without furnishings, except for a bare mattress upon the floor.

One day, Laurel simply walked away. Unattended, relishing the outdoor privileges she had enjoyed for years, she walked through the gate, across the countryside, and into the city.

There was no search for this woman, now middle-aged. No one really missed her. Although it might be said that her doctor did. For a time. He initiated a cursory search, concerned that some danger might have befallen Laurel. But when the search turned up fruitless, nothing more was done to find her.

The doctor fought pangs of conscience for quite some time, but other than him, no one even gave Laurel a second thought. She held no place in the memories of family, friends, or those whose paths she had crossed. There was no one to mourn Laurel Swan's disappearance, no one to miss her.

Laurel was considered a non-person, a "madwoman" who lived on the streets of various cities in the center of the country for many years. How she traveled from city to city, no one knew—or cared. She would simply disappear from one place and show up in another.

Now she was in Valeria.

Chapter Fifteen

Laurel awoke early, stretched and emitted animal-like grunts as she rose unsteadily to her feet. She shivered terribly as the cold morning air struck her aging body.

Suddenly, Molly was filled with compassion. Her fears of the night melted away as the first streaks of dawn edged the horizon. *This woman is too old to be living like this,* she thought. *She will die this winter if someone doesn't watch out for her.*

Molly didn't know that Laurel had survived many a brutal winter on the streets. Sometimes it did seem like she wouldn't be alive come spring, but somehow, she always was. Some years, she would simply disappear when the winter was its coldest—to where, no one knew. Then with the first hint of spring, Laurel would again appear.

Molly felt the same stirrings of caring for Laurel that she felt for the women who had come to the clinic—those whom life had failed and ignored. She stood up from her spot by the fence, stiff with the cold and the cramped position she had been curled in during the night. She walked over to Laurel and gently took her arm.

Laurel pulled quickly away, looking at Molly with fear in her eyes akin to that of a cornered animal. Molly backed off, remembering clearly how many times she had pulled away and fled when an unfamiliar hand grabbed her. But Laurel didn't flee. She just stood as if stunned. Again, Molly walked over to her, gently took her arm and said, "Come with me."

Tears gathered in Laurel's eyes—from the cold or the unfamiliar show of kindness, one couldn't say, but she walked alongside Molly as they made the trek to the spot just outside of town where Molly was warmed the night she arrived in Valeria the preceding spring. There, the two women warmed themselves over the fire in a trash barrel, crowding together with the others already thawing their bodies chilled from the previous night's frigid air.

Laurel stayed by Molly's side that entire day, and several following days. Although the nights continued to be bitter, the days were warmed by sunshine, and by the afternoon, they were fairly pleasant. The two women, one dressed in her too-large black coat with red-plaid fabric draping from the torn pocket, her brown-gray curly hair blowing freely in the stiff late autumn breezes, the other wrapped in layers—a jacket, a coat, a pea-green crocheted shawl, topped by a scarf.

Laurel's head was covered with a floral scarf, fringed on the edges, tied firmly in a knot beneath her prominent chin—an appearance reminiscent of sepia photographs of immigrants entering Ellis Island before the turn of the twentieth century. Laurel's girlhood beauty was a long-gone thing of the past. Her bones protruded in all parts of her body, her face accented by caved-in looking cheeks beneath high cheekbones. Her bony pointed chin made the rest of her face seem even more sunken.

Molly would often throw her head back and breathe in the sharp fresh air. It filled her lungs and heightened the color in her cheeks. Sometimes her eyes would sparkle with pleasure; at other times, they would fill with unbidden tears of longing and sadness.

Laurel never threw her head back, or smiled, or looked at anyone—anyone but Molly. She clung to Molly like a lost puppy that had finally been found—and befriended.

Molly was rarely seen without Laurel the chilly days of early winter. The cold seemed to settle in early, and shopkeepers, as well as shoppers, talked about the bitterness of the weather, projecting a "long, hard winter."

Laurel was like a child, barely able to care for herself. Molly pulled or pushed her into secluded areas for shelter, the effort of protecting her newly found friend seeming to lessen her own deteriorating condition. Her concentration on Laurel appeared to diminish her own battle with her demons. No more than once or twice a week did Molly's screams cut through the cold night air.

The others watched warily as Molly mothered Laurel, treating her like an aging grandmother for whom she was responsible. When the day temperatures rose to an enjoyable level, Molly and Laurel would walk through one of Valeria's many parks, always with Molly leading the way. On those days when it never seemed warm, or freezing precipitation pelted their ill-clad bodies, Molly would seek shelter for herself and her friend. Often they were chased from their chosen spots, but Molly would find another. Some days they would wander on and on, as unwanted as stray animals.

This went on for several days. Laurel seemed to need Molly for her survival; in turn, Molly's strong need to give was fulfilled by Laurel.

One morning after a particularly cold but beautiful night when

Molly had lain awake for hours looking at the stars stretched across a cloudless sky, Laurel was gone. Molly thought, surely, Laurel would appear again sometime during the day, but she didn't.

Molly—and the others—never saw the severely troubled aged woman again. Nor did they hear that she had been discovered frozen, dead, or injured anywhere on the streets of Valeria. She was simply gone—disappeared.

Molly missed her friend. She had been someone who needed her, someone to give some purpose to her life. Molly became more silent, more separate from the others.

Molly grieved for Laurel for a long time.

Chapter Sixteen

Molly was cold—more cold than she could ever remember being. She wore all her clothes, all those that she had once crammed into the gala Christmas shopping bag. Those plus the coat Johnny had located to protect her from the elements that relentlessly gripped the Midwest during the winter months.

Her torso appeared padded; her size undeterminable.

And yet she was cold.

The wind had switched during the night, and it had picked up in intensity, whistling around corners and carrying aloft anything light enough to be airborne. Windows rattled, and hanging signs creaked as they swayed back and forth in the strength of the northwestern gale. Trash cans rolled noisily down alleys, and debris took flight.

Yesterday was cold, yes, but not like this. It was November, and all remnants of late fall had disappeared in last week's snowfall. Snow still blanketed the ground. It had seemed pretty then, this introduction to winter.

As the snow gently fell, Molly had walked in the park. The park lay abandoned by those who took refuge behind closed doors, gathering around fireplaces and in warm kitchens, hiding from the onset of winter, glad it was Sunday so the demands of their jobs didn't force them out from the comforts of their homes. The streets were nearly empty last Sunday, that day of the first snowfall, with only churchgoers and children leaving their footprints in the smooth, pristine whiteness enveloping Valeria. The churchgoers, the children, and Molly.

The churchgoers out of need or habit, the children out of pleasure, relishing this first opportunity to drag out their sleds. Their noisy laughter could be heard from every hillside in town, as they braved the chilly snow until near darkness and parental calls forced them back indoors.

Molly had always loved the first snow—its beauty, its softness, its blinding whiteness. This first snow had been carried on the gentlest of breezes, and the large, wet flakes landing on her upturned face felt, to her, like kisses.

But today the snow was not pleasant. It was frigid and ice-crunchy, its wetness frozen by the tremendous drop in temperature.

Molly huddled in a doorway, her teeth chattering, her eyes

tearing as the brutal wind whipped her hair around her hatless head. She turned up the collar of her coat, hunching up her shoulders and shrinking her head down until the wooly fabric brushed against her aching cold ears. She stamped her feet, partly to remove snow that had crusted around the edge of the soles of her shoes—shoes that barely covered her feet and left her ankles unprotected.

"Get out of here, you piece of human garbage," roared Leland Emerson, owner of the watch-repair shop upstairs in the building where Molly had taken shelter in the doorway, shoving her brusquely out onto the sidewalk as he fumbled with his keys, locking the door for the night.

Leland Emerson, an obviously unhappy and unpleasant man, disliked many things in this world, but topping the list were the street people. "Worthless, no-good bums," he called them. His loud mutterings suggesting what should be done with these creatures dirtying his street could be heard as he walked briskly to his car, eager to get out of the cold.

Molly nearly lost her footing when she was shoved, but staggering, recovered and continued down the street. Passers-by gave her a wide berth as they increased their distance from this disreputable-looking woman, shaking their heads in disgust as they judged her staggering as drunkenness.

Keeping her head down, bucking the merciless wind, Molly glanced up only enough to avoid bumping into others, knowing she must seek shelter. She started towards the old depot, then noticed a line snaked around the corner of an enormous church. She had noticed the church before, had admired its antique-looking beauty, and had been enthralled by the melodious ring of its bells.

She looked at those in the line, hugging the stone walls of the building, trying to shelter themselves from the bitter winds. She saw that many were dressed like her—in rags and castaways. Most were men, but ten or twelve women were scattered throughout—and an occasional child. The desperate wails of an infant competed with the roar of the biting wind.

Molly joined the others in line, following the last person, the one furthest from the door offering shelter. She kept her eyes down. They all had their eyes down—except for the children. The children looked around quizzically, perhaps wondering how they, like all these other people, happened to be standing in this long line going nowhere,

101

as the harsh wind whistled around them, freezing their runny noses and making tears stream down their cheeks.

All of a sudden, the line began to move rapidly, and soon, Molly was within reach of the door. As she approached the interior of the church, the rich smell of food reached her, and she nearly reeled.

Molly had found, not only refuge from the cold, but food as well. Twice weekly the historic Morningside Presbyterian Church opened its doors to the needy and provided a soup kitchen

The soup was wonderful—thick broth filled with small cubes of meat and teeming with vegetables—onions, potatoes, carrots, celery, and cabbage. Large chunks of crusty bread were piled in baskets on the long tables where they all were seated, and huge urns of steaming hot coffee sat on a table at the edge of the room. There were stacks of small cartons of milk for the children.

The crowd was nearly silent as they spooned copious amounts of hot soup into their mouths, satisfying their hunger pangs for the time being. Little ones gulped their milk, laughing at each other as they sported "milk moustaches."

When Molly first sat down, she was shivering so violently from the cold, she could hardly get the soupspoon to her lips. Her first three attempts resulted in most of the hot liquid spilling back into the bowl.

She set her spoon down and placed her hands firmly around the bowl, letting the heat seeping through warm her. Then she leaned so close to the steaming bowl that her chin nearly touched her soup.

Only when the warmth had begun to course through her body and her shivering subsided did she again pick up her spoon and eat. By the time she finished the soup and a large mug of coffee so hot it burned her tongue until it tingled, Molly was warm.

She smiled.

Most of the crowd lingered as long as possible after completing their meal, not eager to again brave the relentless cold. They would vacate their spot at the table to make room for others, but would then mill around the door, taking a longer than necessary time to re-button coats and pull on gloves and mittens—if they were among the fortunate that had them.

Some headed for missions they had just now heard about, hoping to claim a bed for the night.

Molly simply slipped outside, again enveloped in the penetrating cold. But before she left the basement dining room of the church, she walked up to a kind-faced woman wearing a large white apron. She looked as if she might be in charge—maybe one of the cooks.

When the woman glanced her way, Molly said, "Thank you." For a brief second, she raised her eyes and met those of the woman. Then she quickly looked down again and slipped out the door.

Molly joined the throngs lining up outside Morningside Presbyterian seven subsequent times that winter. She'd go for the always hot and wonderful soup—whenever she could remember to do so.

Or whenever she was reminded—when she spotted the line snaking around the lovely old church.

Chapter Seventeen

"This seems so strange, Jake, maybe not even right—having a memorial service for Merritt when we don't even know that she's— that she's . . ."

"Dead, Helen. We're not sure Merritt is dead. But we're not sure she isn't, either. I feel we have to bring some closure to her life. I don't know. It just makes her seem so unimportant if we don't— just a name no one seems to be able to find. Like a misplaced book or something."

Helen's brown eyes glistened with tears as she sighed and said, "I know, Jake. It just seems so sad—too sad."

Helen was not an attractive woman. Her eyes were perhaps too large, appearing to protrude, her nose, long and thin, and her mouth wide and full. But everyone always commented on her kind face. You just couldn't care as much as Helen Barney and not reveal it in your face.

"We don't know where Merritt is, Helen, and we'll probably never know. We don't know why she left, we don't know where she went—and we don't know if she's still alive.

"But we can't just ignore her. Barry Davis was my best friend. And you and I both loved Merritt from the first minute we met her. You couldn't know her and not love her. And dear God, she went through so much."

Jake's eyes, too, glistened with unshed tears.

"There's no way this can have a good ending, honey. Not unless we hear from Merritt, and I really don't think that's going to happen."

Jake Barney put his arms around his wife and drew her tightly to him. For a few moments they stood, silent and sad, thinking of the friend they had lost—not even knowing where.

So Jake and Helen joined a small group of Merritt and Barry's closest friends in the chapel of St. Agnes Academy—the same chapel where Merritt and Barry had been married many years before—to observe the life and probable death of Merritt Hall-Davis.

Chapter Eighteen

Christmas was in the air, and the streets of Valeria gleamed with festivity. Garlands and wreaths adorned the lampposts flanking the downtown streets, and store windows displayed brilliantly lighted Christmas trees and other seasonal decorations, in addition to myriads of wares—suggestions for filling Christmas-list requests.

Many of the homeless joined children pressing their faces against store windows, sometimes awed with the lovely merchandise exhibited there, other times filled with sadness, as they recalled days when such finery was an integral part of their lives.

Shoppers were given little respite from the bitter cold introduced a few weeks earlier. They stamped their feet as they waited impatiently for crowded buses at bus stops, their puffs of breath visible like steam in the frosty air.

The homeless suffered in the relentless cold. It wasn't uncommon for one or two to fall asleep, unsheltered, in an alley or doorway, too unprotected and too scantily dressed to withstand the frigid temperatures. They would be found dead in the early-morning light. When news of the deaths spread throughout the street people, a fear gripped many, and they would wander the street all night, too frightened to lie down—too frightened to close their eyes for fear they might never again open them.

It was the general opinion that people who resided on the street didn't care about life, had given up and would just as soon die as not. That idea couldn't be further from the truth. In fact, this was a group that fought hard to stay alive. Their efforts paralleled those of early mankind when every hour of every day was spent finding food and shelter.

There were some benefits for the unfortunates during the days preceding the Christmas holidays. They could travel amidst the crowds navigating the streets, protected from the wind, drawing warmth from the masses.

And the masses were more generous, more giving. Handouts were not uncommon, although money was not really what they needed. They needed warmth and food. The many homeless afflicted with mental illness had no idea how to use the money to buy a meal— if they could find a restaurant where they'd even be allowed in the door. It may have once been knowledge they possessed, but weeks, months, and years living on the streets without proper nourishment and medication erased that ability.

Even though Molly suffered from mental disease of great severity, she had been living on the street for only a short time, not nearly as long as many of the others, and she did recall how to enter an establishment serving food. When she was given a five-dollar bill by a kindly well-dressed woman who "tsk, tsked," shaking her head as she walked away, having demonstrated her Christmas spirit by placing the bill in Molly's hand, Molly searched the side streets for a small diner.

Managers in the first three pushed her out the door before she was even fully inside. Shoves, combined with, "Get the hell out of here," and, "We don't serve your kind," placed her right back on the sidewalk. In one instance, almost on top of a stylish middle-aged woman who drew away as if she had been placed in mortal danger.

But Molly didn't discourage easily. She still held within her the drive and persistence so much a part of Merritt Hall.

She tried a different side street, about ten blocks from her earlier efforts, and approached a small restaurant squeezed in between a barbershop and a used-furniture store. It didn't look like much, but the smells that escaped when a pair came through the door, bundled tightly to ward off the cold, made Molly's mouth water. She cautiously peered in the window, seeing only an older couple at a table, deeply immersed in conversation, and a woman behind the counter.

The woman behind the counter wore a peach-colored uniform covered by a not-very-clean apron. Her hair, obviously dyed, was much the same color as the uniform. Peach. Her small round mouth, outlined with a thick layer of dark-red lipstick, stood out on her round pudgy face. But the mouth smiled when it spoke to Molly as she entered.

"You're welcome to spend a minute or two in here, dearie, away from the cold. In fact, take a seat at the table over there," she added kindly, nodding towards a small table set back from the door. "I'll give you a cup of coffee, but I can't afford to feed you. Like to. Just can't afford to."

"I have money," said Molly, as she sauntered over to the back table.

"Okay," said a surprised Frannie, her name sewn in orange thread on her uniform. "What'll it be?"

106

Molly looked at the menu, trying to figure in her head, what she could afford—plus coffee, plus tax. Not too long ago, she would have had the ability to do so instantly, but months without proper care had diminished what once were her outstanding mental skills.

But at least she could read and still had full understanding of her financial limitations.

Frannie studied the woman before her while Molly studied the menu. To Fran, Molly seemed to be a contradiction—matted hair, filthy clothes, unclean smell. Nonetheless, she appeared to have an air of gentility about her—the way she held her head, the way she spoke. When Molly looked directly at her, Fran thought she had never seen such beautiful eyes. *What in God's name happened to this woman?*

If Frannie had seen Molly when she wasn't having one of her rare "really good days," she probably wouldn't have questioned her place on the street, but today Molly was having an exceptionally good day.

Except she was cold and hungry—very hungry.

"This is all I have," she said as she laid the five-dollar bill on the table.

Frannie looked at the bill with surprise, but tried not to reveal her astonishment. The homeless usually didn't have money to pay for meals. Although the five wasn't a lot, at least it allowed her to feed this woman. She'd fed a street person once before—one without money, a tiny old woman who could barely stand. Sam, the cook and owner, was furious—said he wasn't running a charity kitchen, and if she gave away his food again, she was "out, out, out."

She knew Sam's bark was far worse than his bite and was fairly sure he wouldn't fire her, but she wasn't about to test it. At least not at Christmastime. She needed the money to buy presents. She may not have a lot, but how Frannie loved to buy Christmas presents.

"Well, the hot beef sandwich is quite good. The gravy isn't greasy, and the mashed potatoes don't have lumps. Not too many, anyhow," she added, smiling. "And the ham and cheese sandwich is very good—it's my favorite. I can give you a bowl of split-pea soup with that. And remember, I said the coffee is on me."

Tears stung Molly's eyes. She had become so unaccustomed to kindness, it affected her deeply. "I guess I'll try the ham and cheese— and the soup. And thank you," she said, raising her tear glistened

107

lavender-gray eyes to meet Fran's. "You're most kind."

Fran walked back to the kitchen to give the cook Molly's order, more confused than ever by Molly's softly spoken words of gratitude. And those eyes. Why she's beautiful!

After devouring her tasty and nutritious meal, Molly left the diner, but not before saying, "Thank you," to Frannie once more. She felt good—full and warm. The soup was steaming hot, and she drank three cups of coffee—all three, Frannie's gift. Her spirits were soaring as she disappeared down the street.

It was snowing again, a light snow, swirling about the heads of hurried shoppers, heads ducked low, scowls lining their faces. They pulled their coats more tightly around themselves and walked more briskly, eager to reach their destinations, to get out of the snowfall.

Not Molly. She was warm now, warm and fed, and free to enjoy Mother Nature's beauty. She whirled around like a small child, enjoying fully the beauty outside and her feeling inside. For the moment, she seemed oblivious to the fact that she was alone, homeless, and dirty—living on the street.

Strangers had shown her kindness—and it was almost Christmas.

Chapter Nineteen

Molly wandered the street alone until late that night, hesitant to relinquish her feelings of euphoria. The streets became emptier by the hour as shoppers went home, piling their packages in cars or dragging them wearily onto buses. Shopkeepers locked their doors, torn between elation over their hefty sales-profits that day and their all-encompassing exhaustion.

As the night went on and the streets became deserted, Molly, too, was becoming very tired. The snow had become heavier with nightfall, and it seeped down her neck and inside her shoes.

Molly really wasn't sure where she had wandered; she had walked far throughout the city, probably miles. She wished she had stayed closer to the familiar; she wished she would see Johnny—or Gert—or even Louis. Someone she knew. Anyone.

She missed Laurel and wished with all her heart that Laurel was still following her, that she could still hear her screams as they nestled closely in the night. If only Laurel were with her now.

The night became too still. And eerie. The only cars she saw now were patrol cars, and Molly didn't want one of them to stop her. Not even to bring her to a warm jail for loitering or the like. Whenever a car approached, she ducked in a doorway, out of sight, made easier by the falling snow.

Just as she emerged from one hiding place, she noted a church on the corner. A large church, a different church from the one that served soup to the needy. The church was well lit, sending welcoming beams to Molly, now badly needing shelter from the storm.

Molly walked apprehensively up to the door, hoping it was unlocked, but not really expecting it to be. She gently tugged on the heavy door. To her surprise, it opened! She eased herself inside, not wanting to startle anyone who might be worshipping at this late hour.

But the church appeared empty. Molly saw no one as she sat down in a back pew. She looked around her, looked at a scene so familiar to her—lighted votive candles, their small flames barely moving, but enough to cast a red glow on the wall behind them. Statues of saints lined the outside aisles; and over the ornate altar, a cross with the Christ hanging in obvious agony—a marked contrast to a large crèche where the baby Jesus slept, just to the left of the middle aisle.

The scene flooded Molly with memories. Memories of holding Megan's small hand, as together they viewed the beautifully carved statues of the holy family and the other figures completing the Christmas story in the front of St. Ignatius, where she and Barry often worshipped together—or at St. Agnes, which held such an endeared spot in her memories. The memory of herself as a small child, standing with her parents, David and Lavinia Hall, viewing the same, flitted through her mind.

A small sob escaped her lips and echoed in the massive empty church sanctuary.

For a while, she just sat, as still as a statue herself. When she could fight sleep no longer, and her heavy eyelids closed, she lay down in the pew and slept.

Molly had no idea how long she had been sleeping—and for a moment, where she was. But she heard the heavy doors open and close, and she heard murmuring behind her. A pair came in from outside, and a rush of cold air came with them. They walked to a front pew where they knelt to pray, paying no attention whatsoever to the disheveled woman in the back pew.

The sky was just beginning to lighten, slightly visible through the stained-glass windows, depicting, in glorious color, scenes of Jesus and the apostles.

Molly suddenly felt frightened, enclosed. She had very little recollection of yesterday and how she happened to be huddled in a pew of this magnificent church. But she felt she didn't belong, and she hastened out the door into the frigid air of early dawn.

She wended her way back through the city and returned to the area that had become familiar to her since she first arrived in Valeria last spring. The snow had abated during the night, making it easier for Molly and the others to navigate the streets, searching for food or anything else available to satisfy their needs.

By mid-morning Molly had seen Old Johnny and Louis, Gert, and Danny. She felt relieved when she spotted them—as if she had been on a long trip alone, and now was returning home.

The remaining days of the Christmas season didn't bring Molly another day as eventful as the one when she ate in the diner and spent the night in the church. She thought of that day only fleetingly; it seemed as if it had come from another time, another place.

But from time to time, she would envision Frannie's kind face and the wonderful warmth of the pea soup; she would feel the awe that had encompassed her when she entered the church. These she stowed among her good memories—which, from time to time, she was able to relish.

Chapter Twenty

Molly knew she needed warmer clothes. Her feet were cold all the time now, and she feared she would lose toes—or worse—if she couldn't manage to keep them warmer and drier. She looked at the feet of the others and saw they all wore similar footwear—boot-like lace-ups. Varying states of wear, black or brown, but always covering the ankles, often halfway up the wearer's legs. The size didn't matter, as long as they were big enough. Any extra space was taken up with multiple pairs of socks, or even rags—sometimes newspaper. Anything to add to the warmth.

So Molly began her mission to find shoes—shoes so different from the many pair filling the shoe compartment of her large walk-in closet back home. Those were for fashion; these were to be for warmth.

Her search took her up and down alleys, looking through boxes of discarded clothing and dumpsters. Day in and day out she continued her search. She came close several times. Once, pulling a brown leather work-shoe from a dumpster, she excitedly dug for its mate, but to no avail. One shoe wouldn't do her any more good than none. So discouraged, she carried her search to yet another alleyway.

Finally, after more than a week of rummaging unsuccessfully through garbage and trash, she came across a pile of boxes along a curb in an older residential part of Valeria. A handwritten sign on the boxes indicated they were to be picked up by a Salvation Army truck.

Molly was uneasy about searching through these boxes, different from the ones in the alleys. It felt a little bit like stealing. But she was desperate. Her feet were so wet and cold, she had to continually stomp them to keep the circulation going.

She carefully raised the flaps of the boxes and peered inside.

The first contained only sweaters; some appeared warm and heavy, and others were dressy, trimmed in faux pearls and beads. The second box she peered into was full of small appliances—an old toaster, an iron, a beat-up blender.

When Molly was beginning to feel that she would again be disappointed because there were no shoes, she opened a large box next to the second one—the one with the appliances. This container was stuffed with hunting gear—camouflage shirts and pants, a heavy wool plaid shirt, fur-lined canvas gloves, woolen socks, and there, on the bottom of the box, a scarcely worn pair of hunting boots.

Molly quickly yanked them from the box, and then, before again folding down the flaps covering the remaining articles, she grabbed the woolen socks and the plaid shirt, and quickly stole away.

She looked around her as she walked hurriedly in the direction from which she had come, but it didn't appear that anyone had noticed her theft. The street was still, the only sound, those few brown leaves clinging stubbornly to branches rustling in the cold winter wind.

When Molly was safely back in a deserted alley, she sat down on the stoop to a vacant building, removed her wet and worn shoes and donned, first, the woolen socks and, then, the boots. They were large—large enough, in fact, to accommodate a couple more pairs of socks, which Molly added over the next few days. But they covered her feet well and kept them reasonably warm and dry.

Molly was delighted with the new addition to her wardrobe.

Molly weathered the changing elements with forbearance—even with a gusto that would have awed those who knew her as Merritt Hall and as Dr. Merritt Hall-Davis. Her endurance was spectacular, considering she had previously lived the life of the affluent, and she wasn't robust.

Sometimes for days and days the voices would torment Molly, invading her once well-ordered mind with taunts and threats. Many nights she found no respite, and some days were equally tortuous. Oftentimes, she would lie huddled until the day ran into night, her head pounding in pain, multicolored flashes exploding behind her eyelids, the voices screaming in her ears—until she fell into a nearly catatonic-like sleep.

The other homeless who had come to welcome Molly's presence during the many months she lived among them feared Molly's episodes and kept their distance as her screams ripped through the silence. But when her deep sleep followed, they would close their ranks around her as if guarding her from further invasion by demons.

Molly was a loner. Although she drew a sense of security from the familiar homeless and sometimes enjoyed their company, most of the time she preferred to be by herself. Many of those living on the streets in Valeria shared her inclination to tackle the world alone. As they strolled hour after hour up and down the "less desirable" sections of town, most would cast furtive glances at those around them, looking for anyone who, to them, spelled danger.

Others, apparently not giving their safety a second thought, would walk close to the buildings, eyes downcast, either too afraid to meet others eye-to-eye or too embarrassed to do so. How many had left lives of ample sustenance—even affluence—behind them? No one knew, no one could tell. No one cared.

Surely no one knew the woman known as Molly was once a brilliant doctor and wealthy—an heiress.

Chapter Twenty-One

Molly awoke stiff and sore—and very tired. It had been a bad night. Her head throbbed, and her stomach growled with hunger. She hadn't eaten much last night because her head ached badly, and she was nauseous. The thought of eating the bunch of shriveled carrots and the overripe banana she had intended for her supper gagged her. As soon as dark had enveloped the streets, with only the soft glow of the street lights illuminating the darkness, she had crawled behind a pile of cardboard boxes, curled up and let sleep overtake her. Anything to escape the pounding pain in her head.

Sleep brought relief from the pain, but none from the torment of the voices. In the morning, as Molly sat up gingerly, she opened her eyes only slightly lest the light of day again start the pounding pain in her temples. The light was still dim, morning just beginning to make its appearance.

Frost sparkled on the surface of the boxes, and the wetness of the early morning gave Molly a chill. She pulled her coat tightly around her and slumped down again beneath the boxes. Her hand went to the cross around her neck, and she clutched it tightly. It gave her solace; it made her feel connected to whom she was, maybe even to whom she had been.

When Molly again emerged from her cardboard haven, morning was in full swing, and the entire alleyway where she had been resting was bathed in light. She heard voices coming from the street in front of the building and knew she needed to quickly disappear. Herb Mason didn't know Molly—and several others—often sought refuge beneath the boxes he carelessly threw out the back door of his appliance store each week. And Molly didn't want to be the first one to be discovered.

Herb was a mean-spirited man, and it was likely he would have the boxes hauled away daily if he, for one moment, thought they were serving to help those "goddamned street bums," as he so vocally described the homeless of Valeria. He once pelted rocks at an elderly man he found sitting upon his back-door stoop, injuring the old man, who fled, blood pouring from the wound on his forehead where the rock had hit its intended target. Herb was fairly sure he had rid himself of them all after the word of his prowess at rock throwing spread on the street.

Herb was a bit confused when a found a shriveled bunch of

carrots and a rotten banana beneath a pile of boxes when he cleared them out later that day. "Now how in the hell did these get here?" he wondered aloud as he kicked the discarded food aside.

Now fully awake, Molly quickly stole away from behind the appliance store, knowing the first item on her day's agenda was to find something to eat. She had eaten nothing since the stale bread and cookies she found outside *Percy Lyons' Bakery* yesterday morning. Percy threw the discarded baked goods out for the birds that nested in the fields behind State Street where his bakery was located, but Molly decided she needed the bread and cookies more than the birds did.

Molly liked Percy Lyons, the baker. Once when she first came to Valeria, before her appearance was as wild and disarrayed as it was now, Percy had given her a cherry turnover. She had been looking in the bakery window, eyeing the delicacies showcased there, when Percy opened the door and held out his hand—a hand holding a mouth-watering turnover wrapped in a paper napkin.

"Here, take it," he said kindly. "And please don't stand against my building," he added, with an attempt at a gruff voice. Before turning back into his place of business, he looked at Molly with just a hint of a smile.

Molly had reluctantly received the gift with a soft-spoken, "Thank you." Then she did as Percy asked, and walked away from his building.

Every time Molly walked by Percy's store—especially when she smelled the delicious fragrance of the bakery every morning she was in the area—she remembered the kind gesture Percy had shown her. He was not one of those she feared.

Molly had a "sweet tooth"—always did have. It was probably one of the reasons she enjoyed hovering around the bakery, and why she stole the treats meant for the birds. She was willing to dust off the dirt of the ground to enjoy their sweetness.

But Molly found nothing behind the bakery today, so she continued her wandering for anything to satiate her hunger pangs.

Finally, behind a small breakfast spot, a waitress was bringing out the garbage left from the early-morning diners. The garbage was "fresh," some of the discarded food still warm. With relish, Molly removed an untouched waffle from the bag the moment the waitress walked back in the door. The waffle was oozing with butter and honey and was just what Molly needed to raise her energy—and her spirits.

She couldn't imagine why anyone would leave the waffle untouched. Maybe it was just more than the diner patron wanted—one of two waffles, or maybe three, she reasoned.

After devouring her breakfast, Molly walked. She had awakened alone this morning and walked alone. She had trouble shaking the weariness that washed over her when she awoke, but the feeling of a full stomach increased her sense of well-being, and the more she walked, the better she felt. Her head cleared, and the voices were, for the time being, forgotten.

Molly walked farther and farther, her pace picking up as the distance from the familiar spot where she had spent the night increased. She soon realized that she was in a part of Valeria she had not seen before. It was as empty as a ghost town following the days of the gold rush. The buildings appeared uninhabited, and no cars or trucks rumbled down the streets.

She saw not a soul, heard no sounds except the roar of traffic in the distance and the mournful honk of the horns on the boats traversing the nearby river. The ghost-town like qualities of her surroundings gave Molly a chill, and she shuddered as she pulled her coat more tightly around her.

Molly reversed her direction and quickened her steps even more as she hastened to return to the familiar inner city from which she had wandered. Suddenly Molly felt she was not alone. She turned around and quickly surveyed her surroundings. Decrepit buildings with boarded windows and burned-out remains of brick and wooden structures. Cracked sidewalks and streets with holes so large and deep they appeared like bottomless chasms. But no people. Molly could see no one—not behind her, not to either side of her.

Why do I sense I'm being followed? she asked herself fearfully. *I just know someone's there.*

Molly felt uneasy, like an animal being tracked. She picked up her pace even more and soon was running, her breath coming in quickly drawn gasps. Again, she glanced over her shoulder, but saw no one there—only a mangy-looking dog, a little brown and white Spaniel, limping slightly, favoring one of its front legs. Then she saw a flash of bright red, as if someone had quickly darted around the corner.

Her attention was again drawn to the small forlorn-looking dog

117

following her. From somewhere within her, Molly drew a strength, an understanding most would have denied she any longer possessed. Her fear of moments before, even the sighting of a "flash of red," was swept aside. Her focus was on the small animal trailing a short distance behind her.

"Here little friend," she coaxed, bending down on one knee and beckoning to the dog, forgetting her own fears. "Let me have a look at that leg."

The too-thin brown spotted pup cautiously inched its way towards Molly, its tail wagging rapidly as Molly gently lifted its leg into her lap and knowingly felt along the small brown leg. As her fingers carefully probed the paw, the dog yelped and pulled its leg from Molly's lap.

"Whoa there, little one. You have a sore paw. Here," she again coaxed gently, "let me have another look. I won't hurt you," she assured him with a voice of authority and command of the situation she hadn't experienced in many months. She carefully turned the paw over in her hand. "What do we have here?" she asked as she noticed a thin sliver of glass imbedded in the Spaniel's paw. She tightly grasped the end and quickly pulled it out. Again the dog yelped and pulled its paw from Molly's grasp, but it didn't run away. Instead, it lay down at Molly's feet and began to vigorously lick its paw.

"That's right, that's just what you should do. You'll need to provide your own medicine, little one—I don't have any. Not anymore," she whispered, a touch of sadness in her voice. She felt old and tired as she rose to her feet and turned to continue on her way. The dog remained where it was, continuing its "self-treatment"— continuing to lick its paw.

Molly again sensed she was being followed, and again it filled her with uneasiness. *Why would anyone follow me? I haven't caused any trouble, haven't harmed anyone. Just helped that poor little hurt dog.* As she hastened on her way, she glanced furtively over her shoulder every now and then.

She turned quickly near the end of a long block—a block with nowhere to hide. As she turned, she saw a man. She easily recognized him as Eddie, his too-short trousers dangling inches above his ankles, his unkempt long black hair blowing across his forehead, a bright-red handkerchief hanging from the back pocket of his overalls.

As soon as Eddie saw he had no doorway in which to hide, no

alley in which to escape, he thrust his hands in his pockets and walked slowly towards Molly, his eyes firmly locked on the ground.

"Sorry," he mumbled contritely as he reached the spot where she was standing, waiting.

"For what?" she demanded.

"For following you," he mumbled in a whisper.

"Dammit! Don't do that any more. It scares me."

"Yer nice. You helped that puppy." Eddie spoke with sincere admiration.

"It was hurt. It needed my help. All I did was pull out a shard of glass. Nothing much." Molly seemed embarrassed by Eddie's praise.

"What's a 'shard'?" asked Eddie, his eyes finally raised to meet Molly's.

For a minute, Molly stared at him as if not understanding his question. A memory quickly jumped into her mind, but she couldn't identify the people—a little girl and a woman in a long black robe. *"What's* discrete *mean?"* the little girl had asked. *Who was that little girl—and who was the woman in the long black gown?*

The memory was fleeting, and in a flash, it was gone. Molly felt very tired. She looked at Eddie and explained, just like someone might explain to a small child, "A shard is a thin piece of glass. It was stuck in the dog's paw. He's fine. Now leave me alone."

With a renewed quickened pace, but bent over, a picture of exhaustion, Molly continued her journey down the street, back towards a more familiar part of the city. As she hurried away, she heard Eddie's soft voice call after her, "Yer nice. And you know lots of words."

Eddie was a quiet, unassuming sort. One had to wonder how he survived on the street. He never asked others to share their finds, but was always eager to share his own. This created some problems for him, particularly where nourishment was concerned. His chances of survival seemed best when he was alone. Alone he could devour his stale bread or discarded leftovers without insisting that he share with the others.

Most of the time, Eddie's eyes were downcast, and he would twist his ever-present red handkerchief nervously in his hands when he spoke. He suddenly had taken a great interest in Molly, beginning on the day he followed her and watched her administer care to the injured Spaniel. As often as he could, Eddie got close to Molly, and in a voice barely above a whisper, said, "Yer nice."

Molly tried to avoid Eddie. His incessant adulation made her uncomfortable on her good days, and on her bad days, she forgot who he was, and his close presence frightened her.

The longer Molly was on the street, the more heightened her paranoia became. She was terrified when someone approached her too closely. Often she would creep off into a corner and huddle, her back against a fence, her knees to her chest, her head bowed, and her belongings clutched tightly, as if her survival depended on their closeness.

I'm afraid. Oh, Daddy, I'm so afraid. Like a litany, her confession of fear repeated in her thoughts, over and over—an admission to her long-deceased father. Never afraid of the dark as a child, now she sometimes trembled with fear when the shadows of dusk overtook bright skies, and the boldness of daylight was swallowed by the darkness of night.

One day, when Molly again thought she was being followed, she grabbed a stick lying on a nearby grassy plot and swung it around, ready to attack the unwitting spy. But there was no one there—no one to attack, no one to dissuade following her.

Molly felt better, though, with the stick gripped firmly in her hand. *I like this. I like this a lot.* She smiled as she walked along, her stick leading the way.

Molly was never again seen without her "walking stick." Those who met her eyed it warily. Many felt its blows and respected the power of this small woman they knew only as "Molly."

Eddie was afraid of Molly's stick; but then he seemed to be afraid of most everything. He was truly a gentle soul who shed tears easily and often. He cried with joy when he found a bag of sugared doughnuts "just like his mama used to make," and wept with fear when he was shoved aside, when someone decided to take what he had.

Molly was walking across the no-longer-used railroad tracks, taking a shortcut to one of the old parks on the outskirts of Valeria. This park was rarely used any longer, and being beyond the maintenance area of the city, was unkempt with weeds overtaking the once grassy fields. Molly loved this park—the open air, the solitude.

She knew Eddie was following her, and it made her angry. *I need to be alone,* she thought. *Why can't he just leave me alone?*

Eddie had started out far behind Molly, but picked up his pace as she crossed the tracks. He didn't want to lose sight of her. Sometimes when he tried to follow Molly, he would let her get too far ahead, and he'd cry when he could no longer see her.

Why doesn't she like me? this mournful lonely man would ask himself. *She's so nice. She liked the puppy with the hurt paw. She likes Johnny. She lets him stand close to her sometimes. But not me. Why?*

As he struggled sadly with his self-questioning, Eddie began to run, and soon was so close to Molly, he could reach out and touch her.

Molly raised her stick and turned. As she began to lower it, she looked into the fearful eyes of Eddie as he stopped dead still, cowering in his tracks. She slowly lowered her weapon and was filled with an overpowering sense of sadness.

She began to walk again, slowly, and soon Eddie was beside her. They walked in silence, this man who so wanted not to be alone and this woman who craved to be, but with all the impact of her mentally debilitating illness, still felt compassion and caring for another who needed her.

Molly and Eddie walked together other times after that, without ever a word passing between them. Eddie seemed to be contented just to be by her side, and Molly was willing, for the time being, to concede some of her privacy to permit it.

Chapter Twenty-Two

Eddie found a friend—a friend other than Molly. His name was Jasper. Jasper's complexion was sallow, dotted by dark brown freckles across his cheeks, forehead, and nearly bald head. Tufts of white hair jutted out in a line running from ear to ear, across the back of his neck—appearing like a tonsure of a monk. His eyes were green with yellow flecks and sparkled with intensity. His voice boomed when he spoke, as if he were in a position of authority.

Actually, he *had* been. Jasper Coleman had been the headmaster in a prestigious boys' preparatory school in the Northeast by the name of Fraternal Arms. Unfortunately, Mr. Coleman had taken the name of the institution too much to heart, and when he was found showing far too much fraternal interest in two twelve-year-olds entrusted to his care, he was asked, in a not-too-kindly manner, to leave immediately.

And so he gathered up his books, his framed diploma, and the photos of his wife Edith and their two daughters, Abigail and Eloise. He tossed his belongs carelessly into his gleaming white Mercury and drove away from the school where he had spent his entire career life—first as an instructor of English literature, then as headmaster.

It took almost as long for Edith to throw him out of their home in elite Westchester Hills as it had for the Board of Regents of Fraternal Arms to slam the door in his face. Edith had too long been in the upper echelon of society in Hermitage, this small city where the school was the most respected, most revered, institution in its midst.

"Get out of my sight, you dirty old man," Edith screamed at him as she threw his suitcase out the door after him. "I don't ever want to see you again," she added, just before she slammed the door and locked it.

And she never did.

Jasper drove to the home of his daughter Eloise at the other end of town, but by the time he got there, Edith had already phoned her with the tale of what a disgusting loser her father was, and Jasper's prolonged ringing of the doorbell went unanswered.

As he turned away from the door, he briefly saw the little round face of his grandson, Michael Jasper, at the window. The face disappeared suddenly—probably as his distraught mother yanked him away. And his daughter would be very distraught.

Eloise Coleman Taylor had always been "Daddy's girl." She idolized her father. Following in his literary footsteps, she was an English-literature instructor at the Hermitage Community College. But she had always quaked in the throes of her mother's wrath. Jasper knew Ellie—as he so lovingly called his youngest offspring—could never muster the courage to defy her mother.

So Jasper sadly walked back to his car—this time with his head hanging low, not so much in shame as in sadness. He wanted to see Ellie, to hold Mikey. He needed them. He loved them.

There was no point in trying to call his other daughter, Abby. She lived hours away in a New York City suburb, and even if she had been close by, Jasper knew she'd never take him in. Abby was Edith all over again—a social climber who cared far too much about what other people thought. She and her mother would have a grand old time running him into the ground as they tied up phone lines between Hermitage and New York City.

Jasper knew he should be experiencing some feelings of guilt or shame over what he had done. But dear God, he hadn't hurt them—would never hurt any of "his boys." He just admired them, their flawless smooth faces not yet marred by facial hair that had to be tediously scraped away each and every day; their voices still high and sweet and just occasionally breaking, as the lower tones predicting future manhood broke through.

"They were so beautiful, I just wanted to see more of them," said Jasper to himself, justifying his removal of the boys' clothing. "You can hardly see the boy beneath those damned suits," he went on, disparaging the formal uniform of the students at Fraternal Arms.

Jasper sighed and tears came to his eyes—not tears of shame, but tears of sorrow. *I'll miss the boys so much.* And he would. In spite of Jasper's errant ways, he had been a good headmaster, disciplined but kind, with a smile and intense laughing eyes. The boys loved him—and he had been a superb English-literature teacher.

He sighed again as he pulled into the parking lot of the local YMCA. A few heads turned as he parked. The "Y" was housed in an old brick building with the beginning signs of neglect and decay. Those who walked through the doors usually didn't leave gleaming new white Mercury's in the lot behind the building.

Jasper stayed at the YMCA for three weeks. He hadn't planned to stay that long, but he really didn't know where else to go. He had

123

tried repeatedly, but unsuccessfully, to talk to Edith and Eloise. "Please, Daddy, please don't call," entreated Eloise in a choked voice. Not wanting to cause the child he loved so dearly any more heartache than he already had, he didn't try again.

His wife wouldn't even answer the phone.

Jasper had lived in this area all his life. He was, himself, a graduate of Fraternal Arms, having left Hermitage just long enough to earn his degrees from an Ivy League university not far away. The thought of leaving, even now, was not an easy decision for him to make.

But Jasper knew he couldn't spend the rest of his life "vegetating" in his sparse room at the Y, so when the third week of his stay drew to a close, he again gathered his belongings and brought them to his car. Just as he lifted his suitcase to toss it into the trunk, he had an indescribable pain in his chest and couldn't breathe. The suitcase dropped to the ground. Jasper fell on top of it.

A pair of young men, also residents of the Y, came upon Jasper's inert body and were certain he was dead. They ran into the building, breathless with fear, and called an ambulance.

Jasper wasn't dead, but close, and soon he was racing away on a stretcher, the ambulance siren loudly announcing its path as it careened around corners and came to an abrupt stop at Hermitage Memorial Hospital.

Jasper Coleman had had a massive coronary. The skilled physicians at Hermitage Hospital saved his life, but his heart had stopped beating for too long a period of time, and when he recovered, Jasper was not the same man he had been. He appeared older—many years older. His speech was halting and slow, although still loud and authoritative, and his mind was most definitely not the same. No longer was he a brilliant expert on English literature.

Edith, his wife of thirty-five years, never did come to see Jasper at the hospital. Oh, she knew he was there—Hermitage wasn't that large. But she figured, if he died, good riddance. In fact, she had him served with divorce papers while he was still flat on his back in the hospital bed. She wanted everything—the house, the furniture, the bank accounts. All of it.

Jasper didn't contest anything. *Let her have it all*, he thought. *I'm probably going to die anyway, so what good is it to me.* So he signed his name relinquishing all his worldly possessions to Edith

Mayer Coleman. Except for his Mercury—that and the small cache of belongings in the trunk of his car.

Eloise—Ellie—*did* come to see her father three times when he was at his worst, when he wasn't expected to live. "Oh, Daddy, please don't die. I love you. I don't understand why you did what you did, but I still love you."

When it appeared fairly certain that Jasper wouldn't die, she didn't come again. Eloise Coleman Martin really *did* love her father. He had been the bright spot of her entire childhood. Not the least bit interested in social climbing as her mother and sister were, she withdrew to her books. There father and daughter found a commonality that created a strong bond. They spent hours and hours talking of tales of wonder and excitement. Eloise lived vicariously through these stories and gained a new appreciation for life. She was a lovely woman, tall and blonde like her mother, but deep and studious like her father.

But when her husband, Delbert Martin, an attorney for the city, threatened to leave her if she didn't stay away from that "sick pervert," her father, and he'd take Mikey with him, Eloise stayed away.

She, too, never saw Jasper again.

When the doctors informed Jasper that they could do nothing more for him, he again crawled into his car and left Hermitage. Having no idea as to his destination, Jasper headed west. He was weary, sore, and broken-hearted—and he had become a muddled old man.

But he was alive.

Almost half-a-dozen years had passed between the time Jasper Coleman watched the lovely maple trees plentiful on the outskirts of Hermitage disappear from his view and the morning he showed up on the streets of Valeria. No longer recognizable as the once-respected headmaster of a prestigious school, Jasper was impoverished, unkempt, and not well. The gleaming white Mercury he had driven with such pride was long gone. But his green eyes still gleamed with intense fervor for life, and his voice still boomed with authority when he spoke.

Eddie looked at Jasper shyly, his eyes beneath long dark lashes studying the newcomer.

Jasper was aware that he was being scrutinized—could hardly be unaware of it. Eddie was watching his every move adoringly. Jasper was flattered by the younger man's attention, and something stirred

125

within him. Not the old feelings of sexual arousal that had been paramount with his attraction to downy-faced boys. Those inclinations had died years ago. No, these feelings were more akin to the fatherly feelings he had once had for some of the less popular boys at Fraternal Arms—those less attractive youngsters who often didn't fit in with the mainstream of the well-liked students.

Eddie certainly wasn't attractive, noted Jasper. That head of dark hair flying everywhere gave him an almost animal-like appearance, and those ridiculous too-short overalls with that disgusting red handkerchief hanging out the back pocket looked almost like a costume a child might wear to a Halloween party. But his velvety blue eyes were stunning—and entreating.

"What's your name, son?" Jasper asked Eddie in his booming voice, the question sounding much like a demand.

"E-E-Eddie?" he responded, stuttering question-like, as if he were unsure of his own name.

"Let's go for a walk," said Jasper, gesturing for Eddie to join him. As they ambled slowly down the street, Jasper put his hand gently on Eddie's shoulder—as a father might.

The two men became friends, nothing more than friends. Nothing more was needed by either of them. One called the other, "son."

Eddie no longer followed Molly. His need for companionship had been fulfilled.

Chapter Twenty-Three

Molly's feelings were mixed when Eddie ceased to be her shadow—part relief, part sadness. Yes, Eddie had been a nuisance. He invaded her privacy, and his incessant following often unnerved her. But at times, his presence buoyed her ever-sagging spirits, and the loneliness that cut through her like a razor-sharp knife had been somewhat lessened by the sound of his footsteps.

Of course, there were times when she was totally unaware of any of her surroundings, or of other people, including Eddie. These were times when the voices so sharply berated her, she was aware of nothing other than their shouts ravaging her very soul.

At those times, Molly was lost to everyone—most notably, to herself.

Sometimes, when the voices were silent, Molly would sit and stare at her own hands. She would try to recall memories when those hands clasped those of another—of her very handsome husband, of her lovely young daughter. At times, she could even recall her hands gently touching those of a patient distressed by an illness—or apprehensive about an approaching treatment.

Now her hands were red and deeply lined, the nails broken and dirty. Dreadfully dirty. But Molly liked to look at her hands. They spurred memories—comforting memories.

What happened to me? Where is the girl who others called "Mimi?" My life was so good—until the voices. What if what they say is true! What if it's my fault they're all dead!

When Molly's thoughts trailed along these lines, she would fold her small hands into fists and pound on whatever surface was nearby—her own lap, a wooden park bench, a brick wall or concrete stoop. She would pound until tears of pain welled up in her eyes and uncontrollable sobs shook her body.

After these outbursts, she would grab her stick and swing it wildly from side to side as she walked, and mumbling incoherently and staring at the ground, she rapidly covered the terrain of the streets of Valeria.

Molly's recollections became dimmer and dimmer, and soon, when she stared at her own hands, it didn't evoke memories. She saw only red chapped hands with broken fingernails and the filth of the street.

Almost seven years had gone by since Molly first appeared on the streets of Valeria, Indiana. Seven years of confusion, danger, hunger, and illness.

***

Riley MacRae enjoyed cruising with his new partner, the rookie cop, Kenny Myerson. Myerson's sense of humor and "aim-to-please" attitude vaulted the young man fresh out of training to the top in Riley's estimation. Kenny's sharp blue eyes took in all the surroundings as his senior partner pointed out the high spots of the area—today, the parts of Valeria most frequented by the homeless.

Kenny Myerson's head all but swiveled on his neck as he viewed all that Riley indicated, the rookie not wanting to miss a word of his instruction, his indoctrination to the streets of Valeria. As he listened intently, interspersing Riley's words with an occasional humorous quip, someone appeared out of nowhere in the passenger-side window, Kenny's window.

The slush of early spring spattered up from the tires of the patrol vehicle, soaking the elderly man who was running alongside the car, wildly waving his arms. "What the . . .? Watch out MacRae, that nut looks about ready to jump in front of us!"

Kenny Myerson was right. Just as Riley MacRae hit the brakes, sending the car into a slight slide on the slippery, slushy street, Johnny ran right in front of them. Somehow, the car avoided hitting him. The full stop occurred in time—just in time. There wasn't the space of a finger between the cruiser and Johnny's old bent body when the car came to a complete halt.

"Johnny, are you out of your mind!" yelled Riley as he jumped out of the car.

"You know this guy?" asked Kenny as he, too, got out, shaking in his boots. For a minute there, Kenny had been certain they'd be running down a bent old man whose age appeared to be somewhere in the neighborhood of one hundred.

"Ya gotta come, Off'cer. Ya jist gotta. She's dyin', I jist know she's dyin'."

"Just a minute, Johnny. Who's dying? And where?"

"Molly. She needs an amb'lance. Right away. Hurry." Johnny headed for the alley, hurrying as quickly as his aging body would allow. Riley followed, motioning for his partner to come with him. Kenny ran around the car, stepping fully in a pile of slush along the gutter as he did so. "Damn," he muttered under his breath, hating the cold slop now inside his shoe, but excited by the pending adventure as he jogged to catch up with his mentor.

Johnny reached the inert body of Molly first, with Riley close behind. The old man knelt down and placed his ear next to her mouth. "She's breathin', but not much. Sounds kinda like garglin'. Get her an ambl'ance. Please, off'cer. I know ya called one for me, a time back. Molly's gonna die if'n ya don't."

Johnny choked on the last words, and tears streamed down his cheeks. *I'll be damned,* thought Riley, *old Johnny loves her.*

"Kenny, call 911. Get an ambulance here—let's see, 300 block of West Appleton. Back in the alley. Pronto!"

Kenny did as he was told—immediately. Then he stood back and watched the drama unfolding before him. All but sobbing now, the old gent was crouched down beside the old lady stretched out on a pile of cardboard, wrapped in what appeared to be a couple of coats. Since the old guy wasn't wearing a coat, Kenny presumed one of them was his.

Riley also knelt beside Molly, took her pulse, turned his head and laid his ear down on her chest—and shook his head as he raised it. "It doesn't sound good, Johnny. Her breathing is really labored. How long has she been like this?"

"Coupla days. Mebbee three. I told her I'd go with her ta find a place for help, but she jist shook her head and ran away when I said it. So yestaday I ain't said nuthin' 'bout it. But she had a bad night. Real bad. And this mornin' I cain't get her ta wake up. Is she gonna die, off'cer? Is she?"

"I hope not, Johhny. Molly's a nice old gal, and I know you don't want anything to happen to her. Here's the ambulance now," Riley said as he stood and backed away from Molly, still asleep—or unconscious—and gently raised Johnny to his feet. In doing so, he noticed for the first time that Johnny wasn't wearing a coat. Riley reached down and lifted from Molly's body what he was certain was Johnny's garment, and handed it to him.

"You'll probably need this tonight, Johnny, and Molly won't. They'll provide her with blankets at the hospital. In fact, the ambulance will have some for her right now; she'll be kept plenty warm."

Johnny reluctantly took the coat from Riley MacRae, and with tears still streaming down his face, and his nose dripping in concert with the tears, Johnny backed away from the scene, saw that Molly was being cared for by the medical emergency personnel, turned on his heels and disappeared down the alley.

"This one's barely alive, MacRae," said one of the medical personnel. "You really know how to find them, fella," he added as he secured an IV in Molly's arm and an oxygen mask on her face. His partner wrapped her feverish shivering body in several blankets.

"Yah, I know. But do the best you can for her, will you guys? I promised someone she'd get the best of care. I'll follow you in— give what particulars I can at the front desk."

"You bet," said the ambulance driver with a smile. As always, the compassion that Riley MacRae put forth impressed those with whom he interacted.

As the ambulance sped away, Riley and Kenny made their way back to their car. "Hope you're not disappointed, Kenny. That was hardly a 'crime adventure' going on back there."

"Disappointed? Heck, no. I was impressed—and touched. Is everyone in Valeria that kind to the homeless?"

Riley snorted, "Hardly. But they're people, Kenny. People who've either made bad choices or life has handed them a bad hand. Maybe both. I don't know. I just know they're people, and I feel it's part of my job to be sure the city cares for them as well as they're able to. The way I look at it, we're servants of the people. So we're their servants," he added laughing as he slapped the rookie affectionately on his back.

Riley knew he had just given Kenney Myerson a lesson in humanity—humanity according to Riley MacRae.

Chapter Twenty-Four

While Riley filled the desk personnel in on what little he knew about Molly—primarily making it very clear that she was a non-paying patient, a charity case—Molly was wheeled to an emergency-room cubicle.

"My God, but she reeks," declared nurse Hannah Dreighton, burying her nose in the sleeve of her royal-blue uniform. "How can any self-respecting person let themselves 'go to the dogs' like this? It's disgusting," she added as she peeled Molly's filthy clothes off her body and threw them in a pile on the floor.

Hannah was fresh from nursing school and treasured all things clean and appearing "nice." Especially herself. Her complexion was flawless, her long blonde tresses neatly pulled back into a ponytail. Long lashes, enhanced by liberally applied mascara, accented her emerald-green eyes, and bright-pink lipstick outlined her full and sensuous mouth.

Her fellow nurse, Diana Blake, wondered what had inspired this girl to become a nurse. She seemed to be devoid of compassion, although she had to admit, Hannah *was* a hard worker.

"Maybe she had no choice," claimed Diana as she tenderly helped undress Molly, adding the clothing she removed to the pile on the floor.

"Nonsense. Everyone has a choice," argued Hannah.

Was I ever that naive? Diana asked herself. Her short, wavy, mostly gray hair, with countless wrinkles to match, gave credence to her as an older and far more experienced nurse than her newly graduated counterpart. Not wanting to divert her attention from their patient, Diana decided not to argue the point with Hannah.

"Find a large plastic bag," she instructed an aide who had just entered the cubicle. "Her clothes need to be kept together."

"What in the world for?" asked Hannah, surprised at Diana's request. "Surely, she's not going to wear those dirty rags when she leaves!"

"And just what do you propose she *does* wear? A hospital gown? Or are you going to outfit her?" Diana wanted to bite her tongue as soon as the words were out of her mouth. She didn't mean to be sarcastic, but the lack of Hannah's compassion and understanding was wearing on her.

Diana looked at Molly, noted her shallow and labored breathing and wondered, realistically, if what she wore when she left the hospital wasn't a moot point. By the looks of her condition, she may not be leaving.

Nurse Diana Blake had cared for many of the homeless who made their way to Valeria's St. Benedict's Hospital. She was well aware of the large number who didn't make it. Years of living without adequate shelter to protect them from the erratic climate here in this part of the country, as well as improper diet, left them extremely susceptible to disease. Their bodies simply didn't have the resistance to hold disease at bay or the strength to survive the illnesses they did succumb to. A large number were too far gone to save by the time they reached the hospital.

It looked to Diana that this woman most likely would be added to those numbers.

After Dr. Brad Hosfeffer examined Molly and judged her to have pneumonia, and silently concurring with Nurse Blake that her condition was so severe, she more than likely wouldn't survive, he instructed that Molly be taken to a room.

As he wrote in her chart, he said, "See if you can clean her up a bit. But carefully, mind you, and be sure she stays warm."

Dr. Hosfeffer was a young man, not ten years older than Hannah Dreighton, but his compassion for the unfortunates was as deep and sincere as that of Diana Blake.

For days, Merritt Hall-Davis, known now for nearly seven years as Molly, lay near death's door in a warm, comfortable bed, well nourished intravenously, surrounded by caregivers, in an antiseptic environment. She didn't speak, didn't even open her eyes. She simply slept, unaware of her surroundings, fighting for her life, although she was oblivious to the battle.

Finally, on the fifth day since Johnny had hailed Riley MacRae and begged for his help, Molly opened her eyes.

Nurse Blake was bending over her, checking her vital signs when she saw her eyelids flutter and open. Molly looked straight at the kind soft brown eyes of the nurse, but only for a moment. She slowly lowered her eyelids and again drifted into a deep sleep.

Diana watched the sleeping woman for a moment. *You have the most beautiful eyes I've ever seen*, she silently told Molly. *What is your story, my dear? I wonder—will you ever tell us?*

Chapter Twenty-Five

After several days of excellent care, Molly's physical condition improved, and the fears and dire predictions regarding her survival vanished. She no longer slept all the time, and when awake, she became very difficult to manage. She tore the IV tube from her arm and the oxygen mask from her face. She shouted at the nurses and babbled incoherently, as the voices in her head plagued her mercilessly. At night, Molly alternately sobbed and screamed hysterically—much like a terrified child wanting to go home to his or her own bed.

The nurses wanted to release her—immediately. The doctor in charge wanted otherwise; he ordered Molly to be moved to the psychiatric unit. Sedated and restrained, she was placed on the sixth floor of St. Benedict's where, now that her physical problems had been resolved for the time being, her mental and emotional problems could be addressed.

Dr. Zachary Small's brow wrinkled in deep concentration as he studied intently the chart he held, the patient identified only as "Molly," followed by the notation, "homeless." Dr. Small's pale-blue eyes squinted behind his thick rimless glasses, and the shock of red-streaked-with-gray hair draping over his left brow bobbed up and down as he nodded, making comments to himself.

"Did you say something, Dr. Small?" inquired the tall intern beside him.

"No, no, I'm sorry, Dr. Hermann. I'm afraid I'm often guilty of mumbling to myself when I'm thinking hard. Quite an admission for a psychiatrist, don't you think?" he added, smiling.

Dr. Kendall Hermann smiled as well. He had the greatest respect for the senior doctor and considered it a great privilege to be working with him.

"May I ask whose chart you're studying? Somebody special?"

"Probably as non-special as we might ever see. A homeless street person, known just as Molly. Have no idea who she really is, where she's from. Not even a really clear idea how old she is. Age accumulates so rapidly when your life is as tough as it is for these people who call the streets their home. I'd guess her to be about fifty—although I could be several years off, either direction.

"She was brought in with pneumonia about a week ago. More

dead than alive, I understand. Apparently Molly wasn't ready to give up her life yet, however." Dr. Small's round jowled face lit up with a slight smile.

He respects this woman, guessed Dr. Hermann. And his guess was exactly right.

"Are we going to be able to help her, doctor?"

"Hmmm?" asked Dr. Small, again absorbed in pondering over Molly's chart.

"I'm going to try, Kendall. Of course I'm really not sure what's wrong with her. And we're unable to do any great amount of testing. She's been totally uncooperative. Won't let anyone near her— screams, curses, cries—begs out loud for voices to go away. And then, at other times, she's totally withdrawn. My guess is a number of things have affected her mind. I suspect, however, that the number one problem is schizophrenia.

"What do you think, Dr. Hermann? If you were having to diagnose this woman based on the meager information we have, what would you say?"

"I'd agree with you. I'd suspect schizophrenia as the lead culprit. Sounds like parts of her brain are receiving too much dopamine— the voices—and she's probably hallucinating, too. Likely other times, her brain isn't getting enough of the chemical. That would account for her zombie-like withdrawal."

"Very good. And what would you do about it?"

"I'm not sure there's anything we *can* do about it. We don't know how long she's been this way, what's been done for her in the past. We don't even know if she'd *let* us do anything for her."

"True. Are you willing to just give up on her then—send her on her way?"

"No, no, but there is a certain feeling of futility in deciding treatment for her."

"I agree, but let's say we decide to do something, try something. What would you try?"

"I'd try an aripiprazole—you know, to adjust the brain's 'thermostat.'"

"Its thermostat?"

"To keep the dopamine more stable—not let it get too high or too low."

"You know what, young man, that's exactly what I'd do. Let's
134

try it."

Dr. Kendall Hermann gleamed with pleasure from the praise bestowed on him by his mentor, his idol. Grinning from ear to ear, he said, "Okay."

Dr. Small's face turned serious as he said, "We both know this is just a 'shot in the dark.' But I'm willing to try, to see if we can possibly restore some modicum of quality to this woman's life. Somehow I believe her mental state is at the bottom of her living on the street."

So Molly received medication for her condition—something she hadn't had since losing her purse shortly before arriving in Valeria years ago. When the purse disappeared, so had the pills that helped her to think clearly, that lessened the attacks by the voices.

Molly slept well last night; the voices were silent, and her usual fears were abated as the bustling noises in the hall foretold a new day in the busy hospital. She had been awake, lying very still for some time, observing everything around her. There was a strange familiarity about her surroundings, even though Molly really wasn't sure where she was—or how she got there.

Even the smell seemed familiar.

"Well, good morning, dearie. Don't you look good today—kinda peaceful and all," greeted the nurse, Melanie Pearson, smiling as she noted Molly's stillness and quiet demeanor. That hadn't been the case the other half-dozen mornings she'd come on duty since Molly arrived on her floor, in her unit. Yesterday the nurse was filled with dread as she entered Molly's room; her chart told of the stormy night she had had, and the shouts rolling down the hall as Melanie walked towards Molly's room confirmed the chaos.

But today looked to be different. *Dr. Small will be so pleased. So will that tall handsome intern, Dr. Hermann,* thought Melanie Pearson. *They seem to have some high hopes for this one.*

Molly kept her eyes on the nurse as she took her vitals, but she didn't say a word. In fact, Molly hadn't said a word since she collapsed in the alley—with the exception of her pleas to make the voices stop. She watched as Melanie opened the door of the small locker-like closet assigned to Molly.

The closet was empty except for a bundle lying on the bottom— a bundle wrapped in a large plastic trash bag.

"We need to get you a few things, dearie—soap, towels, robe," said Melanie as she closed the closet door. "What we need isn't in

135

here. I'll be back shortly," she promised, smiling brightly at Molly as she exited.

Molly looked at the closet as the nurse left the room. She threw back her covers, sparkling clean and smelling slightly of antiseptic, stepped out of the bed, crossed the room to the closet, and opened the closet door. She removed the plastic bag and hurriedly removed the contents, putting on her old, soiled clothes as she pulled them out of the bag. She didn't even take off her hospital gown. Molly was accustomed to layers, and the gown simply became the first layer.

The bag with Molly's clothes had followed her from the emergency-room cubicle, to her room in the respiratory wing, to the psychiatry floor. The clothes were still filthy, they still reeked, but they were hers. She smiled as she pulled them on—all of them.

When fully dressed, Molly opened the door to the room and walked out. No one noticed her, this strangely dressed woman walking down the hall to the stairway exit. All were too engrossed in reading chart notations from the preceding night, preparing for their duties of the day.

Molly walked down the stairs—all six flights—and opened the outside door to face a cool but sunny day. Her smile matched the glow of the sunshine. She had been warm, she wasn't hungry, it didn't hurt her to breathe, and she didn't cough anymore. And, for now, the voices were silent.

Molly hurried on her way, eager to find her friends, her family, the community of others who resided in doorways, empty buildings, and cardboard boxes. The others who lived on the street.

She was eager to "get home."

Drs. Zachary Small and Kendall Hermann were dismayed when they learned of Molly's unscheduled departure. Dismayed, but not surprised. It was more or less what they expected. They had seen some improvement from the drugs they'd given Molly over the past few days, but only slight improvement. She had been unattended for so long, any real progress would take months, maybe years. And they knew Molly would never give them that kind of time.

Molly found her way back before dark. Gert spotted her first and nodded at Johnny. The old gent ran to Molly's side. He didn't say a word but handed her big "protection stick" to her. Molly grasped it tightly. She nodded to Johnny as if saying, "Thank you for keeping it for me," but she said nothing. Nor did he. But the face of each bore a look of contentment.

Chapter Twenty-Six

Molly gathered her treasures and stuffed them into an old bag. A cloth bag that had, at one time, been a pillowcase, a pillowcase embroidered with yellow daisies and pink hearts.

It had once been gleaming white, perhaps starched crisply, its whiteness and colorful embroidery adorning a bed where some girl or young woman laid her head. Or maybe an older one, a charming grandmother who spent her time baking cookies and embroidering hearts and daisies on pillowcases.

Now it was dirty-gray and torn, but Molly held on to it tightly; it held all that she had in this world. She knew she was fortunate to have a bag made of cloth. Most didn't. Most had only paper bags to store the possessions that others had discarded as no longer of any use, but to those living on the street were gathered as treasures.

Regularly, the paper bags would tear, just as her long-ago Christmas shopping bag tore, and all they held would roll onto the dirt or broken concrete paving the alleyways and old streets. Sometimes the unfortunate owners never found all their treasures again. Some would roll under dumpsters and boxes scattered everywhere along the way. Some things were immediately snatched by others, increasing their own store of treasures by adding what had so recently belonged to their fellow street dwellers.

Molly's belongings were not numerous. Content with the garments she wore, and usually wearing multiple outfits at the same time, her bag contained only a few articles of clothing. She didn't treasure clothing, except for shoes. Molly liked shoes. But it was hard to find shoes cast away by others that didn't hurt her feet.

The hunting boots she found her first winter on the streets of Valeria were worn to barely-hanging-together shreds of leather a few years ago. The boots had served her well for a long time, but day after day of carrying Molly as she walked the streets in all kinds of weather, they eventually fell apart. They were replaced by others, but none so nice or in as great shape as that first pair—the pair that were to have been picked up by the Salvation Army truck.

Most of the time, Molly wore old lace-up work shoes— generally, without the laces or with the laces untied. Often, the ones she found were far too large, but she stuffed newspaper in the extra spaces until they fit.

Early last spring, Molly found a pair of tennis shoes that really looked nice. She thought they were lovely, and they nearly fit. So she threw the old work shoes into her bag and wore the tennis shoes day in and day out. After only a few weeks, however, her feet poked through the canvas, and the thin rubber soles wore through until she was walking the streets in her stocking feet. Again, she put on the old lace-up work shoes and carried the tennis shoes in her pillowcase bag.

Molly never wore the tennis shoes again, but she kept them. They were a part of her store of treasures.

Once, Molly found a coat she liked—really liked. It had been carelessly jammed in a box, lying on top of several pairs of shoes—fancy shoes in many colors, with high heels and buckles or other adornments across the toes. Sadly, Molly couldn't wear the shoes, although she tried on each and every pair. They were much too narrow and weren't serviceable for the life she led.

But the coat she kept. As she pulled it carefully from the box where it had been stuffed, she sucked in her breath—just like a little girl opening a package containing the perfect doll, the one she had been dreaming about for months. When Molly held up the coat, she glanced around, thinking surely it must have been a mistake. No one would throw away something so lovely. But as she furtively glanced around, she saw no one. Not one person came running down the alleyway declaring the coat was hers—that it was discarded by mistake.

Molly slipped her arm in one sleeve and then the other, shivering with delight. She pulled it closed and with reddened hands, carefully buttoned all three shiny silver buttons and pulled the collar of long gray fur up around her red, wind-burned face.

The coat fit Molly perfectly, just as if it had been tailored for her small body. Although Molly wore layers of clothes, she was nonetheless a petite woman. The additional clothing made up, in part, for the unnatural thinness resulting from her meager diet as a street person.

The garment was woven of soft gray wool, and Molly liked to stroke the coat's softness—just like the cat with long gray fur she had loved years ago.

Sometimes, when moments of clarity forced their way through

Molly's memories, she recalled sitting in front of a fireplace crackling with warmth, her feet curled cozily beneath her, the cat stretched out beside her on a long white sofa. Her hand would absently caress the small furry head, then stroke down, again and again, until she could feel the low rumble that was a purr.

Stroking the coat made Molly feel just like she had when she stroked that cat. Filled with peace and contentment.

But others saw Molly's coat and wished it to be theirs. They watched her wrap it around herself when the winds whistled down the barren streets in the wee hours of the morning, or when she leaned over a burning trash barrel to warm her gloveless hands, as large flakes of snow fell, sizzling in the ashes of the blaze. They watched too closely as she turned up the fur-trimmed collar and laid her head down, pillowed on a small pile of cleaning cloths—cloths thrown away, too torn and dirty to be of any use to their owners, not knowing that their discards served perfectly as pillows for those sleeping outside unprotected by the cover of walls and roofs.

Hidden from view one moonless night, they watched as Molly's lavender-gray eyes disappeared behind closed lids, and her shoulders rose and fell with the breathing of deep sleep.

Then they pounced on her—three of them. The greediest of those who lived on the street.

One held his hand over her mouth, not feeling her savage bite as her teeth sank angrily into his foul-tasting glove, while the other two yanked the coat from her body. To be sure those nearby wouldn't hear her shouts, the meanest of the trio struck her in the head with a heavy metal object. A crow bar, maybe, or a tire iron kept just for such occasions. He struck her behind her left ear, not too hard, but hard enough.

Molly became as limp as the pile of rags Old Johnny carried around with him in his tattered clothes basket. A basket with holes so big, sometimes Johnny would leave a trail of long-ago discarded worthless remnants of fabric in his path.

Just for good measure, one of Molly's attackers kicked her savagely in the ribs before they ran, her lovely gray coat bundled in the arms of the front runner.

"Geez, Ted, don't kill the old lady. We gotta git outta here. Fast. Before any of her cronies sees us."

So they ran, leaving an unconscious Molly with a small trail of blood trickling from behind her ear down onto the ground beneath her head.

Molly awoke slowly and moaned softly as she regained consciousness. As soon as she was aware her coat was gone, her moans escalated into cries like a wounded animal. Intermittent with her cries of rage were sobs, and tears coursed down her dirt-stained cheeks.

Her coat. Her beautiful coat was gone!

No more could she stroke its gray softness, conjuring up warm memories which otherwise escaped, fleeing swiftly into nothingness.

Molly's cries were heard by the others sleeping in the semi-shelter of doorways and piled boxes. They gathered around her, keeping their distance, wary of the screaming old woman whom they knew could explode in a feral outburst of temper at the slightest provocation.

But Johnny didn't watch from a distance. He wasn't afraid of Molly. Taking one of his rags, he wiped away the blood that already had stopped flowing from behind Molly's ear. She pulled away from his touch but stopped screaming. He helped her to her feet and guided her to an accumulation of boxes, piled just so to keep the whistling wind at bay. Gently, he helped her lie down again and placed the cloth speckled with Molly's blood carefully beneath her head. He removed his coat and covered her—just as he had the night she arrived in Valeria.

Old Johnny—incredibly old now, stood watch while Molly again drifted into the silence of sleep.

The three thieves were never seen on the streets or back alleys of Valeria again. They were smart enough to realize that Molly's friends would kill them if their identities were discovered.

Never again did Molly treasure any of her possessions. None, that is, except the gold cross hanging around her neck. And perhaps, her gray felt hat.

The cross no longer shone brightly as it had when presented to the nine-year-old Merritt Hall, and most of the time it went unnoticed among those who mingled with Molly. Very few even saw the cross as it hung buried beneath the dirty collars of the layers of clothing Molly wore. Those who *did* see it had the good sense to turn their eyes the other way.

News on the street travels fast, and everyone had heard about the time Molly bit Old Johnny's finger to the bone when he had dared to reach out and touch her cross. His right index finger stiffened after Molly bit him so savagely, she severed nerves, ripping his flesh to the bone. The finger remained stiff and crooked.

No one had touched the cross since. Everyone seemed to know it was special to Molly in an extraordinary way, and she would fight like a wild animal to keep it.

Johnny had forgiven Molly a long time ago. It was his own fault, he decided. He never should have touched her beautiful shiny piece of jewelry.

But damn, it was pretty!

Molly's hat was a more recent addition to her treasures than her cross, but she had worked hard to make it her own—just a few weeks ago.

***

Breathing hard, with perspiration glistening on her brow, Molly stopped and leaned against the rusty and torn chain-link fence surrounding the long-abandoned warehouse. She had been chasing the hat for more than three blocks now, and every time she caught up with her new find and reached for it, another gust of wind lifted up the fedora and sent it rolling even further down the alley.

Molly eyed it lying not three feet from where she was standing catching her breath. It was beautiful. Gray felt the color of a mourning dove. The burgundy-colored band around the crown was like the red ring surrounding the small necks of the birds she so loved—the birds that always soothed her with their incessant cooing. Tucked in the band was a small feather. A gorgeous light-gray feather.

Carefully, she took two steps towards her target, expecting it to again take flight on the wings of the wind that had been swooshing all day, lifting paper and debris swirling from the streets to lofty heights.

Quickly, Molly reached over and grabbed it. Her hat—her beautiful new hat. She placed it quickly on her head, as if she feared the wind would snatch it from her grasp. Pulling it down securely, as far as it would go, Molly smiled.

There was no one to see her smile, but so delighted was she with her new find that her face lit up with a broad grin, ever so briefly reminiscent of the happy joy-filled woman she had once been.

No one ever again saw Molly without her hat—her precious mourning-dove hat.

141

Chapter Twenty-Seven

Molly was gone. She had never before left the limited area where she lived on the streets of Valeria since arriving in the cold spring rain years ago—except for her stay in the hospital. Those who had grown accustomed to seeing her daily were alarmed, and soon the word spread on the streets that "old Molly was missing."

Johnny, in particular, felt her absence. He had been her self-appointed guardian for years now, and had never even imagined the streets without her. Molly had given some purpose to his life, and without her, he felt aimless.

In the past, Molly may not have been around for a day or two—usually when the weather was unbearable, and she had found shelter in an old building off the beaten path. But her absence this time was stretching into days—many days.

It had been a bitter cold night, and Molly was very tired. The voices inside her head had been on a tirade for days, and night after night, her sleep was interrupted by her own screams. She was wandering the back alleys, cold and miserable, shivering severely. Some of the buildings along the alley were empty, their dark emptiness adding to the mournful quality of the night. Others were filled with light and life; warmth emanated from within each time a rear door opened. Sounds and scents of people celebrating life rode on the warm air seeping through the opened doors.

Parking lots backed up to some of the establishments, and Molly stumbled across one of these. The lot was full from the alley to the building. She spotted a truck—a beat up old truck, painted in various shades of dark-blue, with a pile of folded tarps filling the back. Molly was attracted to that truck, to those tarps. They held promise of warmth, of protection from the bone-chilling cold.

She walked up to the truck and peered inside the back. What a wonderful bed—warm, with covers. The tarps smelled overpoweringly of paint and turpentine, but Molly, so often surrounded by unpleasant smells, didn't notice.

Just a short nap, she thought. *I'll grab a few winks while I get warm and then be on my way.*

With great effort, she boosted herself into the back of the truck, wincing as she banged her knee resoundingly against the hard edge of the truck bed. Tears welled in her eyes from the sharp pain, surely to be followed by a large spot of black and blue, but Molly didn't utter a sound. She didn't want to take a chance that she'd be discovered, although that was highly unlikely. No one lingered in the parking lot just off the alley where Molly had been wandering— the lot behind a bar shaking with loud music and raucous laughter. The frigid temperatures didn't invite lingering.

Like a small animal, Molly burrowed beneath the pile of tarps. Soon she was asleep, her breath billowing in small visible puffs, so cold was the night air beneath the black starlit sky.

Woody Burk, his western hat sitting jauntily on top of his mass of dirty straw-colored curls, staggered out the back door of the bar at just past one o'clock in the morning. Smoke curled out from the room as the door opened, and yells of, "Close the damn door," followed him out into the frosty night air. Woody quickly wrapped his red-plaid fur-lined jacket around himself and muttered something about the "god-awful cold."

"Wait up, Woods," yelled his brother Bobby, struggling to don his own jacket, shivering as the frigid air hit him when he rushed out into the dark night. Bobby ran up to Woody just as he was crawling in the truck, grabbed the edge of his jacket, and said, "Let me drive, Woods. Pa said I was to watch, and if you had too much to drink again, I was to do the driving."

"No way in hell, Bobby. This here's my rig, and only I drive it."

"But Pa said, Woods," objected the younger of the Burk brothers.

"Well, Daddy's boy, I really don't care what he said. *I* do the driving. Got it? Now, do you plan to ride, or are you hoofing it home?"

Sullenly, Bobby walked around to the passenger side and quickly got in—not without apprehension. He valued his own neck and knew what a reckless driver his big brother was when he had been drinking. Bobby glared at his older brother, his dark-brown eyes flashing with anger and not a small amount of fear. "You just be careful, okay," Bobby said, brushing back his unruly black hair and jamming his cap firmly on his head.

"Yessir," said Woody with an exaggerated mock salute as he pulled away with a screech and careened his way down the road. Woody Burk maneuvered his truck, recklessly jerking from side to side of the poorly lit traffic-way leading out of town. Soon the truck was speeding carelessly down a dirt road that led to the Burk's home far past the city limits of Valeria.

The sudden lurching of the truck awoke Molly, and she poked her head out from beneath the tarp. She was bewildered, her deep sleep removing, for a moment, any recollection of how she happened to be bouncing about in the back of a truck driven by, what seemed to her, a maniac.

The sharpness of the cool night air soon awoke her completely, and she remembered how the cold and her weariness had prompted her to take refuge under a pile of tarps in the back of a truck. She now doubted the wisdom of her choice. In fact, she was terrified.

"Dammit, Woody, slow down," demanded Bobby, hanging on to the truck's dashboard for what he felt was his dear life.

"Sure, little brother," said Woody as he pressed harder on the gas pedal, and the truck bounced more swiftly down the rough road.

"Woody!" screamed Bobby this time.

"Okay," laughed Woody as he came to a screeching halt in the front yard of their home. The sudden stop catapulted Bobby forward, and his forehead banged into the windshield so hard that, when Bobby's hand went to massage the blow, it came away sticky with blood.

"Damn you, Woods! Just damn you!" Bobby screamed loudly at his brother as he bounded out of the truck and slammed the door.

"Shh, Bobby. You're going to wake the old man. Oh, oh," he muttered under his breath as he noticed the lights in his parents' bedroom flick on. "Now there'll be hell to pay."

Bobby had already made his way to the house, his hand clutching his forehead. Woody dragged behind, suddenly much more sober than he had been when he exited the bar.

Molly had clutched the side of the truck during the wild drive, and her fingers, poorly covered in tattered gloves, were so cold, they were totally numb. The air was incredibly cold, and the wind whipping in her face during the speedy ride had brought tears that now felt frozen on her cheeks.

She longed to seek comfort again under the pile of tarps, but didn't dare. She was sure if she were to be enveloped in the warmth, she would again fall asleep and risk discovery. Molly wasn't sure what she feared, but the drive had been terrifying, and the hollering exchange between the two brothers anything but pleasant.

144

Molly knew she needed to distance herself from the truck, but she wasn't sure which way to go. The moon was barely a sliver and offered no light to guide her way. Light from the windows of the house illuminated only an area directly below them, and Molly had no desire to tread that close to the house, where now three voices were raised in a loud exchange.

Crawling down from the truck cautiously so as not to further hurt her bruised knee, Molly stole quietly away from the vehicle where she had sought shelter, away from the house teeming with warmth and light—and anger.

She walked blindly into the freezing darkness.

Chapter Twenty-Eight

Molly knew she was lost. And she was so cold—so unbearably cold. She would have liked to just lie down and freeze to death, although that was unlikely, since winter was in its early stages.

Molly didn't keep track of the seasons—or the months, or time. She just knew that not too long ago, she was enjoying warm days—days with multicolored leaves floating down on her pathway, crunching under her feet as she wandered across Valeria. Now the temperature barely hovered above freezing, and the wind blustered in from the Northwest, whistling loudly through the trees.

She wandered, cold and confused, with no idea how to get back to Valeria; she knew no landmarks, had no way to judge the distance. She wouldn't have been able to see a landmark if she *had* known one. It was far too dark.

So she walked until she stumbled, and then pushed on again. There were trees everywhere, and she continued to bump into them with nearly every step. Deep piles of leaves brushed above her ankles, their crunching the only sound breaking the stillness of the night. Once or twice, she heard the whooo-whooo of an owl from a distant tree.

Finally, Molly felt she could go no farther and slumped down beneath a tree and leaned, exhausted, against its rough bark. Although still shivering with cold, the effort of the walk had warmed her somewhat, and as she sat on the ground underneath the tree, she scooped leaves onto her body, covering herself to her waist. She liked the earthy, loamy smell. She lay down on her side, resting her head on her bag, and scooted down further beneath the thick bed of leaves, covering all but her face.

And so she slept, covered in leaves, her head resting on her bag of worldly possessions, her stick clutched tightly in her hand.

The wind had died down by the time the pale light of dawn graced the horizon, but the damp coolness remained. Molly shivered anew as she brushed off the leaves clinging to her clothing. Pulling her coat around her, she stood unsteadily, grabbed her bag and stick, and looked around her.

The faint light cast by the just-rising sun hadn't yet erased much of the darkness as it filtered through the trees. The woods had an eerie quality about them, and Molly shuddered. She recognized nothing around her, and fear gripped her. She didn't know what to do, so she began to walk. She trudged along what seemed like a path—a path barely discernible beneath the fallen leaves.

As she walked, the sun rose higher in the sky, lighting the woods and warming the early morning air. Molly's step became lighter and more confident. The sun sent warmth through her veins, and a feeling of peace arose within her.

Molly knew she needed to find something to eat. The discomfort from the cold had so encompassed her the night before, she had neglected to find anything for her dinner before seeking shelter in the truck. Now hunger pangs gnawed at her insides, and when she stopped to survey her surroundings, the rumbling of her stomach was loud amidst the quiet of the woods.

Continuing on her trek away from the house harboring the reckless driver and his nagging younger brother, Molly walked farther and farther into what appeared to be deep woods. Everywhere she turned, Molly saw nothing but trees—trees in their various stages of shedding leaves. Some were still covered in dingy brown leaves stubbornly clinging the their branches; others were totally bare, ready for winter snows. She was grateful for those bare, allowing shafts of sunlight to flood her path.

The sun was now fairly high in the sky—as high as it gets when the shorter days of winter overtake the bright rays of early autumn. Molly had been wandering since early dawn and was having great difficulty getting any sense of where she was going. All directions looked the same, and she was so hungry—so very, very hungry.

As she was beginning to stagger, lightheaded from hunger, she came upon a clearing. It was a picturesque spot, inviting, with a small creek rippling along one edge. Thin ice clung to its edges. Logs were arranged in a circular fashion around a burned-out campfire, its embers cold. Leftovers from a cookout were strewn about—papers, cans, bottles, and a bag, which when Molly opened it, was found to contain leftover food.

Tears flooded Molly's eyes. She was filled with gratitude for her good fortune. Now she could satisfy her hunger and then, perhaps, be able to find her way out of this seemingly endless maze of trees.

First she strolled over to the creek, and dipping her hands in the frigid flowing water, she brought some to her lips. Although it chilled her, the water also soothed and invigorated her. Cupping her hands, Molly drew some more and drank deeply. She splashed some water lightly on her face.

Then she came back to the circle of logs and picked up the bag containing food apparently deemed not worth saving. Opening a package of hamburger buns, she tore off a large piece of bun and jammed it into her mouth, chewing and swallowing rapidly, making room for more. She yanked open a previously unopened bag of potato chips and hastily ate several handfuls. She rolled down the top of the package and deposited the remaining chips in her cloth bag. The two remaining hamburger buns, she stuck in her pockets—nourishment for a later time. The other bag contained cookies—most reduced to only crumbs. Pulling out pieces large enough to keep, she stuck them in her pockets, along with the hamburger buns. Gathering the discarded papers, cans, and bottles, she filled the now-empty food bag and neatly deposited it in a rusty trash can on the perimeter of the site.

An observer would have thought it strange that a dirty old woman who had lived on the street for years would correctly discard refuse at a picnic site. Somewhere, deep inside Molly, a memory stirred so that she knew it was the right thing to do.

Having satisfied her hunger, Molly resumed her journey. She walked and walked, leaves crunching beneath her feet, low branches and twigs slapping at her as she walked by, sometimes scratching her face. If the assault of the branches hurt her, she didn't show it in any way. She didn't cry out, didn't even grimace. She only pushed harder to her goal—getting out of these woods.

Just when the shadows lengthened as the sun again lowered close to the horizon, Molly finally exited from the maze of trees; it ended abruptly. She could now see ahead, the horizon visible in the fading light.

Molly had accomplished her feat. She was free of tree upon tree upon tree.

Now she saw nothing. The landscape was as barren as the woods were tree-filled. In the far distance, she could make out a house. A thin trail of smoke rose sluggishly from the chimney. Molly feared she might have returned to the site of Woody and Bobby Burk's home—that she might have traveled in a circle. With that in mind, she put the house behind her and walked in the opposite direction. The walk was easier now, the grass short and yellow-brown, dormant

148

until next spring. But as the twilight began to disappear, the bitter cold again took control. Molly gathered her coat tightly around her and ducked her head into the wind.

Just before total darkness overtook the fleeting day, Molly saw the off-and-on flash of a neon sign. "Dew-Drop Inn," the sign read.

Molly had no intention of dropping in, but she felt more secure knowing she was coming upon a town. For tonight, she would find somewhere to sleep, an abandoned building or even an alley. Someplace protected from the cold wind.

And tomorrow, she would try to find her way back to Valeria—back to her "home."

Chapter Twenty-Nine

Molly awoke from a dreamless sleep. Even the voices had left her alone while she slumbered among a pile of boxes behind a grocery store. She rose stiffly from her cardboard shelter and, stretching, surveyed her surroundings.

Molly had found her haven behind the store shortly after she came to the motel she spotted in the distance. She ambled past the Dew-Drop Inn, warily walking on the opposite side of the street, invisible in the shadows. She didn't know where she was; she didn't know whom she could trust. Living on the street had taught her to trust no one—no one but her own kind.

Looking around in the early morning light, Molly examined the buildings around her. Low buildings, nearly all of them. None appeared to be over two stories high, except for a courthouse in the center of a square situated just opposite the front of the furniture store where she had taken refuge. The Wilford County Court House was established in 1894—so claimed the sign in front of the building, on the front edge of the spacious lawn surrounding the historical structure.

Encased in shiny copper, the cupola topping the building reflected the colors of the sunrise, appearing to be pink rather than the metallic hue of copper. Scaffolding hung tremulously from the roof along one side where repairs were being made.

Molly sat down among the boxes that had served as her bed and pulled a hamburger bun from her pocket, squashed and crumbly. Hungrily, she ate her breakfast, saving the other bun and her chips for later in the day. Then realizing she was thirsty, she gathered her bag, clutched her stick, and began a search of her surroundings.

In almost no time, Molly found herself at the other end of the small town. The streets were extremely clean, flanked by tree-lined boulevards. She hadn't gone far from the square when she reached residences—homes with yards well kept and attractively landscaped. Not ostentatious nor particularly large dwellings, but appealing and attractive homes.

As she viewed her surroundings, Molly experienced such a profound sense of longing, she doubled over as if in intense pain. She had claimed no real home in so long, and the place she had long regarded as home—Valeria—was God only knew how many miles from here.

She felt hopelessly lost.

Molly decided she had nothing to gain by turning around and returning to the center of town. The town's small size and perfection made her feel uneasy, and she jumped with the noise of each passing car. She had not seen one single street person as she explored what appeared to be the center of the city—the area around the courthouse. No Johnnys, no Gerts, no Eddies or Jaspers. No Mollys.

So she returned to the highway and began her walk—the opposite way from where she had entered the night before. As she wandered away from the town, she glanced back at the sign posted at the edge of the outskirts—*Watkins, population 1,264.*

Molly had spent the night in the small burg of Watkins, Indiana, thirty-four miles from Valeria.

Shortly after Molly left Watkins behind her, she turned away from the highway she was following and began anew a trek across the countryside. This part of the landscape was not covered with trees like she had encountered immediately upon leaving the Burk home. But it was hilly, and Molly soon became weary as she walked up hills and down.

The sun hid beneath afternoon clouds, and a cool breeze strengthened as the sun sunk lower in the sky. The air felt damp, and Molly feared rain was on its way—or worse, sleet!

She walked faster, although as the day waned, her energy seemed to slip away. Just as it seemed she couldn't drag on another step, Molly spotted an old ramshackle building that appeared it might have once been a storage shed of some sort. She mustered her last spark of strength and ran—sprinted across the dry brittle grass of the countryside and fell through the open doorway of the building.

Molly tried to pull the door closed. It apparently had been open for a long, long time, and its rusty hinges groaned as she tugged and tugged. At first, it appeared that the old door wouldn't possibly budge, but finally, her continued efforts were fruitful. The creaking door eased closed—just before the rat-a-tat of a sleet storm pelted the weathered old building.

Molly plunked down on the dirt floor of the shed and gasped for breath. She was totally spent from her running and door-tugging, and her chest heaved with her labored deep breathing. When she had gained control of her breathlessness, she sat back and surveyed her surroundings. Dirty, old, and tumbledown, but intact. None of the sleet beating relentlessly against the aging wooden planks was leaking in. In its day, this had obviously been an airtight, well-constructed shed. Now it wasn't airtight—the wind whistled around the ill-fitting door and the dirt-encrusted, cobwebbed-draped window. But it was sleet-proof. And for that, Molly was indeed grateful.

Molly smiled as she sat back, and pulling the last remaining hamburger bun and the chips from her pocket, she ate her supper. She hadn't taken a break from her journey for lunch, and she was famished. Although the bun was a squashed ball of bread and the chips nothing but a mound of crumbs, to Molly it was a feast.

The sleet continued until its snow-like pebbles blanketed the landscape. When it was quiet and daylight faded, Molly curled up on the dirt and broken-board floor of the shed, and resting her head on her bag, she fell into a deep sleep.

For the second night in a row, the voices were silent.

Molly awoke to a day overcast and gray. There would be none of yesterday's rays of sunshine to warm her journey. Although she was sorely tempted to remain in her protected haven, she knew she had to find food. Not even a crumb from her stash in the pockets of her coat remained. It was imperative that she trudge on.

So gathering her bag and clutching her stick firmly in her hand, Molly left the shelter of the old building. Closing the door behind her, she again wended her way across the countryside—each step bringing her farther and farther away from Valeria.

Chapter Thirty

For more than two weeks, Molly wandered in the same area. She knew she must be going in circles, because twice she found herself back at the tool shed, the building isolated from any other sign of life. The first time, the time she spent the night in the shed protected from the driving sleet, she had walked an entire day before she came to another building—to a source of food. That time she had come upon a small settlement—a post office, a combination gas station and grocery store, and a small foul-smelling diner.

Molly raided the garbage can behind the diner for food. At the time, she hadn't eaten in thirty-six hours, and the spoiled produce she was able to salvage satisfied her hunger and only slightly nauseated her.

The second time she came upon the tool shed, she stayed only briefly, taking a momentary rest from her travels. The third time, she didn't stop—just spied it in the distance, affirming her concerns that she was, indeed, walking in circles.

She walked away from the shed, not going in the same direction she had the first two times. She didn't go farther from Valeria. Instead, she retraced her earlier footsteps, back towards the Burk place. Much like a lost dog would find its way home.

She had lost the anxiety she experienced after her harrowing ride in the back of the truck with Woody Burk at the wheel. Any remaining fear she had was overpowered by the strength of the homesickness she felt for Valeria and her "family" there. So step by step, she let her instincts guide her back through the woods, back to the Burk's.

After a long hard trek, she arrived at the Burk place just after dusk. She slowly crept closer to the house—but not too close. She didn't like what she had heard from this house before, and she had no desire to place herself in the hands of these antagonistic people.

Molly rested beneath a tree, far on the edge of the property on the side she was coming from. Lights shone from every window in the house, and a small spiral of smoke swept up from the chimney. Molly was too far from the house to hear any voices this time, but from time to time, she saw shadows move across a lighted window, as those inside moved around living their lives.

Molly continued to sit under the tree—waiting, shivering with cold. In time, the lights in the downstairs rooms of the house were turned off, and finally, those in the rooms upstairs followed—one by one. She waited a while longer, until she was certain all those inside were sleeping. Then she carefully crept up to the truck and looked at the mud-encrusted tires.

A slight moon hanging low in the sky helped her see what she was looking for. She wanted to see which way the truck had come from the last time it left the road and turned into the Burk yard. The tread was deep on the tires of the old beat-up truck, suggesting they were many times newer than the vehicle.

She was in luck! The tire marks showed up well on the thin layer of snow dusting the country road. In the moonlight, the marks were very clear, and she could plainly tell from which direction they came. So with her bag thrown carelessly over her shoulder and her stick swinging back and forth in front of her, guiding the way, Molly started down the old dirt road, the moonlight brightly shining on the snow, illuminating her path—hopefully, towards Valeria.

Molly walked well into the night. When she could no longer drag herself another step, she crawled off into a thick copse of trees and lay down. Sleep quickly overtook her, but it wasn't to be a restful slumber. The voices assaulted her mercilessly, and her screams shredded the silence of the cold moonlit night.

When Molly awoke, she felt as weary as she had before lying down—and nearly frozen. In addition, she was muddled and confused. She wasn't certain where she was or where she was going. Last night's well thought out plan of finding her way back to Valeria had disintegrated in the night's terrors.

It was only by sheer chance that Molly found herself back in Valeria. She had been gone for two and one-half weeks. It was now the dead of the winter.

Chapter Thirty-One

By the following year, most of those Molly had originally met as her "street family" had departed—either dead or disappeared. The familiar group was smaller; their numbers had dwindled. Some of those gone had been Molly's favorites.

Jasper and Eddie both had died—Jasper quietly succumbing to a heart that really hadn't worked right for a long time, Eddie dying of a hard blow to the head, a blow that really wouldn't have been necessary. Anyone who had wanted the bright-blue blanket Eddie found in the dumpster could have had it for the asking.

Kind, giving Eddie. That's just the way he was.

But no, someone had taken the blanket by force, stealing quietly up to him as he slept, silencing his gentle charm forever with a massive rock found at the site.

So now Eddie was gone, taken away in an ambulance summoned by the policeman who found his bloodied homeless body. Why an ambulance, none of the others could understand.

It was too late to help Eddie.

Louis, too, was gone. Probably dead, but no one was sure. He had been terribly sick. Even his ever-present protruding belly had dwindled. His body seemed to deflate over a period of weeks—as if he were a balloon slowly leaking air.

One day, he was gone—simply gone. Since he had always been anti-social, some who had known him speculated that he crawled away somewhere to die alone—like a stray animal.

Others never gave his disappearance a second thought.

***

The day was bright and mildly cool—an invigorating day. Most of the street people had been scattered for weeks, each going his or her own way before the cold weather hit Valeria. It was difficult to say where they went.

Some stretched their journeys into neighboring towns, and some of those never returned to Valeria. Perhaps they found life easier in another place.

Maybe they just kept going until they returned to where they had come from.

Maybe they had become tired of living on the street.

This year, Molly didn't stray more than six or eight blocks from where she had spent the stifling summer days when heat would rise in waves from the sizzling streets, and the air was fetid with dirt and decay. She welcomed the cool breezes of another early fall, even the chill that sometimes moved her to wrap her own arms tightly around her body, warming herself in her self-given hug.

Not that Molly wasn't wearing enough clothing for warmth. Even at the height of sweltering summer, she continued to wear her clothes in layers, as if hiding her identity deeply in cover upon cover.

Tonight, the twilight was picturesque; pink and lavender clouds drifted across the round, red sun. As it reflected like a prism off the storefront window, Molly watched the colors. She saw a woman in the reflection.

A woman she didn't recognize.

Merritt long dead in her eyes, she saw only the street person called Molly.

She returned her gaze to the sidewalk, swiping the stick she was carrying from side to side, much like a blind person feeling her way, hidden in non-seeing darkness. But Molly could see. She could see perfectly. With her eyes.

With her mind, she saw little much of the time, and seemingly comprehended nothing.

She wandered down the street, ambling slowly as if carrying several decades of age with her. Her body was bent from countless hours of staring down, her skin wrinkled from constant exposure to the elements.

In truth, Molly was only middle-aged.

Rounding the corner and entering the alleyway, she stopped to sit on a doorstep. She probably wouldn't be able to stay long. If Neville Martin, the proprietor of the shop just to the other side of the worn and beaten door, were to emerge, she would be shooed away, accompanied by curses and threats.

She stayed but a moment—a moment to rest and think. Molly thought a great deal. When the voices would let her. Then she thought and thought.

Sometimes—on rare occasions—she even remembered.

As the evening gave way to night, Molly wandered to the edge of town, something she rarely did anymore. On the edges of the city, she felt less safe. There were fewer people, fewer of the street

156

community.

Tonight she felt the pull to the wooded edge of town, however, a pull to a park resplendent with rustling trees and the fragrance of fresh air. She walked slowly up to a park bench and sat down.

On a facing bench, just to the other side of a winding path, two young people sat lost in an intimate embrace.

The young woman looked up and saw an unrecognizable figure sitting across from them, huddled, wrapped in ill-fitting clothing, a hat pulled far down, almost covering eyes that were fixated on some spot on the ground. The young woman couldn't tell if the figure was man or woman, but seeing Molly and hearing her barely audible mumbling, she was afraid. She gasped.

At first, the young man thought the gasp an expression of great ecstasy, an indication of the effect his lengthy kiss had upon her. But then, she moved her lips from his to his ear and whispered, "Andy, there's someone over there. I'm scared. Let's go. No, don't look," she warned as he started to turn his head. "Let's just go," she pleaded.

Hand and hand, the young couple eased their way around the back of the bench, where moments before they had been focused only on their proclaimed love for one another. As soon as they had cleared the bench, they began to run down the path, away from the park.

The figure on the bench never looked up, never even moved. She had no curiosity about the feet pounding on the path. She continued to stare at a spot just beyond her feet, mumbling words that only she could possibly know the meaning of.

There she sat until the moon that had been brightening the autumn sky began to drift towards the horizon, heralding the beginning of morning light.

***

The evenings were turning cool again, and often, although not every night, the homeless in Valeria would once more gather outside town by the old depot and warm themselves around a fire in a barrel. Reminiscent of the traveling homeless during the Great Depression. At first, there were only a few, but then, more of their numbers sought the refuge and camaraderie of the group.

One night, a new couple joined them. Oliver and Maggie.

Oliver was tall and slim, with thinning brown hair streaked with gray. In spite of his filthy clothing, he had an almost distinguished look about him. His smile was shy, and when he smiled, his watery blue eyes twinkled merrily.

Maggie's appearance was directly the opposite of his. She was short, round, and solemn. Very, very solemn. Her dirty blonde hair was so long, it brushed the sash she wore around her waist, and her doe-like brown eyes glared warily through colorless lashes.

Oliver and Maggie were the youngest couple to join their throngs in quite some time.

And they didn't stay long.

Oliver drank heavily and constantly, anything alcoholic he could find—or steal. Not that drinking was that unusual among those living on the street, but when Oliver drank, which was most of the time, he became mean. Sober, or even nearly sober, he was quiet and very solicitous towards his companion, Maggie.

When drunk, he mistreated her brutally. At first, just verbally, then, physically. Her pudgy round face was often badly bruised. But no matter how much he abused her, she never left his side. Nor did she complain. Neither did she smile. Almost never.

One night, when Oliver was mean-drunk, he yelled at Maggie loudly, calling her names. "Maggie, Maggie, you no-good bitch," he screamed again and again.

After the fourth or fifth time, he struck her with his doubled-up fist, sending her sprawling across the old railroad tracks. As he stood over her with his fists raised above his head, ready to strike again, he was hit from behind with a large rock.

Bellowing with rage as blood trickled down his neck, staining his gray-brown hair with scarlet, he turned, ready to strike his assailant.

But the rock-thrower was already by the side of his companion. Her words, the first anyone had heard Molly speak in a long time, sounded so unlike her that the others were dumfounded.

"It's okay, Megan. Mommy's here. I'm so sorry you're hurt, but Mommy'll make it okay. Shh. Shh. Hush now, honey, and go to sleep."

Molly cradled Maggie's head in her lap and gently stroked her brow. In her muddled mind, she was comforting her daughter Megan, when Megan was just a child. Hearing the now prostrate woman referred to as "Maggie" had prompted memories.

All, even Oliver, were quiet. For a moment. Then Johnny and

Evan broke the silence, and almost in unison, glared at Oliver and ordered, "Out."

"Take yer babe and leave. 'Less she don't wanna leave with ya," said Evan. "We's good folk an' don' hurt each other. Yer not one a us, so git," he said, pointing his forefinger down the track.

Stumbling, Oliver grabbed Maggie's arm, pulling her to her feet, pushing Molly aside in the process. "Okay, okay. Guess we know when we're not wanted."

The pair disappeared into the darkness.

Molly was inconsolable. "Megan, Megan," she screamed, her cries echoing into the otherwise quiet night. Nothing anyone said eased her cries. She wrapped her arms tightly around her knees, rocking back and forth, her moans piercing through the still night air like coyote howls across the prairie.

Molly's friends gathered around her, making soothing sounds and begging her to be silent, but she would not. One by one, they pulled away and wandered off into the night.

The community of the homeless of Valeria survived by *not* drawing attention to themselves, and Molly's cries made them uneasy.

The last to leave was Johnny. Old Johnny had long ago appointed himself Molly's guardian. His attention bore the signs of true caring—and also of old-fashioned chivalry. But he, too, feared unwanted attention, and when he found there was no way to console Molly or to end her attention-drawing wails, he faded into the night.

Chapter Thirty-Two

Shortly past midnight, when Molly had already wept, screamed, and moaned for hours, a patrol car drove up. The driver approached and restrained the distraught Molly, and firmly, but not unkindly, shoved her into the squad car. Recognizing the unkempt and disheveled woman as one of the "regulars" of the street, the policemen drove her to a shelter in the center of Valeria and handed her over to Jessica Rose, the guardian of every homeless woman in the area.

"This is the one known as 'Molly,' Jess," said Lonnie Bates, the elder of the two who had responded to the report of Molly's cries. "Hope you can do something for her. Sounds like she's in a helluva lot of pain."

"I'm sure she is, Lon, but we'll probably never know why. I'll make sure none of it's physical, though, and see what I can do for her.

"Thanks, guys," she said, nodding at the two patrolmen appreciatively. She knew many of their cohorts would have tossed the homeless woman in jail for disturbing the peace, but like Riley MacRae, Lonnie Bates was one of "the best of the best." He really wanted to help the street people—a group that, although not growing, seemed to be ever-present in Valeria.

With her hand on Molly's elbow, Jessica guided Molly over to a cot and sat her on the edge, the entire time making soft "shhhhhing" noises, trying to comfort this very distressed woman. But for a long time, nothing she said could quell the shrill screams of "Maggeeee!" and heart-wrenching sobs that seemed to come from the depths of this woman's soul.

Jessica sat with her arm around Molly's shoulders until their heaving decreased and her sobs lessened. How long this took, Jessica didn't know, didn't care. She had an incredible level of empathy for those whom life seemed to have abandoned.

The more they hurt, the more she cared.

Soon the only sound was Molly's deep breathing, bordering on sighs.

"My dear friend," said Jessica, taking Molly's slender hand in hers. "I don't know what hurt you so, but you are completely exhausted. Please lie down now and get some rest. We'll figure out what to do for you tomorrow."

Finally quiet, Molly sat immobile as Jessica spoke. That is, until Jessica reached up to remove Molly's hat, saying, "Let's just get you comfortable now—take off your hat and shoes, and . . ."

Her words were cut short by Molly's screams as soon as her hands touched the revered hat. Jessica quickly pulled away, recognizing immediately the hat was off limits.

"Okay, okay, I'm sorry. The hat stays. But will you please let me take off your shoes?"

She eased Molly back, gently guiding her hat-adorned head to the thin flimsy pillow, swung Molly's legs up onto the bed, and carefully removed the old, worn, mud-encrusted shoes.

When Molly's screams and sobs had ceased completely, she closed her eyes, and within moments, succumbed to deep sleep.

"I wish I knew your story, Molly," spoke Jessica softly, tears misting her eyes. "Maybe I could be of more help if I knew."

With a step reflecting a combination of sadness and determination, Jessica Rose walked to her own cot at the other side of the room and lay down, fully clothed, and soon gave way to her own total and complete weariness, joining her newest resident, Molly, in deep sleep.

***

Who was Jessica Rose, and how did someone with a smile that looked like it should be on the face of a beauty queen and a figure to the slight side of a model's happen to be managing a shelter for women?

All who knew Jess, as she was fondly called by most, marveled at her cheerfulness, her dedication, her caring. She walked with a spring to her step, always wore a smile, and extended a helping hand to the down and out women who came her way.

Most presumed she was just one of those individuals who had so much happiness, she had to spread it around; she just couldn't hide it.

Only those who looked into Jessica's eyes—really looked—saw the intense sadness beneath their gray softness, saw the grief so painstakingly hidden by this highly energetic woman who gave so much of herself to those whom others had discarded.

Until nine years ago, Jessica Rose was Jessica Huntington—Jessica *Rose* Huntington, to be exact. A successful young Minneapolis lawyer with plans to marry Gaylord Patterson III, "Gay," son of *the* Gaylord Patterson, Jr., Minneapolis' famed criminal attorney. A spring wedding was planned. A huge spring wedding, to be held in one of the city's largest and most elegant churches, followed by a country-club reception. The society wedding of the year. Everyone who was anyone would be in attendance.

Everyone except Jessica's mother.

Jessica's mother wouldn't be welcome. Gay's father, and his mother, Amanda Delft Patterson, were not about to be embarrassed by the likes of Katie Huntington, town drunk and oftentimes, street dweller.

"How can I *not* have my mother at my own wedding, Gay? I love her. She's the only family I have since Dad died."

"Be reasonable, Jess. Of course you love her. She's your mother. But half the time she's so potted, she doesn't even know you. And you have to understand how Mom and Dad feel.

"If it were up to me, I'd want her there as much as you do. But, darling, you know the likelihood of Katie being sober enough to even show up is pretty slim. And can you imagine putting her in the same room as an endless supply of champagne?

"This is to be our special day, Jess. I don't want to give Katie the opportunity to ruin it for us. And my parents don't want the embarrassment of their new daughter-in-law's mother parading her drunkenness in front of all their friends," he added, harshly. "You know how Mom and Dad are about their society cohorts. They're very important to them," he added, trying to shift the blame for his insensitivity to his parents.

"And my mother's very important to *me*," argued Jessica. "After all, it's to be *our* wedding day, not theirs!"

Her cheeks flaming with anger, and with hot tears barely in check, Jessica left the room where she and Gay had been planning to spend this bitterly cold evening in front of the fireplace, warmed by a roaring flame and their love, talking and planning the upcoming nuptials. She ran to her car and sped away, driving far too fast for the frosty streets and her troubled state of mind.

Miraculously, she arrived home safely, leaping from her car as soon as it skidded to a stop in the driveway of her rented old Victorian-style house on the shores of Lake Harriet. She could barely get the key into the lock on the door, she was shaking so. Running into her bedroom, she flung herself across her bed and sobbed for what seemed like hours.

How can he be so heartless, she thought. She wondered how she could have missed his ability to be so cruel—cruel and non-caring. *Did I fall in love with the real Gay?* she asked herself. He had always seemed so loving, recognizing and responding to her every mood.

But this—this pompous concern about appearances. I can't live with that.

Weary, her mind in a quandary, she prepared for bed and crawled in between the cool comfortable sheets, warmed by her favorite quilt, an heirloom created by her maternal grandmother. She fell into a restless dream-ravaged sleep.

A shrill ring awoke Jessica. At first she thought it was the alarm clock summoning her to begin a new day. Then realizing it was the phone, she reached for it and picked up the receiver, thinking it must be Gay, apologizing, admitting how heartless he had been.

"Hello," she said, her voice husky with sleep and hours of tears.

"Miss Huntington?" the official-sounding voice on the other end asked.

The voice was most definitely not Gay's.

Suddenly, she was filled with dread.

More awake now, she answered in *her* official-sounding voice. "Yes, this is Jessica Huntington. And who is this?"

"This is Sergeant Waters of the Minneapolis Police Department. Your mother was found in an alley off Hennepin Avenue tonight. An ambulance brought her to North Memorial, but Ms. Huntington, I don't think they'll be able to do much for her. She was damn near frozen stiff, and . . ."

Jessica threw down the phone before the sergeant even had a chance to finish. She quickly donned the clothes she had discarded on a chair the night before, and combing her hair with her fingers as she dashed out the door, she jumped into her car, praying it would start quickly on such a frigid night. Her teeth chattered, and shivers ran up and down her spine as she turned the key.

"C'mon, c'mon," she coaxed.

Almost as if her ten-year-old-but-what-a-great-buy Audi could understand her pleas, it turned over on the second try, and Jessica sped off into the night, headed for the hospital to face what? Dread was pulsating through her entire being, and tears tracked down her cheeks.

Oh, Mom. Please be okay. Please.

But even as she pleaded with the Divinity, whom she addressed far too little these days, she knew her mother was gone.

An orphan. She was now a twenty-nine-year-old orphan, as frightened with the aloneness as a five-year-old.

Jessica pounded the steering wheel in anger and fear as she sped down the highway for the second time this night. Traffic, fortunately, was light. As she pulled into the hospital parking lot, she glanced at the clock lighting up the dashboard and noted it was 3:27 a.m. Grabbing her purse, she slammed the car door and ran to the emergency entrance.

The hospital corridor was eerily quiet—nothing like the last time she was here. The difference between predawn hours and the middle of the day, she supposed. She wished she hadn't hung up on that policeman so abruptly. She had no idea where to go—what room, what floor, what anything.

"Can I help you?" came a voice from behind her. She whirled around and faced a friendly looking young man dressed in blue scrubs topped by a white lab coat. A hospital name tag identified him as Mark Brooks. Seeing a friendly face and hearing a friendly voice, Jessica gave way to the emotions that she had barely kept in check. "I'm looking for Mrs. Hu . . . Hu . . . Hun . . ."

Jessica couldn't say her mother's name.

She rubbed the back of her hand across her burning eyes like a small child, took a deep breath and said, barely audibly, "I'm looking for my mother."

"Could you tell me her name, please?" Mr. Brooks asked kindly.

The dim corridor shimmering through her tears, Jessica took another deep breath, looked at the friendly face, and said in her best lawyer voice, "Mrs. Huntington. Kate Huntington. I received a call from a Sergeant Waters saying they had found her in an alley off Hennepin, and . . ."

"I know, I know," said the friendly voice as he placed his arm gently across Jessica's shoulder. "Come over here and sit a moment so we can talk."

He guided her over to a reasonably comfortable chair covered in dark-green faux leather. Many a soul had sat in that same chair awaiting news of the fate of a loved one. It sagged in the middle, and

164

Jessica sunk down like a small child, a pose fitting the way she felt.

"She's dead, isn't she?" asked Jessica.

"Yes," responded the friendly voice with compassion. It was almost as if he shared the grief Jessica was feeling. So different from the last time she was here, when her mother had been attacked, the victim of a street brawl. Then, she was met with derision and clicking tongues.

Jessica wondered if they saved the truly caring help for the night—to somehow lessen the terrible fear exacerbated by the nocturnal stillness and darkness.

"She just wasn't strong enough to handle such bitter cold," he explained. No accusation, simply a statement of fact. "Let me take you to her."

Jessica nodded and let herself be guided by a gentle hand on her elbow, to see, one last time, the mother she had adored all her life, the mother who herself had once been a brilliant lawyer. Long before most women even considered entering that field.

The mother whose losing battle with addiction took her to the street. The street where she died.

Jessica Rose Huntington left Minneapolis the week after she buried her mother. Gave up her law practice, stored the furnishings she had so enjoyed buying for the lovely old Victorian house where she had lived for the past two years. She mailed the key, along with rent for the remainder of her lease, to the house's owner, packed up her Audi with all it could hold, and headed for Valeria, Indiana.

Jessica never even called Gaylord Patterson III to say good-bye.

***

"Well, Jess, it's just as you might have expected," said Dr. Jim Baylor in his soft voice as he turned from examining Molly—not a small feat as she kicked and scratched at him with every move he made. "She's probably dehydrated, anemic, carrying God only knows what kind of infections, and most likely afflicted with schizo or some other dementia.

"The usual stuff for our friends on the street."

He sighed as he said the latter and looked at Jessica. "I don't know what you can do for her, Jess. There was a mild sedative, as well as some pretty strong vitamins in that injection I managed to slip into her arm. No doubt what she needs badly is one of the new miracle drugs for her dementia. But for those to work, it takes a regular regimen, and that's never going to happen. She's not ill enough to hospitalize, and it's my guess that the minute you turn your back today, she'll be back on the street.

"If not today, tomorrow."

Jim Baylor knew Jessica Rose's story and understood her deep empathy for the women living on the street. He knew, although totally disagreed, that she blamed herself for her mother's death. Many a night he held her as she wept for the mother she lost in such a sad lonely manner, her head buried in the mass of black curls on his chest, heaving with heart-wrenching sobs. They had a very deep personal relationship, sometimes romantic, sometimes just friendly. Both wondered from time to time if they should allow it to go further.

This time it was Jessica who sighed. "I know, Jim. It's just that . . ." She let her unfinished sentence hang in mid-air.

Jim Baylor knew what she meant. Knew that she felt if only she could save this one, maybe she would be vindicated for not helping her mother more.

"Just don't let her break your heart, Jess. Look at all you're doing for these women," he said as he glanced around the room crowded with cots, several still occupied with those sleeping soundly, deep sleep induced by exhaustion and deprivation—and often, drugs.

Again he sighed, and closing his black bag, he rose, gently smoothed back Jessica's ash-blonde hair, kissed her lightly on the forehead, and headed for the door. "Call me when you need me, kiddo," he called back as left.

Jessica knew she would. She always did.

Molly slept until mid-afternoon. As Dr. Baylor had predicted, while Jessica was in her office tending to business matters—such as trying to shuffle her finances so she could pay the rent on the shelter another month—Molly walked out the door.

Jessica didn't see Molly again for several months. She had never sought refuge in Jessica's shelter before, and it took time for her to seek it now.

Chapter Thirty-Three

"Okay, Harri-ETT," said Jessica, taking great care to emphasize the final syllable of the woman's name, just as Harriett wanted it. It was a simple concession to this woman, too old and too ill to be living on the street.

But there she was just the same.

Harriett was old, large, and black. Her eyes, such a dark brown they appeared as black as coal, were cloudy—filmed—and Jessica was certain she was far closer to blindness than she was to being fully sighted.

Diabetes took its toll rapidly when there was no proper diet and no way to monitor medication. Or there was no medication *to* monitor.

The last time Harriett received pills she should have taken regularly, the vial dropped from her bag as she pulled out a pair of socks, rolled down the gutter, and disappeared through a grate. She watched it disappear, then turned her attention back to her socks, totally disinterested in her loss.

Her feet, discolored and often raw with open sores, did interest her, however. They hurt. Whenever she could get her hands on a new pair of socks, she added them to those she already wore. On occasion, her feet were cushioned and protected as best they could be by three or four pairs at a time.

It was hard to keep your feet dry living on the street, hammered by driving rains or soaked by drizzles lasting for days.

Once Harriett learned she could count on Jessica Rose at the women's shelter for new dry socks, she was a regular visitor. "Harri-ETT, she need socks," she'd proudly declare, her nearly toothless grin never betraying the pain she must be feeling. Jessica would help her remove her shoes, torn, and cut out where they weren't torn, and her grimy and often wet socks.

Jessica grimaced as she gently pulled the socks away from the woman's badly damaged feet. "Harri-ETT, you need to have a doctor look at these. This is serious business."

Still grinning, Harriett shook her head. "No doctor. No hospital. Jes' socks." Jess looked at her sadly, shook her head and carefully pulled new socks on the woman's swollen and discolored feet.

"Thank you. You such a nice lady."

The words were always the same. And each time, she would take Jessica's hand and gently pat it, a token of her appreciation for the help Jess gave her. Then Jessica would help her stand, and Harriett would shuffle towards the door, a picture of pain and gratitude.

One morning, just as she was helping Harriett to her feet, Jessica saw Molly drift in. Harriett saw her too. "*She* crazy," declared the old woman as she hobbled towards the door, giving a wide berth to her fellow street dweller.

Jessica had not seen Molly in several months and often wondered if she would ever see her again. She began to think Molly had left Valeria, had joined the numbers of the many who simply disappear.

But here she was.

Molly looked straight at Jessica, walked over to a vacant cot, lay down and promptly fell asleep.

"M'am," started Ruth Baker, one of the volunteers whose help Jessica could not do without.

As Ruth started towards Molly, who already was asleep, Jessica said, "No, Ruth, just let her be. I've been trying to find her for months. Lonnie Bates brought her in once last winter.

"Her name is Molly," added Jessica, with something akin to fondness in her voice.

"But Jess, shouldn't we at least take those filthy shoes off the blanket?"

"Huh-uh. I don't want to disturb her. Blankets wash, Ruthie. I'm just so glad to see her again. The last time she was in here, she was nearly inconsolable. I wanted so much to help her, but I never had the chance. She walked away as soon as she had the opportunity."

"You can't help them all, honey," said Ruth gently, as she walked back to the small cramped kitchen section of the shelter, ready to put in many hours of preparing meals for these women, many of whom seemed to have no one else in the world except Jessica Rose.

Often now, Molly would wander into the shelter, lie down on the first empty cot she came to, and clutching her bag of belongings, instantly fall asleep. She left as soon as she awoke, speaking to no one, most of the time her eyes focused on some nameless something in front of her, on the ground.

Once or twice, she'd raised her eyes and met Jessica's. In those few seconds, Jessica felt a bonding with this woman decked with many layers of clothing and a dirty felt hat pulled down nearly over her eyes—eyes that were the most beautiful Jessica had ever seen.

Jessica tried several times to engage Molly in conversation, to offer to find help for her or to have Dr. Baylor give her some medication to help. Molly didn't refuse. She didn't even shake her head in disagreement.

She just stopped coming. For a while.

Then she would return and again collapse into incredibly deep sleep, her snoring sometimes accentuated by her cries.

The pattern was repeated several times over a period of many months. Jessica began to look forward to seeing Molly, to the days when she'd turn around and there she'd be, fast asleep, her hat pulled down so far it nearly hid her face.

One day when Molly was deep in sleep, lying on her back, her face turned up towards the ceiling, Jessica pulled up a chair by her bedside and sat down.

"What in the world are you doing?" asked Ruth, as she came up behind her friend and mentor.

"Oh, hi, Ruthie. Just watching Molly. She's so small—and beautiful, really. Look at those hands, those long fingers."

"Jess, you're a hopeless romantic," said Ruth with a smile. It was one of the things she really loved about Jessica—this ability to see beyond the homeless woman who was in front of her. To see who she really was—or who she once might have been.

She knew Jessica could see more in these women from the street than *she* could. Jess envisioned caring mothers with broods of noisy, happy children, or socialites with their hands on the arms of their prominent husbands, or professionals in snappy business suits—even successful attorneys like her.

Even though Ruth didn't have that ability, she felt great compassion for the women who filled their cots nightly, who partook of the food she prepared—plain, but wholesome and plentiful food. She knew Jessica would so like to have this small sound-asleep woman accept the food they offered, but so far, all she had been willing to accept was a bed.

And that was at unexplainable intervals.

She probably comes because she feels Jessica's caring. Ruth

169

smiled as she watched Jessica gently touch Molly. *Love that strong is bound to have power*, she mused, sighing.

Ruth worried about her friend when she saw her become so attached to one of the women who frequented the shelter. Every time it happened, Jessica got hurt. Ruth was certain this would be no exception.

I wonder who she really is, what happened to bring her here to Valeria, to the street, thought Jessica as she watched Molly sleep. She was certain she would never know, and she was right.

Molly came three more times. After that, Jessica never saw her again.

Chapter Thirty-Four

It was a clear day, but cool, with a blustery wind tossing debris about like anchorless boats in a hurricane. Molly shivered and pulled her coat more tightly around her. As she rounded a corner, pressing closely to the buildings, seeking protection from the wind, she felt a tug on her coat.

Molly jumped and uttered a startled, "Wha…?" She looked down, more surprised than ever when she saw a little girl clutching the hem of her tattered coat.

The child was small, probably no more than five or six years old. A bundle of auburn curls surrounded her small face, topped with a royal-blue fur-trimmed hat. Her tiny ears, not covered by the hat were red with cold, as were her tiny gloveless hands.

Molly took the child's small hands in hers and rubbed them briskly. "Why child, where did you come from? And where are your gloves? Your hands are like ice."

The little girl didn't respond, only smiled up at Molly, her eyes tearing with cold, her little nose running. Molly searched through her bag for a cloth she might use as a handkerchief. Finding a small red-checkered square of cloth—not clean, but not as unclean as most of the contents of her bag—she squatted down to wipe the little nose.

"Now blow," she directed. The little girl obediently did as she was told.

Then Molly tugged hard on the sides of the child's fur-trimmed hat, pulling it down over her little cold-nipped ears. "There," said Molly, "that should keep your ears warm." The hat now covered her forehead as well, and in order for her to look up at Molly, the little girl had to tip her head far back. But she didn't complain. In fact her face still held the same angelic smile that adorned it when Molly first saw her little "sleeve-tugger."

Noting the top two buttons of the child's coat were unbuttoned, Molly momentarily removed her gloves, holey with at least half the knitted fingers ripped through, and worked the top two fur-covered buttons through the buttonholes on the little blue coat.

Molly glanced down at the little girl's feet, and seeing the patent-leather dress shoes she was wearing, said under her breath, "Someone really didn't care if you caught your death of cold, taking you out on

171

such a chilly day without proper clothes."

Molly looked around, still not seeing anyone the child might have been with—or anywhere she might have come from. This was mostly an abandoned section of town, with only a minimal amount of foot traffic and an occasional car or truck driving along the nearly empty street.

"Can you tell me where you came from, honey?" asked Molly in a soft but gravelly sounding voice. The child said nothing—only continued to smile.

Shadows lengthened as the day was drawing to a close.

"Well, I'm not leaving you here. You're coming with me. Here, stick that hand in your pocket and leave it there," she ordered. Molly took the child's unpocketed hand and clutched it firmly in her own.

The pair—an old street woman clothed in layers of ragged clothing and a small girl dressed elegantly in patent-leather shoes, white tights, and a fur-trimmed hat and coat—wended their way across Valeria seeking shelter.

Their steps were slow, Molly's usual hurried gait impeded considerably by tiny footsteps struggling to keep up with her. The wind had died down with the coming of dusk, but Molly and her small companion were both thoroughly chilled, the child shivering almost uncontrollably as they finally reached their destination—the old train depot at the edge of town.

Molly reached into her coat pocket, brought out a bent nail, and inserted it in the keyhole. At first she had difficulty getting the nail in the hole she was shaking so badly, but using both hands to steady herself, she finally made her makeshift key work, and the door to the depot swung open. Molly took the child's hand and gently pulled her inside.

The dingy room was nearly barren and, of course, had no heat. But although it was cold, it was less cold than outside. The child sniffed the smell of dust and disuse, and sneezed. She was still smiling, although her nose was again running—profusely—and tears from the cold were streaming down her ruddy cheeks.

Molly carefully lifted the little girl's hat from her head, and auburn curls tumbled down, folding around her cherub-like face. Molly again took the red-checkered "handkerchief" and wiped the little face.

"I don't know where you belong, little one, but I guess I'll worry

172

about that tomorrow. Now, let's build you a bed."

Molly took two sections of cardboard piled along one wall and laid them side-by-side. Next she piled several layers of folded newspaper on top of the cardboard. Then she slipped off one of the two skirts she was wearing and laid it over the newspapers. She pulled an old partly unraveled crocheted black shawl from her bag, and rolling it up tightly, she placed it on one end of the "bed."

"Now honey, you lie down here, with your head on this end," said Molly, pointing to the rolled-up shawl.

The child did as she was told, her auburn curls shining against the blackness of the old shawl. Molly covered her with her coat, wrapping it tightly around the child's small body. Bending down to kiss her pink cheek, she said, "I wish you'd at least tell me your name, child."

The little girl giggled as her weary eyelids closed over her lovely lavender-gray eyes, and she said, "You know, Mommy, it's Megan."

Early morning light was streaking through the dirty windows. Molly stretched and yawned. She was chilled through and through. She reached to pull her coat more tightly around her, to capture what little body heat she had retained underneath her newspaper covers.

But she wasn't wearing her coat. Alarmed, she sat up abruptly. Next to her bed of cardboard and newspaper, crisp and yellow with age, was a perfectly laid bed—cardboard neatly piled, layers of newspaper neatly stacked on top of the cardboard, and on top of that, her skirt and her coat. At the top of the coat, neatly rolled was her shawl, the one she usually carried in her bag.

Molly grabbed the coat, sending the shawl flying onto the floor. She buttoned the one button still remaining on the garment and wrapped her arms around herself, rubbing up and down, warming herself. Soon she was feeling much better, much warmer. She picked up the shawl and skirt and stuffed them back into her bag.

There was no sign of her small "companion" of the night before. Nor did Molly have any recollection of her. She didn't even wonder why her coat and shawl lay, unused, beside her on a neatly fashioned cardboard and newspaper bed. Molly was not one to question anything. The inquisitive child that had been such a strong trait within Merritt Hall-Davis died long ago.

Chapter Thirty-Five

The newcomer was a scrawny girl. Just a kid really. Her large hazel eyes, framed by long lashes of reddish-gold, were flecked with gold and green.

She knew her eyes were her best feature.

Her too-small nose was upturned like a pixie's and sprinkled with a smattering of freckles, and her mouth, also too small, displayed large square teeth. The girl's large teeth appeared out of place in their tiny opening, much like the teeth of a first-grader when new ones arrive to fill the gaps left by baby teeth fallen out and placed under a pillow to test the generosity of the "tooth fairy."

Her long stringy hair was pulled back from her small face and tied with a bright yellow scarf. It was difficult for those who saw her to state the color of the long tresses trailing down her back. Her hair was many colors.

One piece was bleached blonde and lay side-by-side with another dyed nearly black. Some parts were a mixture of both—the almost blonde and the almost black. A few small strands of reddish-gold, the same color as her lashes, trailed beneath the garish multi-colors of the top layers.

Her black lace-up boots were many sizes too large. Consequently, she walked with a gait reminiscent of that of a circus clown—halting and clumsy.

Her long skirt wrapped around her legs as it was caught in the howling wind. The skirt was of a gala print of tropical flowers and plants, astoundingly bright in the midst of the drab surroundings of the street.

Over a fishnet knit sweater, dark forest-green in color, she wore a three-quarter length brown tweed coat. A filthy brown tweed coat. The coat and the shoes seemed not to be a part of the original ensemble. It appeared as if she were trying to fit in, to look like she belonged among the homeless.

Like she belonged on the street.

The waif-looking girl sat down on the doorstep and folded her arms across her chest, protecting herself. And yet she didn't act afraid. Somehow she seemed to sense she had nothing to fear from these people who made their homes in doorways and under bridges, whose bedrooms were often nothing more than boxes that had recently held furniture and appliances.

After a few minutes, she stood up, gracefully, almost with dignity. She seemed unsure of what to do with herself. Then she spotted an old fruit crate, upturned it to serve as a chair and again sat down. Her long skirt billowed around her. She looked up shyly, her hazel eyes questioning beneath their red-gold lashes.

They seemed to be asking, "Can I stay?"

Gert, still wandering the streets of Valeria in her wildly bright clothing, had maintained her interest in the name of any newcomer to their midst. Her gravelly old voice broke the silence that had been hanging heavily since the girl appeared around the corner. "Ya gotta name?" she inquired.

"Petey. Just call me Petey," the girl said with a smile.

Only one of the others smiled in return, but the tenseness of the silence had been broken. Not that anyone was saying anything more. They just went on about their business—huddling together for warmth, searching through the dumpsters and barrels for anything that would satisfy their needs.

Bertram returned Petey's shy smile with one of his own. His teeth were chipped and as gray as the old porcelain sink heaped amongst the trash piled behind the burned out remains of *Bob's Bar and Grill* at the end of the alley. Bertram was new to the homeless group in Valeria. He had shown up one morning about four months ago and quickly melded into the group. He seemed always fearful, and rarely, if ever, ventured off by himself. No one was certain why, but thought perhaps the fact that he had been badly beaten when he arrived made him fearful of being alone, of being unprotected.

Both his eyes were blackened the day he arrived, and his left arm had obviously been broken. It still dangled at his side, barely usable.

But Bertram had a winning smile.

Once she was asked her name, Petey knew she was accepted. She was now one of those most frequently referred to as "those dreadful street people."

Petey looked around at the people she had selected to be her new cadre of friends—her new family. Most, but not all, were old. None was even close to her age, her not-yet-having-finished-her-second-decade-of-life age.

She studied them all.

Lowell was the youngest of the group gathered when Petey arrived. Younger than the others, but not nearly as young as she was. She smiled at him, too, but his coal-black eyes simply glared at her in return.

Old Johnny—now very, very old—was so bent over, Petey thought he looked like the gnomes in the fairy tales her mother read to her every night not so many years ago.

For just a brief moment, thinking of her mother brought a stinging sensation behind her hazel eyes, but she recovered quickly, blotting out all thoughts of anyone other than the group around her.

Petey continued to survey the group and stored her observations in her memory. Of the two women, Gert and Molly, Gert was the flashiest. She was also the most talkative. Gert was rarely quiet, and it was not unusual for the others to walk away from her to seek silence. But she was a good sort, and the others seemed to accept her in spite of her constant chattering.

The homeless are generally an accepting group, embracing those who society-at-large have rejected. Petey noted how diverse this group seemed to be. No two resembled another—not in appearance, not in behavior.

Gert fascinated Petey. Gert's behavior was like that of a beauty queen, yet she was old and nearly feeble, sometimes hardly able to stand. But a smile still lit up her grayed wrinkled face much of the time, and her gravelly crackled laugh often rode upon the silence. Gert would stare—just like she was staring at Petey now. And while she stared, she usually chattered.

Petey would later learn that Gert stored her jewelry and make-up in the black plastic marble-bag tied around her waist on a piece of rope. A broken piece of mirror, which she refused to share with anyone, completed her collection. She truly enjoyed her hoard of valuables and was firmly convinced of her own beauty.

Gert scrutinized the new arrival so carefully that Petey became uncomfortable and looked away.

Petey looked at the one called Molly, but Molly didn't return her gaze. Molly's eyes appeared locked on something far in the distance, totally oblivious to the new person who had just arrived in their midst—apparently totally oblivious to any of her surroundings.

Petey turned and looked in the same direction as Molly, but she could see nothing to attract such ardent attention. When she turned back to look at her again, she saw Molly was now looking down at the ground, kicking away at an ant hill with the toe of her scuffed lace-less brown shoe.

Molly's hair was still a mixture of gray and brown, but now mostly gray, tendrils of curls jutting from beneath the gray felt hat she wore pulled down, nearly covering her eyes. Petey noted that she was a small, almost delicate looking woman. Her body appeared padded—padded with layers of clothing.

The top layer today was a navy-blue print skirt, short enough to show the brown one underneath. Beneath them, she wore khaki-colored pants. All were held up with a cracked brown leather belt—tied, not buckled. Her top layers were covered by a man's suit coat, buttonless and gray-striped. Her top blouse, showing as the coat hung open, was once white. Now it was as gray as fresh cement churning around and around in a cement mixer.

Petey watched Molly for a while, not wanting to again meet Gert's critical eyes. Molly's hands intrigued her. They were surprisingly pretty. Petey wondered if she had ever been a model for nail polish or something—something that would show off her hands. *If ever she talks to me, I'll ask her,* Petey decided.

Molly continued to kick the dirt, the little ants long since having scurried to safety. Petey wished she could hear and understand what Molly was saying, but it was truly mumbling, likely not intended to be heard and understood by anyone but Molly.

Just as Petey stood to try to find somewhere to relieve herself, Molly looked up and met her gaze squarely. Her eyes! *She has the most beautiful lavender eyes.*

Petey took a step toward her and opened her mouth to say something, but Molly's glance was fleeting, and before Petey could speak a word, Molly again looked down, kicking the dirt and mumbling her meaningless words.

Chapter Thirty-Six

Petey regarded Molly as a challenge. The pull she felt towards the obviously demented woman was much like that of Jessica Rose. Molly had magic in her eyes.

Granted, most of the time her eyes were so dead, they appeared nearly opaque. In fact, when Petey first arrived on the streets of Valeria, she thought perhaps Molly was blind—or going blind. She had watched the way Molly walked down the streets and alleyways waving a stick from side to side, feeling, rather than seeing, her way.

It took weeks for Petey to understand, to realize, that this seemingly strange habit for a sighted person was simply one of Molly's ways of protecting herself.

Because Molly locked her eyes on the ground most of the time, she was easy prey to someone approaching her unseen. It did not, however, take long for an offender to feel the blow of Molly's stick as she swung it around the moment she felt a touch.

It was a formidable weapon, and the strength behind the blows made many a receiver of them question just how old this "old street woman" really was.

Petey kept to herself much of the time, just as many of the others on the street did. She liked Valeria. She felt almost invisible as she wandered the streets, few paying any attention to this pretty but shabby girl. Oh, she heard a few clickings of tongues and saw some shakings of heads, but in general, she remained unnoticed.

A girl barely old enough to go out on a date without a chaperone, wandering the streets of the city unnoticed and alone.

Once, when she first left home, before coming to Valeria, Petey had hitched a ride with a trucker as far as Westmoor, and there she had a real scare. She covered every inch of the town in one evening, and although it was an attractive little place, she decided it was too small and—well, too perfect. The fairy-tale hometown. *No thanks*, she thought, *I've already had the dream life—the boring pointless dream life.*

She saw a Greyhound Bus Depot down the street, and having decided she'd head out, Petey walked towards it, doing just a mite of window-shopping along the way. She thought she probably should feel some regret, some pull towards the mall-shopping trips she had gone on every weekend with one her many friends.

She felt no regret, but it was fun looking just the same.

The bus depot was a sleepy little spot. Rather "seedy" looking with cigarette butts thrown carelessly on the floor and crumpled paper overflowing from the trash receptacles. An elderly man was sprawled out on one of the two benches, his head thrown back, the rhythmic cadence of his snoring filling the room. The lone ticket salesperson was only slightly more awake.

After purchasing a one-way ticket to Columbus, hoping to find a more interesting, exciting life in a larger city, she wandered around the small waiting area, trying unsuccessfully to alleviate the boredom of waiting.

She stopped in front of the bulletin board, completely covered with notices of lost pets, garage sales, and for-sale items—and missing-children flyers. She gasped aloud as she looked straight ahead at her own likeness. There, on the bus depot bulletin board, was a picture of her—a missing child. The poster was squeezed in between a computer-printed notice of a lost poodle, "Sweetie Pie," and a handwritten card claiming a "truk—eksellent condition" was for sale for only three hundred dollars.

How Petey hated the photo on the poster. Her cheerleading photo from last year's yearbook. Big smile, big bouncy hair-do, big school letters across her sweater. "Miss-I'm-So-Important," instead of whom she really was, "Miss-I-Hate-My-Life."

Petey didn't always hate her life. She had everything any fifteen-year-old could possibly want. Great house in the best part of town, replete with all the amenities—perfectly manicured lawn, well tended flowerbeds, long driveway that curved around the back of the house, where it became a basketball court.

And there was an official league-specified basketball hoop, a place for Robbie to practice.

But Robbie wasn't there to practice anymore. Since he went away to the University of Illinois, he hardly ever came home. At least not after the first couple months, not after Mom and Dad got their divorce.

So what if he hardly saw his little sister—the little sister he said he was so proud of and loved so much. Just leave her to try to understand what had happened to her family. Why the Mom and Dad who had been so fun-loving and happy suddenly hated each other.

Her perfect life just wasn't so perfect anymore.

And now, here was that darned photo, coming back to remind her, possibly ruining her plans.

Petey looked cautiously around her. The old man was still snoring away on the bench, and the ticket salesman obviously hadn't recognized her. He hadn't really even looked at her

Maybe traveling by bus wasn't such a good idea, she decided. If there were missing-children posters in a sleepy little town like this, there most certainly would be in Columbus.

She walked out the door, trying to appear casual, her heart pounding. Out on the sidewalk, she walked fast, but not so fast as to draw attention. She took off towards the highway. She'd just have to rely on hitching another ride. Maybe even with someone who was going to Columbus.

Tearing up her bus ticket into tiny pieces, she dropped it down the storm-sewer drain along the curb. She hated throwing away the price of the ticket, but what other choice did she have?

It was late when they pulled into a truck stop outside Columbus. Again Petey's transportation had been with a trucker. The driver was nice and really talkative. Petey wondered how he could stand driving alone all the time with no one to talk to. *He must talk to himself,* she decided.

She was so weary. She hadn't slept a wink because Art, the driver, didn't stop talking long enough. All those many miles—talk, talk, talk!

Mostly Art talked about his family, about his kids. He had seven of them. *No wonder he's a cross-country truck driver who talks all the time*, thought Petey.

But he seemed to adore them, all seven of them. And his wife. Art made his wife sound like a cross between Miss Universe and Reba McIntyre. "A gorgeous redhead with a voice like an angel," he described her, his voice heavy with the accent of his native Texas. "And my two girls—they're purty just like their ma," he added with pride.

Petey then heard the steady litany of his boys—how strong and tough they were. "Real boys," boasted Art.

She suspected that all this family talk was partly for her benefit.

When Art slowed to a squealing stop along the side of the highway just outside Westmoor and beckoned her to come over to his truck, he quizzed her like she was applying for an after-school job or something. Then he lectured her for twenty minutes about the dangers of hitching rides.

"You look about the same age as my Vicki, and if I ever caught her thumbing a ride anywhere, I'd ground her 'til she was thirty," he declared with paternal authority.

Petey was left with the feeling that Vicki would never think of doing anything so terrible. *Well, neither would I if my dad cared about me the way Art does about his kids. Dad probably doesn't even know I'm missing.*

The thought filled her with such intense sadness, she had to brush away a tear she couldn't check before it was too late.

Art saw the gesture. "What's the matter, little one? You okay?"

"Sure," she replied with an air of indifference she didn't feel. "Just some dust in my eye. From standing on the side of the road, I guess."

Art didn't believe her, but nonetheless, didn't question her further. This little bit of a girl sitting with him in the cab of his truck, his "Big Emma," as he had dubbed the vehicle—a truck he loved second only to his wife and seven kids—was hurtin' about something.

If only he could figure out what it was and how to get her back where she belonged.

All the talk of family unnerved Petey a bit, and she halfway expected Art to turn her over to one of the highway patrolmen they saw traveling the same highway on their long trip across the state. But Art was a "true-blue" friend and didn't snitch on her. He just asked countless questions about her family.

She answered with a mixture of half-truths and total-fabrications.

Art figured she was spewing nonsense, but he listened just the same.

When they reached the outskirts of Columbus, Art pulled into a truck stop. "Time to grab a bite to eat," he declared. They had munched on chips and cookies and washed them down with soda pop a few miles back, but Petey *was* hungry. She decided, however, it was time for her to disappear again.

"I'm beat, Art," she said, stretching and feigning a yawn. "Would you mind bringing me something?"

"No problem, kiddo. You just get a little shut-eye."

181

When he returned to Big Emma thirty minutes later, Petey was gone. A napkin bearing the imprint, "Murphy's—best steak on the road," lay on the driver's seat. Written on it in lipstick was a note.

It simply said, "THANX."

Petey hurried away from the truck stop as fast as her rubbery legs could carry her. The small duffle bag she had been carrying for so many miles as she hitched her way, first to Westmoor, then on her way to Columbus, seemed suddenly very heavy.

She needed to put as much distance as possible, as soon as possible, between her and Big Emma—and Art.

Art was a great guy, but too much a family man. She was certain he'd really like to get her to the authorities, and she'd soon find herself on the way back home.

And that would never do.

Petey walked away from the truck stop, away from the highway.

In what seemed like many hours, but was really only two, she found herself on a nearly deserted street in what was most definitely not the best part of town. But a good place to get lost, she thought.

Lost among old dilapidated buildings.

Petey climbed through a space in a boarded-up window in what appeared to once have been a grocery store. Part of a sign remained, reading, "Levy's Gr-ce-ies." Graffiti adorned the redbrick walls, and trash surrounded its foundation.

Throwing her duffle bag in first, she rolled in on top of it. Both landed with a thud that echoed through the emptiness of the building. The room was dark and smelled of disuse and rodent droppings.

But Petey didn't care. Totally overwhelmed by exhaustion, she curled up against the wall, and using her duffle bag as a pillow, fell sound asleep within seconds.

Awakening to the sound of rain beating against the boarded windows and the drip, drip as it found its way to leak through the many unprotected spots, Petey lay, unmoving as she listened for any noises indicating she wasn't alone in her shelter.

Other than the rain, there was silence.

Petey stood up and stretched. She felt incredibly rested, considering the floorboards had been her bed.

She smiled as she thought of her brother. *If only Robbie could see me now—wouldn't he be surprised. He didn't think I'd ever be able to take care of myself. Well big bro, there's no one to take care of me now except myself.*

She could almost hear him. "Connie, honey, just because Mom and Dad are getting a divorce doesn't mean they don't both love you. And don't forget, I'll *always* be here for you, kiddo. That's what big brothers are for."

His words had really comforted her at the time. Now as she thought of them, she felt an intense sadness.

"No," she said aloud. "I can't be thinking of Robbie now."

Her words echoed in the emptiness of the building.

Petey glanced around her temporary home and decided she might just as well camp here for a while. At least it gave her a place to come back to.

Suddenly she was aware of how very hungry she was. Her stomach rumbled, and she felt a bit light-headed. She wished she had been able to wait until Art brought her dinner from the diner.

But she just hadn't dared.

Not wanting to draw attention to herself, Petey decided she'd better freshen up a bit. Then she'd find a coffee shop. Someplace cheap. She wanted to stretch the money she had as far as it would go. Then what she'd do, she had no idea.

She refused to even think about it.

Crawling out the way she came in, she stepped into the dark and dreary rain pelting the streets of Columbus, Ohio.

Petey spent the better part of the summer in Columbus—at first in the same abandoned grocery store she had discovered upon her arrival. But after a time, she decided she needed to get to know others living "away from home" as she was, and she searched for the gathering places of Columbus' homeless. There weren't many that she could find. *Maybe Columbus isn't a very large city after all*, she thought. Then, *but it is—I know it is!*

Avoiding the established shelters, Petey followed those she judged to be down and out, hoping to find others whose life-style she could share.

Sometimes she was fooled, as she watched a "homeless candidate" board a bus or walk to a car. And always, if they approached what appeared to be a shelter, she would keep going.

Petey still feared being recognized from the missing-child posters. Although she hadn't seen any since arriving in Columbus, she didn't take any chances. No bus depots, no post offices, and no

183

buildings that looked as if bulletin boards might hang in their lobbies.

She also steered clear of policemen and patrol cars.

Petey became very adept at finding other homeless wanderers and came to enjoy their companionship. After all, she was just a girl and had a great need to share her days—her life—with others.

One morning she found a real friend, a fellow runaway, as both reached for a box of discarded doughnuts in a dumpster behind an office complex. At first, they grappled for their treasured find. Then they recognized that there were probably enough doughnuts for both of them, that they might consider sharing. So they ran from the alley to the edge of a nearby park, and sitting in the shadows of a lilac bush just as the early morning sky began to lighten, they devoured their find of seven Krispy Kreme doughnuts—three and one-half each.

"Not bad, not bad a'tall," said Petey's newly discovered compatriot. Petey nodded in agreement, her mouth stuffed, telltale sugar coating her lips.

When she finally could, she said, "Hi, I'm Petey."

"And me—Ah'm Angel."

Petey didn't think she looked like any angel she had ever seen pictured, but didn't say so. Angel's hair was black and curly. Very curly. It was cut really short, no more than an inch all over her head. Her eyes were dark and large. Brown, guessed Petey, although they really looked black until you were just inches away. Angel's skin reminded Petey of her dad's coffee after he added the cream. A rich, warm, creamy coffee color. Her voice was soft and low, and heavy with a drawl that declared she hailed from the Deep South. Although Petey never asked her where she was from.

Nor did Angel question Petey.

The girls became good friends and wandered the streets and alleys of Columbus together. Angel taught Petey a lot about the ways of the street. She showed her where to find the best castaway clothes and the freshest discarded food.

Because they were so young, they both knew they were subject to be turned over to the law if they went to any of the shelters scattered across the east end of town. Those, they systematically avoided.

They found other shelter, and often, did just fine without any.

Angel helped Petey change her hair and augment her "suburban-America" wardrobe with other clothing. "You look like a high-school kid," teased Angel one day.

They stole some black liquid dye and hair bleach from Walgreen's one night, and the next morning, they found an old warehouse with a bathroom and did Petey's hair. There was no running water in the bathroom, but some remained in the pipes and served them just fine. The bleach burned and the black covered their hands—for weeks, in fact. They had fun with their beauty project in spite of the physical drawbacks of playing beautician without the proper supplies.

Laughing until they cried over Petey's "skunk-like" appearance when the job was finished, the girls then set out to find Petey some clothes. Soon a brown tweed coat and a pair of work boots enhanced the clothing she had jammed into her duffle bag when she fled from her home. By the end of the day, Petey no longer looked like a high-school kid from suburbia.

The girls were inseparable, and for weeks filled their days walking the streets, rummaging through trash barrels, and running away from the unsavory types who often approached them.

They giggled together just like any other two girls their age. They became good friends, really good friends.

Early one evening each went off alone—just for a couple of hours. Angel said she was planning to meet an acquaintance outside one of the shelters. She wouldn't say why. There was no way Petey was getting that close to a shelter, so they made arrangements to meet later in the nearby park.

But Angel never showed up. When Petey heard through the grapevine of those living on the street that Angel had been found badly beaten and with her throat cut, Petey was heartbroken and filled with terror.

She fled Columbus, again covering the miles by hitchhiking. When she left the driver of the vehicle that had given her a ride, saying good-bye and "thanks," Petey found herself in Valeria, Indiana.

Chapter Thirty-Seven

Petey felt someone watching her. But there was no one around except Molly, and she was staring at the ground. As usual.

Petey was playing a game of dominoes with Bertram. Bertram loved to play games and had found the dominoes, the set mostly intact, in the trash with several other discarded toys. He had no use for a broken doll, headless, or a toy fire engine with no wheels. But Bertram was really excited about the dominoes.

If only he could find someone to play the game with him. Not many of his comrades were interested in spending their time—which was plentiful—matching dots on little black rectangles.

Just when he thought he had exhausted the possibilities of a partner, he asked "the kid," as he referred to Petey.

"I'd love to," she responded with a smile. "I used to play this game a lot with my brother, Ro. . ." Petey caught herself before saying Robbie's name.

They settled into their game, Bertram beating Petey resoundly. Twice during the three-quarters of an hour they spent in their friendly competition, Bertram whispered, "She's lookin' atcha."

The first time he said it, Petey glanced quickly Molly's way, but not quickly enough. Molly was again looking at the ground. The second time Petey didn't turn, but as soon as she and Bertram finished their game, and after she had congratulated him on his "domino ability" and told him she'd match wits with him another time, she slowly ambled over to where Molly was sitting.

For some time, she simply sat there, quietly, not speaking, not moving. Two women—one just a girl, and the other, seemingly old.

Petey had wanted many times to talk to Molly. She liked her. Not that she could begin to explain why—she just liked her.

Molly continued to look at the ground in front of her, her walking stick clutched in her left hand and her bag of possessions at her feet. Molly's back was semi-turned to Petey, who was sitting to her left.

Suddenly, Molly reached over and touched her. The move was so unexpected, it startled Petey. But she didn't move. Neither did she say a word.

Molly withdrew her hand as soon as she touched Petey, but then a few minutes later, she turned towards the girl and again laid her hand on her arm. This time, she didn't immediately take it away. Petey turned towards Molly. Molly raised her eyes and looked at Petey—squarely, eye to eye. And she smiled. Petey smiled back.

Molly has such beautiful, unusual eyes, thought Petey—*and a pretty warm smile. Please let me get to know you,* she pleaded inwardly. Aloud she said only, "Hi. I'm Petey."

Molly nodded and said, "I know." Her voice, although very husky, either from age or disuse, had a lilting quality about it.

Nothing more was said; the two just sat, side by side for a while, Molly looking, not at the ground, but straight ahead.

Petey had noticed other times when Molly did this—looked straight ahead. They were usually very brief times, times when Petey had not been so close to her. Sitting by her side, seeing Molly's head raised and her eyes focused, she seemed very different to the girl.

After a time, Molly stood up and said, "Come with me."

Molly led the way, and Petey followed. They walked side by side, into the countryside surrounding Valeria.

Petey loved it.

They didn't talk much. Petey was reluctant to ask questions—to say too much for fear Molly would pull away from her. She waited until Molly asked a question or made a comment, and then she responded.

How far she had come from the impetuous spoiled teenager who, as Robbie always said, "constantly ran over at the mouth."

"You're young," commented Molly.

"Yes, I am," she responded without revealing her age. Petey didn't know why she didn't want to tell her age—she just didn't. For one thing, it seemed so unimportant here on the street.

And she no longer felt like a teenager.

"You have a father—or a mother?" Molly asked, haltingly, her voice lowering as she said "mother."

"Yes."

"Go home."

"I can't, Molly. I just can't."

Molly looked at Petey directly in the eyes for the second time that day and noted the tears imbedded in the girl's golden-red lashes. Molly sighed, but said nothing further.

In fact she said nothing more that day.

Nothing intelligible.

187

As they changed their course and walked towards the center of the city, Molly began to slump, her eyes again cast down. She swung her stick side to side and muttered. Loudly, almost angrily.

The words had no meaning, words Petey couldn't understand.

After a while, Petey stole quietly away, knowing she had lost Molly's companionship—at least for now.

Petey treasured that first experience as Molly's friend.

***

The days were getting shorter. Shorter and colder. The street people became less visible, as they sought shelter from the approaching winter.

Some acquiesced and joined the throngs at the Salvation Army or the several Mission shelters in the area. Or at Jessica Rose's shelter for women.

But never Molly. Although Molly might visit Jessica's for a brief respite from the elements or for a nap, she never spent a night there after that first time. Nor did she go to any other established shelter.

The voices wouldn't let her.

Petey had no idea where her newly found friend spent most of her nights. Molly just seemed to disappear when shadows lengthened and the sun sank low on the horizon. Sometimes Petey didn't see Molly for several days.

One blustery day, as wind-driven rain pelted everything in its path, and evening approached, Molly appeared next to Petey as the young girl stood shivering in a doorway. Petey had her head tucked down into her shoulders, attempting to shield herself, knowing she needed to break away from her minimal shelter and find something more protective for the night. But she was having trouble controlling her teeth-chattering shivering—and her tears. And she really didn't know where to go.

"Come on, child. You can't spend the night here. This'll be a bad one. I know. I've been through more than a few like it in this place."

Petey was startled to hear Molly's voice; she hadn't heard or seen her approach.

She had seen Molly only once or twice, briefly, over the past few weeks, and when she did, Molly didn't even look at her.

Now here she was, talking to her, comforting her. Just like a

188

mother.

"Oh, Molly, I'm so cold. And wet," she added.

"Not nearly as cold and wet as you'll be if you stay here. Now come with me."

Petey obediently followed Molly, rain pelting their faces, their feet sloshing through the icy cold water in puddles along the way. Before too long, they crossed a series of railroad tracks and came to the old unused depot.

The same spot where Johnny had led Molly upon her arrival in Valeria years before. The spot where she and Laurel had spent cold nights years ago. And the spot where she had brought the small child she had envisioned.

Molly removed a piece of wire from one of her many pockets. It appeared to have once been the hook of a coat hanger. She lost the bent nail that had served as her makeshift key in earlier years.

She stuck one of the ends of the wire in the old lock and wiggled it, working it just right until the door popped open. The lock was apparently the only thing keeping the door closed.

"Now hurry, get inside," ordered Molly as she gave Petey a gentle push. As soon as both were inside, Molly locked the door, keeping it tightly closed. The pounding of the driving rain and the whistling of the wind echoed throughout the hollowness of the empty depot.

Petey stumbled into a large cold and dusty room—a room smelling of filth. But it was dry. Mostly, anyhow. Rain dripped steadily down the wall in one corner, puddling as it gathered on the rotting boards beneath.

In an opposite corner were cardboard boxes, stacks of newspapers—and a cloth bag that looked suspiciously like the one Molly usually carried.

Petey was sure she was learning where her friend spent her time—at least some of it—when she disappeared at night.

"It's not too warm, but it's warmer than outside, and it's mostly dry. There used to be some old barrels out by the tracks where we could light fires and warm ourselves," Molly said wistfully, "but they were removed some time back. Now take off those wet shoes," she instructed as she removed her own, "and wrap these around your feet."

Molly handed Petey some rags from her bag. Petey watched as

Molly wrapped her own feet and followed suit. She laughed as she looked at their rag-swathed feet. Molly smiled.

They didn't talk much that evening. Mostly idle comments about how good it was to be out of the cold rain. As the room darkened, they curled up using newspapers for pillows and large pieces of the cardboard for blankets, and slept.

Some time during the night, Petey was awakened by Molly's screams. "Molly, Molly, wake up. You're having a nightmare."

Molly didn't awaken completely, but the screams ceased.

In the morning, Petey didn't mention the nighttime screams. Nor did Molly. In fact, Molly wasn't talking at all. Only mumbling. After she again locked the door with her coat-hanger key, Molly and Petey each went her separate way.

Petey never again heard Molly say as much as she did the night Molly rescued her from the cold. Oh, there'd be snatches of conversation, and more than once, Molly would show up beside her and say, "Follow me." Then she'd lead her young friend to shelter. But only twice did Petey hear her speak in a series of sentences, talking like a "regular" person—talking like her mother. The first time she advised her to go home and the night she rescued her from the wet and cold.

But Petey didn't care that Molly didn't talk. She didn't even care that Molly didn't look at her most of the time.

She was content just to know Molly was her friend.

Chapter Thirty-Eight

Another wet, cold day. Gray dirty slush turned the side streets into slithery surfaces, and more than one car hurrying too fast to reach its destination plowed into another. It seemed to patrolmen responding to emergency calls that there was a fender-bender on every block. "These damned fools," one officer was heard to say to another, "why they can't learn to pay attention to the conditions is beyond me."

Only the main thoroughfares were clear, plows and heavy traffic having worked together to make them that way.

One of the patrolmen, Harvey Blight by name, was writing up a ticket to hand to an insolent young high-schooler who tried to blame *him* for his careless driving. Harvey was tempted to haul him in—but frankly, he didn't have the time. He had so many other places he had to be, so many other stupid drivers to ticket as they screamed insults at their cars, often kicking them, as if it were the vehicle's fault it skidded on the slippery street and ran into a light pole.

Just as Harvey turned to walk back to his patrol car, having presented a traffic ticket to the young man, who kept saying over and over, "My dad's gonna kill me when he sees the car," Harvey spotted a foot peeking from beneath a pile of cardboard boxes along the side of *Osburne's Furniture Store.*

Harvey gently nudged the foot with his shoe. "Better get up, now." No response. He knelt to shake the foot to awaken whomever it belonged to lying there. Harvey knew Les Osburne would be in to open the store soon, and every time he found a "bum," as he called them, loitering around his place, he'd call the station, demanding they send someone out to haul the trespasser off to jail. Usually him— Harvey Blight. And frankly, this morning he was just too busy to deal with it.

As Harvey touched the ankle, he knew immediately that he wouldn't be awakening the person sleeping here. The ankle and the leg above it were ice cold—no one living could feel so cold.

Harvey pulled off the boxes and threw them behind him. Underneath was a man, an old man. A street person. His completely bald head was uncovered, and his face was blue with cold and death. As Harvey bent to close the dead man's pale, almost colorless eyes,

191

he noticed an old holey clothes basket close by. The basket was filled with rags—Old Johnny's rags.

Johnny had been old for a long time, as long as any who knew him on the streets of Valeria could remember. He apparently had become too old, too uncared for, too fragile to bear the cold any longer.

Word of Johnny's death spread rapidly on the street. There was a sad silence among the street people who had been his friends. He had really mattered to them. They knew the streets of Valeria would never be the same without his bent gnome-like body in their midst.

Molly learned of her friend's death about mid-morning as she was leaving her search for food in a dumpster behind *Bob's Bar & Grill*, in an alley not far from where Johnny's body was found.

Johnny certainly wasn't the first of their numbers to die. Many of the people she met on the street over the years were gone. Many died, others just disappeared, and Molly seemed oblivious to their absence.

Of those Molly first met upon her arrival in Valeria, Gert was the only one remaining, and she, too, had grown very old. She often sat alone now, her jewelry flashing in the light. Although she still sometimes chattered incessantly, there were times when she'd just sit and stare into the distance. Perhaps remembering—perhaps reliving her life on the street.

Gert still loved her flashy possessions, though, the dangling earrings, colorful beads, flashy scarves. And she still wore makeup— lots of makeup. Sometimes Molly allowed her to adorn *her* face with rouge and powder. She never gave her permission, exactly. It's just that Molly didn't stop Gert, the self-proclaimed beautician, as she applied circles of rouge on Molly's weathered, wrinkled face.

Time seemed to have decreased Molly's awareness of nearly everything, incrementally, as year after year, she braved the elements and hazards of her life on the street. She was lost in her own world most of the time, rarely seeming to grasp the reality of the people and places around her.

There were rare interludes, however, when she appeared almost "normal," when she fastened her lovely eyes on another's, when she spoke in complete sentences, her soft voice a surprise to the listener— such as the night she guided Petey to warmth and safety.

But most of the time, Molly's mind was off in another world, muttering sounds rather than words, her gray felt hat—the beautiful light-gray feather lost long ago, and the burgundy-colored band disintegrated—pulled down over her filthy, mostly gray, curls, her eyes downcast, following the stick she swung side to side before her.

But Molly had always felt differently about Johnny than she did any of the others. Of him she was very much aware. Molly loved Johnny. He had been her protector for the many years that she had made the streets of Valeria her home. And hearing of his death filled her with unbearable pain.

Pain like that she had felt when her husband and daughter died—in the far distant past.

Molly disappeared the day Johnny died. She wasn't seen again on the streets of Valeria for nearly five weeks.

Chapter Thirty-Nine

Petey spent days searching for Molly, but saw no sign of her anywhere. She knew Molly was upset over Johnny's death, but he was so old, surely she couldn't have been surprised. And it wasn't as if they spent a lot of time together—Johnny and Molly. Both went their separate ways alone most of the time. *I've never even seen Molly speak to Johnny*, noted Petey.

Petey wished she hadn't been the one who told Molly that Johnny had been found dead, though—that she had seen him carried away. She found Molly gnawing on the heel of bread she had found by the dumpster—her lunch, probably, her meal for the day. Molly acted like someone had punched her in the stomach, gasping and sucking in her breath when Petey delivered the sad news. Then she rapidly walked away, and Petey hadn't been able to find her since.

Tears rolled down Petey's face as she wearily walked away from the old depot—her last spot to check in hope of finding her friend. *Oh Molly, I'm so sorry. I never should have told you about Johnny. Where are you?*

Petey sat down on the crumbling concrete steps that once were used by travelers excited with anticipation as they entered the depot to buy tickets for destinations widespread across the country. The distraught girl cried—for Old Johnny's death, for her missing friend, and for her own loneliness.

***

Molly almost ran from Petey when she heard of Johnny's death. *Johnny. Johnny. Who will take care of me now?* Molly was filled with grief over the passing of her dearest friend. And fear for her own well-being. She couldn't remember ever feeling so alone.

She walked and walked, half running at first, her breath coming in gasps, her vision blurred with tears. *No, not Johnny. Not my best friend.*

After a while, her pace slowed considerably, and yet she continued walking—walking away from town, away from Valeria. The snowy slush of earlier in the day had begun to freeze, and deep frozen ruts lined the shoulders of the highway where Molly began her trek away from Valeria. Trucks whizzed by, just inches away from where she walked, and more than one trucker blared his horn loudly, unnerved by the tottering gait of the old woman making her way along the roadway.

The noise of the horns and passing trucks, along with her state of immense grief, disoriented Molly, and she hastily ran away from the highway, engulfed with terror.

Night was settling in, crisp, clear, and, away from the highway—silent. Molly was shaking with grief, terror, and cold. She walked all night, too fearful to stop. By morning, she had no idea where she was. She only knew that she was away from Valeria—away from the source of her pain.

Molly was running away from sorrow, just as she had done when she left her home nearly a decade and a half ago.

***

"Riley, have you really looked everywhere?" asked Jessica when she hadn't seen Molly in what she felt was an inordinately long time. "She couldn't just disappear!"

"Jessica, of course she could just disappear. You've been operating the shelter for what now—going on nine years? All these women have disappeared from somewhere. Some are running from relationships just too painful to endure, some from a lifestyle they couldn't stand. Some are even running from the law.

"Others—I don't know. Maybe they just disappeared because they were really sick, and no one was watching.

"I'll keep my ears open for word on old Molly, but a whole lot of the older ones seem to be gone. Maybe they just went someplace warmer. It's terribly cold on the streets of Valeria, Jess. Maybe Molly went someplace where she wouldn't be so damned cold."

"But Riley, she could have come here every day to keep warm," Jessica argued.

"I know, Jess, I know," said the caring policeman with a sigh. "I'll try to find her, but I'm not sure I will. All I can do is try."

Jessica asked her friend, Dr. Jim Baylor, for his help, too. Maybe, just maybe, he might have heard something through the medical grapevine.

Again she reasoned, "People don't just disappear."

"Nonsense. You disappeared, Jess. And even with all his wealth and connections, look how long it took Gay-whatever-his-name-is to find you."

"I know, Jim, it's just that I really thought I might be able to

195

help this one. She hadn't always been down and out. I'm sure of it. I had the feeling that she was really somebody once. Somebody beautiful and important."

"You may be right. Many of them were 'somebody' once. And they still are. Isn't that why you do this, Jess? Why you spend your days making a place where they can feel warm and fed—and loved? Because the women really are somebody, not just *things* to be discarded?

"Maybe she simply couldn't cope with the intensity of your love. It's pretty powerful, my dear."

Jim put his arms around Jessica and drew her close, burying his face in her soft hair. She smelled of lavender and springtime flowers. He always marveled at how she cared for herself amidst all this squalor. Soft and feminine, lovely and caring. That described Jessica Rose, formerly Jessica Huntington. And Dr. James Andrew Baylor loved her for it.

All of it.

"I'll do what I can, Jess. But I doubt she'll be found. Molly has to be mighty street-wise to have survived for this long . If she doesn't want to be found, she won't be."

"But, Jim, you saw how demented she is. How can she possibly make plans for what she does? That's what you're describing. A plan."

"I don't know if it's a plan, Jess, or just instinct. I really feel that many of our street people develop a sense beyond what most of us experience. Some of them have had only themselves to rely on—and in a few cases, each other—for so long, they sense a change in the elements, in their surroundings, and especially, in their emotions.

"Remember that night when Riley brought Molly in here in the middle of the night? She was in so much pain—emotional pain—she was like a wild animal. Even though she walked out as soon as she could, she was very aware of the care you gave her. Enough so that she came back—again and again. You reminded her of someone, Jess. Or maybe you reminded her of herself in another time, another place.

"Molly probably was, as you say, someone beautiful and important in another life. But that person likely has been gone for a long time, replaced by someone else who came to be known as Molly—dirty, ill fed, ill clad, addled in mind and spirit."

Jessica tried very hard to accept what both Riley and Jim were

196

telling her. Molly was gone, and it was highly unlikely she'd be able to abate the guilt that had plagued her for the past nine-plus years by giving her the loving care she regretted not giving her own mother.

Chapter Forty

Molly wandered for three days without food, three days without shelter. She saw some homes dotted across the countryside she traversed, many complete with barns and other buildings where she might have sought shelter. But it was as if she were driven by a mission—nothing could stop her or slow her down. Molly had no destination, only the desire to escape her grief drove her on.

Her exhaustion was nearly complete when she came upon a picturesque city surrounded by bluffs flanking a river, covered now in places with a layer of ice. Preston Valley. Molly had walked to a city neighboring Valeria, but that she didn't know. Her walk had been so intense, so devoid of purpose other than running away, she might have been across the country for all she knew. She really didn't care where she was.

Preston Valley was smaller than Valeria, but still large enough to be considered a city. And as such, it did have a population of street people—although it took Molly several days to find their numbers.

Staggering into the city, Molly was the object of wary glances as people studied the small bedraggled old woman who appeared to be on the verge of collapse. No one offered her assistance, but neither did they shout obscenities at her, or threaten her with bodily harm. They simply gave her a wide berth and quickly looked the other way.

Molly wandered through the streets until she came to an industrial area—one with back alleys and dumpsters. There she searched until she found food—fetid garbage. But she was in no condition to be selective and ate until her most intense hunger pangs subsided. She had no idea what she ate, nor did she care.

When Molly finished eating, she crawled behind the dumpster, curled into a fetal position, and fell asleep—her first rest in three days.

A small crescent moon was low in the dark sky when Molly awoke. Night was drawing to a close. She had slept soundly—even the voices had rested. She was hearing less of the voices these days. It was as if they, too, had aged along with her and, wearily, were giving up on their torments. Had it not been for years of undernourishment and the toll taken by the elements, Molly might have had long periods of clear thinking. But she had too long been the victim of her environment.

Also, she had been without medication for more than a decade, allowing her illness to control her.

Something awakened Molly. At first she wasn't certain what, but then she picked up the clanking and churning noises of a trash-removal truck and knew she wasn't safe where she was. Before the truck reached the dumpster where she had been sleeping, she stole swiftly away into the predawn darkness.

Molly's hunger pangs of the night before had returned, and she felt queasy. Perhaps the garbage she had eaten didn't agree with her. Whatever the cause, she knew she soon needed to quickly find a spot to relieve herself.

Looking around as best she could in so little light, she saw no fields close by—or any boarded up old buildings that might possibly have facilities. No all-night diners or bus or train depots in sight.

Why did I leave? I want to be back in Valeria. But Johnny's gone. How can I bear it without Johnny? A sob and small moan escaped her, and unshed tears burned her nose and throat.

Unable to find a facility, and no longer able to contain the urgency rolling through her body, Molly crept to a corner of the alley not fifty yards from where she had spent the night, squatted and relieved herself. Then sickened with shame and saddened with homesickness, Molly again began her walk down the alleyway.

The sun rose in splendor, the day promising to be one of brightness and warmth. Molly found her way out of the warehouse district, following the flow of cars towards what she hoped would be the center of town. She walked for over an hour, head down, occasionally muttering to herself. Every now and then, she glanced up to watch the flow of cars. Then she continued again in the direction where most of them were speeding—on their way to jobs, careers, or pleasurable pastimes.

Molly had lost her walking stick in her unplanned flight, and she felt terribly vulnerable without it.

She came to a stretch of sidewalk, and high office buildings dotted the skyline, the golden-red hue of the rising sun reflecting in their windows. Other people joined her on the walk, taking out keys and unlocking doors to establishments not yet open for business. Some turned into doorways of coffee shops and diners, their folded newspapers tucked firmly under their arms, ready to ingest the news of the past twenty-four hours along with their breakfast.

The smells wafting from the eating establishments increased Molly's feelings of light-headedness. She had, after all, eaten nothing other than last night's refuse in one-half a week.

Bakery smells floated on the morning air, and recalling *Percy Lyons' Bakery* in Valeria with longing, Molly hastened her steps to the source. The sign in flourishing script across the front window read *Monica's Bakery and Boutique*. Molly stopped for a moment and peered in the window. A rack of colorful women's clothing adorned one side of the room. Complementing scarves and jewelry draped from hangers, enhancing the dresses, promoting an entire ensemble for the boutique shoppers.

Along the other side of the store were bakery cases for breads, cookies, pies, and cakes. A trio of women was busy stacking the cases with mouth-watering wares. One stopped in her tracks and stared at the disheveled old woman's face in the window.

Molly hurried on her way.

When she came to the end of the block, she turned right and walked around to the back entrance. There, lying untouched on the top of the trash, were remnants of the early morning's baking that apparently didn't live up to the standards set by the trio inside.

Molly hastily grabbed a loaf of bread with a burned crust and two broken doughnuts, and ran. She ate the doughnuts immediately, scarcely chewing before swallowing. The bread she stuffed into her torn pocket. It was too large to work its way down through the hole and fall to the ground, as so many of Molly's treasures had done when she jammed them into the worthless pocket.

The bread was still warm and felt comforting as the warmth seeped through her clothing. She tore off a piece and quickly downed it, tears of satisfaction filling her eyes.

She spotted a water fountain across the street near the center of what appeared to be the city square. Brick and stone paths bordered by well-trimmed shrubbery led up to the fountain. Her thirst was nearly unbearable. Unusual for cool months, the water was running—although only a small trickle. Leaning over the fountain, Molly drank for a full minute.

When her thirst was finally satiated, she again wandered the streets of Preston Valley. Uncluttered streets and treed boulevards supported its claim as a "clean city," so noted on the signs along approaching highways from all four directions of entry into town. In addition, numerous parks added to its inviting appearance—parks which Molly soon discovered. She walked the paths around and through the grassy areas, resplendent with trees. Sitting on a bench overlooking a mostly frozen pond, she shared her bread with a flock of ducks. Through their loud cacophony of quacks, the ducks expressed their appreciation.

As the sun began its daily disappearance beneath the horizon, Molly left her comfortable perch on the bench and again wandered—this time searching for a secluded place to spend the night. She wandered until there was no light, and still she did not see another person who appeared to be a "street person."

Molly walked until she found her way back to the industrial area where she had spent the previous night. Alone, she again crawled behind a dumpster, and curling around her possession-filled bag, she slept.

Chapter Forty-One

Molly longed for company—even the company of strangers. Although she had essentially been a loner all her years on the street, she felt her safety threatened when she didn't see a single person who appeared to be in the same life predicament as she was.

After two more nights of making her bed behind dumpsters up and down the alley of the industrial part of town, early in the evening, she spotted two men, one of whom looked so much like Old Johnny, she thought Petey must have been mistaken when she told Molly of Johnny's demise.

Molly followed the men. Their ragged clothes flapped in the hefty breeze, and they ducked their heads into the wind, bracing themselves against its chill. When the pair came to the river, they vaulted over the wall that ran along its banks. It wasn't a high wall, obviously built more for appearance, an orderly accompaniment to the natural surroundings along the riverbanks. Molly had no trouble crawling over it. She followed the two down a grassy bank, the grass stiff and brown from the winter cold and snow.

A bridge spanned the river, aligned perpendicular to the spot where Molly had crawled over the wall. When she had wended her way cautiously down the bank, slipping and sliding, twice falling, she came to a stone walkway. Just to her left was the underneath structure of the bridge. This was the destination of the two men—a protected expanse of concrete with pillars to shut out the cool breezes blowing across the river.

Molly inched her way forward onto the concrete floor, the rumble of cars passing overhead. Although total darkness had not yet enveloped her surroundings, she couldn't see clearly, and the black lapping water, coupled with the roar of the traffic overhead terrified her. For a moment she was sorry she had followed the men.

But as Molly walked farther onto the expansive concrete area, she felt more secure, and she was overcome with complete exhaustion. She found a yet uninhabited spot behind a pillar on the edge of the structure, lay her head down on her bag of belongings, and fell asleep.

No one paid any attention to the new resident under the bridge.

Molly awoke just as the sun was a narrow slit along the horizon. It gave a golden cast to a small stretch of the river, a golden band in the midst of the blackness. Molly rolled over, her eyes looking straight up. She saw nothing but darkness.

For so many years, Molly had greeted the dawn and watched the lightening sky above. But here the bridge was overhead, and there was nothing but the dark opaqueness of the concrete. Molly felt claustrophobic, and instantly, she gathered her bag and walked to the edge, watching the golden band grow until the whole river within her view shimmered with the gold and brilliant orange hues of the rising sun.

"Don't fall in, old lady."

Molly turned with a start to see who had spoken to her. It was one of the two men she followed the night before—the one who reminded her of Johnny. But close up, even though the young day was not fully light, she could see he didn't look like Johnny at all. He was as bald as Johnny and similarly bent over, giving him the same gnome-like appearance, but this man was much younger. His yellow eyes shone in the semi-darkness, and although the slight fringe of hair remaining on his head was mostly gray, the long beard covering the lower half of his face was an intense black.

Molly stepped back further from the edge of the concrete floor underneath the bridge.

"A smoke?" asked the man, thrusting a crushed cigarette package towards her. His voice was low and had a menacing quality about it.

Molly shook her head, casting a quick glance at the man as she did so. His yellow eyes looked sinister. She stepped back farther from the edge but away from the man.

He shrugged and walked away.

The others who had sought shelter under the bridge were also dispersing and began to climb up the hill. Some vaulted the wall as if they were athletes in training; others carefully crawled over to the other side—each going his separate way, most likely in search of food.

Molly was the only woman among the thirteen who had spent the night in the shelter of the expansive bridge.

Chapter Forty-Two

Molly wandered the streets of Preston Valley daily; at night she returned to the haven underneath the bridge. It confused her that she didn't see any of the others from under the bridge as she walked the streets, but they seemed to disappear at sunrise. Once or twice, she'd catch a glimpse of someone she recognized from the preceding night or early morning, but then they'd vanish from her line of sight.

Not as familiar with the spots for finding food as she was in Valeria—and with no one to show her—Molly struggled to find adequate nourishment. Just like pioneers of old, she spent a good share of her hours searching for food. Perhaps it was the newness of the area, or perhaps it was because she was afraid to travel too far from the protection of the bridge. The stately structure had come to be something familiar to Molly—and she so longed for something familiar.

None of the other bridge people befriended her, nor did she find any other homeless women—at least not in the part of Preston Valley she covered. Had she dared to wander farther, she would have found a sizeable shelter for women, and another that allowed women as well as men.

Soon, day in and day out became week in and week out. Molly spent each exactly alike. Just before dark, she'd crawl over the wall and down to the shelter of the bridge. Sometimes, if the weather was inclement, she'd stay underneath the bridge for protection well into the day—until it was necessary for her to leave to begin her continuous search for food.

Molly's diminishing nourishment, along with the incredible lonely existence engulfing her, was taking its toll. The frail old woman became frailer still, more stooped, more disoriented, weaker, and thinner. She heard the voices from time to time, and she was often afraid.

But in spite of the speed at which she was failing, Molly would occasionally have perfectly enjoyable moments—moments when she would look above and marvel at the clearness of the sky covering the beauty of this valley. Or she would sit for hours watching the river water change with the colors it reflected, as the hours of the day ticked away from early morning until late night—when nothing was any longer visible beneath the cover of the bridge.

One night after just such a day, when Molly was contentedly taking in the natural beauty of her surroundings, the pangs of hunger overtook her just as darkness was settling upon the river. She had neglected to eat since morning.

The rippling currents of the river, no longer reflecting light, were so black they appeared oppressive, and as a chill crept along her spine, Molly wrapped her coat more tightly around her. She stood unsteadily, stiff from sitting on the concrete, aching from her stiffness and the coolness of the night breezes as they wafted across the flowing water. After standing for a moment to get her bearings, she took off, away from the river and the protection of the bridge, to find something to eat.

Just as she came to the top of the incline, ready to crawl over the wall, a hand covered her mouth, and another wrapped itself tightly around her frail body. Molly tried to bite her assailant, but the grip was so tight, her mouth was forced closed. As she was lifted off her feet, she kicked, but her flailing feet missed their mark. She was dragged into tall grass, farther and farther from the protection of the bridge.

"Now you old bitch, let's see if you're really a woman."

Molly was thrown to the ground so hard it knocked the wind from her, and the pain in her midriff added to her fear and confusion. The man, still holding her down and still covering her mouth, ripped open the front of her coat and both shirts she was wearing. Not having worn a brassiere for many years, Molly's bare skin was now exposed, and she shivered violently.

"I'll be damned—ya are a woman. An ugly old woman. Now let's see if the rest of you agrees."

As he shoved up her skirt and tore open the trousers she wore, he saw that she was indeed a woman.

"No undies. Great. Just makes it easier for me."

As her attacker released his hand from her mouth, Molly screamed.

He struck her—hard. Her head jerked back violently, and darkness overcame her.

No one heard Molly's screams. No one heard the man's animal-like grunts as he released his hate and violent anger within her.

"There," he said as he stood up and zipped his filthy stained

205

pants, kicking her limp rag-like body, "stay the hell off my bridge. Can't you see it's for men only?" His yellow eyes flashed like an animal's as he walked away from his prey.

Moaning in pain, Molly regained consciousness. Her face throbbed where her attacker had struck her, her left eye already swollen shut, her lip split; dry blood caked her mouth and chin.

"Oh," she cried in agony as she tried to sit up. It hurt her to inhale, her ribs bruised or cracked from her assailant's kicks. Molly's bare skin was exposed where he had ripped open her clothes, and she was so chilled and shook so violently, it seemed she was experiencing an earthquake.

Unable to stand—even to sit up, Molly pulled her clothes around her and rolled. Each time she completed an entire roll—seven in all—she cried out in pain. Finally she came to rest beneath a clump of evergreen shrubbery. There she slept, cold, bloody, and broken.

Molly scarcely moved as she slept non-stop for two days and two nights. If anyone saw her or heard her moans, they didn't stop to offer assistance

Just before dawn after the second night Molly had lain deep within the thicket of bushes, she awakened—slightly. She felt something lightly stroke across her cheek, and she brushed it away, sharply sucking in her breath as she touched her check. Her cheek was purple with bruises, and even the slightest touch caused sharp needles of pain to shoot through her jaw.

She felt the soft stroking touch again—this time on her forehead. She fought to open her eyes. One was swollen completely shut, but through the other she could faintly see a shadow. Pre-dawn darkness still enveloped the area.

Molly shuddered with terror, fearing her assailant had returned. But she was too weak to escape, too weak to resist in any way. Through her swollen and bloody lips, she sobbed.

"Shhh. Don't cry," a small voice consoled.

Molly felt a hand grasp hers. A tiny hand. "Go back, Mommy, go back to Valeria."

"Megan, is it really you?"

Again, Molly struggled to see. In the ever-so-faint light, she could see the outline of the small child crouched beside her, gently holding her hand.

"Yes, Mommy, it's me. You need to get up now. You need to go back home—back home to Valeria. Petey needs you," the little voice urged.

Using her hand on the side where she wasn't kicked, and with the child still grasping the other, Molly first sat up, then rose to her feet. She clutched the bushes, fearful she would again fall onto the ground where she had been lying. The earth rocked beneath her, and her body throbbed all over with intense pain.

"I'll help you, Mommy. I'll help you get back."

So Molly slowly dragged herself away from the shadow of the evergreens, ready to begin her trek back to Valeria. She had no idea how—or which direction to go. But the little girl beside her, firmly clutching her hand, promised she would help her.

Molly believed her.

Chapter Forty-Three

Petey, never a very big girl, was now just a wisp of the confident young lady who had breezed into Valeria and made herself at home among the street people living there. Her shoulders slumped, and her eyes were dull with sadness. Her pert face was so drawn, she looked much older than her teen-aged years.

Petey missed Molly terribly, and she blamed herself for her older friend's flight. She had searched every inch of Valeria and wasn't able to find her—not anywhere. Petey was certain Molly was dead.

And it was her fault.

The last clutches of winter were leaving. The ice on the river began its break-up, heralded by ear-splitting noise as some of the larger ice floes crashed into one another. Breezes which had been bitter and bone-chilling when Molly arrived in Preston Valley were warmer and carried with them the hint of spring. Wisps of green sprouted up along the water, as early-blooming willow trees began to leaf, their pale-green supple branches swaying in the breeze.

Molly didn't travel far that first day of her journey back to Valeria. Pain wracked her body, and she was weak with hunger. Only the little hand clasped in hers kept her going.

On the first leg of her journey, Molly walked back towards the center of Preston Valley, putting as much distance as possible between her and the bridge—and the perpetrator of her brutal attack. Then she sought out the fountain in the square and drank and drank. The cold water stung her face, which was bruised inside as well as outside. She had long ago sacrificed most of her teeth to the poor nourishment and lack of hygiene that was the hallmark of life on the street. Two teeth of those remaining had been loosened when her assailant struck her, and the cold water pained those as well. But still she drank, now determined to set out on a journey she might never be able to complete.

Next, she set out to find food, dragging one foot after the other, her hunger and injuries making each step a monumental effort. The child encouraged her each step of the way.

"C'mon, Mommy. You have to find food. That's the most important right now—food."

Molly pulled her coat tightly around her and tied it closed with the piece of rope she wore as a belt, so her torn clothes and body were covered. There was no hiding her damaged face, yet no one stopped to help her or even to ask if she needed help. Her only assistance came from the child. As she tottered, the little girl grabbed her arm.

"It's okay, Mommy. You'll be okay."

Molly turned down a familiar alley and found a dumpster she had slept behind many a night. Refuse spilled out—fortunately, since Molly was in no shape to climb or reach high into the receptacle. Morsels of food were scattered among the refuse, and Molly grabbed them and jammed them ravenously into her mouth.

She could not bring herself to give garbage to her little girl.

"That's okay, Mommy. I'm not hungry. Really. Now let's find somewhere for you to rest."

The pair walked a short distance further to the edge of one of the many beautiful parks that were the pride of Preston Valley. Molly walked to the thickly treed boundary and wearily edged herself down.

"Here, Mommy, lie down. You can use my coat for a blanket. I'm really very warm."

Molly didn't argue—not even when her child offered her coat. Her weariness was all-encompassing. She stretched out and laid her head on her bag containing rags and old clothing. The child smoothed her coat—the lovely royal-blue coat trimmed in white rabbit fur— over her sleeping mother. Then she returned her small hand to her mother's hand.

Molly slept the remainder of the day and all night. When she awoke in the morning of a new day, the child was still there by her side.

With the beginning of each day, Molly would painfully sit up, then stand, and with great difficulty begin anew her arduous hike back towards Valeria. She had no idea whether or not she was walking in the right direction.

Other times, other journeys, she had often veered from the course she needed to follow to reach her destination. But this time, she was headed the right way—as if some unseen radar was guiding her.

Molly and her little companion pushed on, always staying clear of traveled routes, of other people. It was nearly impossible for her to find food on the paths she traveled—only early-spring berries or an occasional apple core or half-eaten sandwich thrown carelessly into the brush that followed the direction of the roads to Valeria.

Thirst became a problem, as the cloudless days remained devoid of the usual spring rains. One day, Molly came across a can half-filled with rainwater, remnants of a shower earlier in the month.

"Drink it, Mommy. It'll help you feel better."

Molly smiled at the child and raised the can to her lips, the rim rust-encrusted, the faded and torn label, *Del Monte Early June Peas*, barely legible. She greedily drank the fetid water, draining every drop. The child watched her, smiling.

"Better, Mommy?"

"Better," said Molly, as she renewed the day's journey.

The days came and went, each like the one before. Molly continued her return to Valeria—to her "home," clutching the child's hand as she dragged her frail body with almost superhuman determination to reach her destination. The pair rarely spoke, except when the child offered her encouragement, prodding to keep Molly going.

Some days were better than others—days when Molly would seemingly draw more strength from reserves she never knew she had. The voices were silent, just as they had been before when Megan was by her side.

Days worse than others spotted the journey. When a much-needed rain came, it came in torrents, driven by wind and preceded by hail. Molly was buffeted by both. Not able to garner the strength to run, she slowly ambled to the protection of a grove of trees and slumped beneath the largest. She laid her head back and her tears mingled with the large raindrops peppering her face. Her hair hung in sopping wet strings about her shoulders, and her gray felt hat—the treasure second only to her cross, dripped as the rain cascaded from its brim.

The downpour was short-lived, but it was towards evening when it stopped, and there was no sunshine to help dry Molly's wet clothing, only a soft breeze carrying the fresh smell of early spring. Spring's fragrance might have been pleasant if Molly hadn't been so drenched. The gentle wind brought her teeth-chattering chills as she pulled her wet coat tightly around her and fell into a dreamless, uncomfortable sleep. The child, completely dry, sat by her side.

In the morning, Molly was stiff with cold and bone-chilling

210

dampness. During the night she had developed a rasping cough, and it pained her to breathe. It was midday before she left the protection of the trees and again dragged herself through the brush.

The sun shone, and its warm rays began to dry Molly's damp clothing, but did nothing to really warm her. Every few steps a sudden chill would quiver through her body, and her eyes were bright with fever.

"Just a little ways more, Mommy," said the child with reassurance, tightening her grasp on Molly's hand.

Petey sat on the edge of a park bench looking up at the cloudless sky. Her small turned-up nose was pink with sunburn. She had been sitting on the bench, in the sun, most of the day.

It was a beautiful day, the sun's warmth greatly appreciated after yesterday's deluge. And that hail! Petey had run for shelter from the large ice balls roaring down from the sky. The hail came on so suddenly, it frightened her. She couldn't remember when she had been in such a storm—at least outside in one.

Even though today was a great improvement, Petey still felt frightened and sad—like a small child afraid of the dark. All the excitement she had felt with her adventure of life on the street was gone.

It left with Molly.

Just thinking about Molly made her more sad, and she blinked back tears threatening to escape. As she rubbed her eyes with the back of her hand, she looked across the park and saw a bent-over old woman walking alone, dragging herself from the field adjoining the park on the north end.

Petey looked away and then looked quickly back. Something was familiar. There was no determined gait—nor stick swinging authoritatively from side to side—but there was definitely something familiar about the woman. The hat!

"Molly," cried Petey, running to greet her friend. She almost knocked her down, she was so exuberant.

There had never been any significant touch between Molly and Petey—only an occasional light touch on the arm. Certainly never a hug. But Petey hugged Molly now—enveloped her in the strongest hug she could muster.

"Molly, Molly, you're back!" she exclaimed, half laughing, half crying.

Molly only looked at her and dragged herself towards a bench. Petey, noticing her friend appeared to be hurt and ill, took her arm and guided her.

The dark purple bruises had faded during Molly's long journey back, but a green-yellow color streaked across her cheek. Her breathing was so labored, she gasped for breath, and her rasping cough shook her frail body.

"You're hurt, Molly, and sick, too," said Petey mournfully. "I'm going to go for help."

"No," said Molly as she placed her hand firmly on Petey's arm. Petey sat down again.

Molly looked at her young friend—looked directly into her eyes. Petey noted again the spectacular color of Molly's eyes, their beautiful lavender hue, now incredibly bright with fever. She thought she had never seen Molly's eyes look so clear and bright.

"Go home, child. Go home."

"I can't, Molly. You know I can't."

Again Molly said, "Go home."

Petey began to cry and shook her head.

Molly repeated her admonishment twice more. "Go home."

Petey was openly sobbing now. "I can't, don't you understand? I thought you cared about me. I missed you so. Aren't you even glad to see me?"

Once more, her voice no more than a whisper, Molly said, "Go home."

Petey bolted up from the bench and ran across the park, and soon she was out of sight.

The child, having left Molly's side when she entered the park, reappeared.

"Oh, Megan, she won't listen to me. She won't go home."

"She will, Mommy. She will when she knows it's time. Now let's find you someplace where you can rest."

Molly slowly raised herself from the bench and let the child again take her hand. Together they wandered down the alley, past *Percy Lyons' Bakery*, past the backs of other establishments so familiar to Molly.

When she spotted a pile of boxes behind the furniture store, she stopped. "These boxes make a fine bed, Megan. Did you know that? A fine bed," she repeated as she carefully lowered herself onto a stack of cardboard.

"Mommy doesn't feel very good, honey. She thinks she'll go to sleep now." Molly patted the child's hand and let her eyelids close slowly over her very lovely eyes.

Chapter Forty-Four

The black and white rolled to a stop at the edge of the street, its light-bar flashing. Sammy Vale and Mike Baxter jumped out.

"There she is, just like the caller said," declared Mike. He squatted his large frame down—all two hundred and sixty pounds—and placed his fingers on the hollow of Molly's wrinkled, grimy neck. "She's dead all right. No doubt about that."

"Do you suppose someone killed her?" asked Sammy, noting the fading bruises on Molly's face.

"Naw, the street killed Molly. A long time ago, I'd say. She wasn't a bad old girl. Might have even been pretty once, but God, what a life she lived. Ate garbage, slept on the ground, got kicked, slapped, and God only knows what else. But one thing—I never saw Molly do anything mean to anyone. She was the kindest old lady I ever saw around here. Always made me wonder who she was, where she came from, what her life was like before.

"But we'll never know. Best I call the wagon. It's the end of the line for Molly."

Petey picked up her pace as she walked away from where she had left Molly's body, wanting to put as much distance as possible between the sirens and herself, her hand tightly clasping the cross and chain in her pocket. Her tears flowed freely now, and she didn't try to stop their steady stream down her small freckled face. She felt hollow inside; her sense of loneliness so overpowering, she could scarcely breathe.

She hadn't realized she loved Molly so much. That she would feel so terribly lost and alone without her. She hadn't felt this way since she was four years old and had been lost at a shopping mall. So frightened. So alone. Just like now. She could still remember how, sobbing, she clung to her mother when she found her. She could almost hear her mother's soothing "shhh's" and feel her hand gently stroking her hair as she said, "It's okay, honey. Mama's here."

Petey drew the dirty cuff of her old tweed jacket across her face, brusquely wiping away her tears, and ran to the closest phone booth. She dug around desperately in the coin slot, but found no change.

She ran to another, and then another. On and on she ran, covering nearly the entire west end of town. Finally, she came to a phone booth just as a man was walking away. Looking disdainfully at the thin disheveled girl with the wild looking hair waiting as he exited the booth, he stomped off, obviously angry. Apparently his intended call was unanswered, because Petey's hand closed around the needed coins as she reached inside the slot. She removed the coins, still warm from their previous owner's touch, and inserted them, one-by-one.

She heard the sharp intake of breath as the operator asked the woman who answered the phone if she would accept a call from Connie Peters. Then the "Hello, Connie—is it really you?"

Petey—Connie—was crying again, this time so hard she could hardly speak. With a halting, sobbing voice, she replied, "Yes, Mom, it's me. I'm coming home. I've had enough of life on the street."

Molly—Dr. Merritt Hall-Davis—had lived on the streets of Valeria, Indiana, for fourteen years, ten months, and eight days.

Printed in the United States
203965BV00001B/526-543/P